# NIMBUS

Nimbus
by Bernard Voss

ISBN 978-1-7372837-0-6 (hardcover edition)
ISBN 978-1-7372837-3-7 (paperback edition)
ISBN 978-1-7372837-2-0 (ebook)


Voss, Bernard.
Summary: Nimbus the red fox loses his mate and begins a new
life in the city.
[1. Animals—Fiction. 2. Foxes—Animals—Juvenile Fiction.]


Library of Congress Control Number: 2021910336


Text set in Linux Libertine
Cover design and art copyright ©2021 by Mariya Prytula


Published by Quisquiliae Books


Printed in the United States of America

# Contents

# Prologue

I dreamed that she wore flowers in her fur—a silly dream, but clear and lingering. It left the taste of clover honey in my mouth. In my dream, Aurora walked slowly, each step deliberate and measured, her narrow paws gliding as if on ice. Later, I found it impossible to remember whether there had been anything but silence. I recalled no sounds, only images and smells. The vixen's brush, full and rosy like the dawning of an autumn day, was adorned with daisies, their stems tied delicately in bows. And the sweetness of their scent blended with the spice of her own. It was foolish, of course, since foxes cannot ornament themselves in this way and—most of all in my Aurora's case—have no need to. We are noble animals, sleek and brilliant and above ostentation. And so this dream—the one I had the day before our wedding—stayed with me as much for its strangeness as for its sweetness.

Foxes are born blind and deaf, shivering and toothless. We whimper but do not know it. Our coats are dull and ashen, the complement to our stunted senses and frail limbs. We survive and grow into the noble creatures that we are by the patient care of our mothers, who lend us their warmth and their milk. Our mothers for their part rely on the daring and craft of our fathers, who spend themselves in the risky business of the hunt so that the vixen, and the cubs in turn, may eat. I was no longer a cub, or—as my keener hindsight tells me—I was about to begin my real growth. Like all foxes, I began my life in dark silence. This is the story of how I came to see and hear.

CHAPTER

1

# A Fox's Wedding

The forest was cold and dark. The trees' bony branches, stripped by late-autumn winds, filtered the moonlight, but from our clearing I saw that fading crescent still barely ruling over its starry court. Tomorrow it would disappear entirely, and in the safe embrace of darkness, Aurora and I would wed. Then, as we began our new life together, the embryonic moon would wax afresh.

Tonight, I had arrived before my beloved. I lay down at the base of a large elm. Leaves crackled beneath me. The air was dry, sharp in my nostrils. My thickening coat felt ready to spark, like the lightning that rakes its way across the landscape, searing and smoldering where it will. I had heard that sometimes lightning inflicted great fires and even razed a dozen generations' growth in a single night. This was so rare, I was told, that I need not fear it in my lifetime. It was part of nature's grand turning, like the cycles of the moon or the seasons themselves.

Some die so that others can live. I thought of all the prey I had already killed in my short life—every mouse, every bird. I felt in that moment that I was ready to die. Should the need arise, I would throw myself to some beast and take joy and pride in letting it rend my flesh and drain my blood for Aurora's sake.

My heart swelled and ached. I wanted to go on feeling heroic things, but some words from my father whispered in my mind. He had told me once that a male fox must give his life in another sense, that he must not only be willing to die for his family but also to live for it. *Nimbus*, he had said, *to love is to perform a thousand trivial and unnoticed tasks, each insignificant in itself and easy to omit.*

This sentiment flooded my breast with a different warmth, but it puzzled my head. Surely, someone with the courage to die, like myself, would be all the more able to weather the small demands of family life. My father's admonishment made the hard easy and the easy hard.

*Well,* I told myself, *he was a wise fox by the standards of his own day, but he's a little out of touch.*

In any case, he and my mother had a different kind of relationship. They were happy enough, comfortable with each other in a boring, domestic sort of way, but they couldn't be expected to understand true romance. They would never grasp the passion Aurora and I felt.

Aurora still had not arrived. She lived to the east across a long field bordering the woods. Humans used it as farmland. This scared off most other predators, but foxes can be brave when advantageous, and we easily adapt. Aurora's family fed on the rodents and insects that lived there. As long as they kept their distance from the humans and their dog, they were safe enough. There were stories, of course, of relatives who had died in seasons past, cousins or a great-aunt or uncle who had been careless or unlucky. Their greed may have urged them too close to the human settlement, or thirst driven them in some drought to cross the great high-way to the south so as to reach the large pond it borders on the other side. Aurora and I would swap the caution-ary tales we had learned from youth, sometimes for fun and sometimes in bitter seriousness.

My own family lived, more safely I felt, on the western side of the woods, which divided Aurora's territory from mine. The woods themselves were common and free to all. It was here that we had first met and here that we continued to meet most nights.

Suddenly my ears pricked up. "Aurora!" I called to the darkness. "This evening flatters you."

"*You* flatter me," she snorted, entering the clearing. "You can't even see me yet."

"Well, I can see you now, and I was right. You're beau-tiful."

"I look like a matted mess with this half-winter coat. Why the time for pairing up has to be the season we look our worst I'll never know."

I nuzzled her shoulder. "I bet it's so that we aren't over-whelmed by physical beauty when choosing a mate. That's a real danger, you know."

She sat and scratched behind her ear with her hind paw. "It's so itchy in this in-between state. You know, now that I think of it, I'll probably look even worse molting in the spring." She sighed.

"Sounds about right," I agreed. "I'm curious myself." Aurora and I were both approaching our first birthday and full adulthood, so winter would be a new experience. My impression of the season was based on the education I had received from my parents. "In any case," I continued, "when the time for actual mating comes, I bet you'll have a gorgeous winter coat."

"Well, I hope so."

"What about me?" I asked, cocking my head slightly to emphasize my jawline. "Do I look rugged?"

"Oh, please." Aurora rolled her eyes. Then she sat up straight and studied me with mock seriousness. "I suppose on a superficial level one might describe the shaggy look as rugged. It's certainly not a proper look for a vixen, but it *could* work on a male."

"I saw my reflection in a frosted puddle the other day, and I think I look strong. The extra fur makes me look bigger, not just fluffier but rough, like a wolf."

"A wolf?"

"Yeah, I mean, not as big, but like the kind of animal you don't want to mess with. You know, dangerous."

"Hmm," she murmured thoughtfully. "Well, once your full coat is in, dangerous or not, I don't want you looking like you have the sort of mate who would let you out of the den totally ungroomed."

"Sorry, love," I said, "you'll never be able to tame me." I pressed my muzzle hard against her cheek.

"That tickles!" she cried, nipping at me so that I pulled away.

"Okay! Okay!" I conceded. "I know you don't like that, but I just couldn't help myself."

Aurora paused, glancing down for a moment. "It's not that I don't like it. Just the whiskers, you know?"

"You're right. I'll try to control myself better." I plopped down again onto the cold leaves. "You know, I had a dream about you."

Aurora lay beside me. "Oh? Go on."

"It was silly," I said and explained my dream.

When I had finished Aurora wrinkled her muzzle. "That's not very plausible. For one thing, how would I tie daisies to my fur?"

"I told you it was silly." I paused a moment. "But I liked how you smelled."

"In a peculiar sort of way," Aurora said, "that's kind of sweet. I hope you think of it when we're cooped up in a stuffy den this winter."

I leaned over and licked her ear, taking care this time not to ruffle her whiskers. "And the next and the next."

"And will we have enough food?" she asked.

I couldn't tell whether she was serious or just testing me. "That depends on where we live, I suppose."

"What about our discussion?"

I hesitated, not wanting to start a fight the day before our wedding. "Moving to the city?"

"Yes," she said. "Time's up. We have to make a decision."

"You know what I think about that. It's not safe."

Aurora shifted next to me, rustling a few leaves. "I grew up around humans. As long as we keep our distance, it's safe."

"You live near farm humans. City humans may be different. You know how dangerous those roads are, for instance. The highway leads to the city. The city must be filled with roads, running together like so many twigs in an enormous nest. Their machines, their metal vehicles, are always speeding down the highway. The city may be even deadlier."

"Of course, I've studied the city!" scoffed Aurora. "The humans don't live on the roads, you know. Besides, there *are* city foxes, many of them, and they always have enough to eat all year round."

I wondered how she could possibly know that but kept quiet. For the first time that night, I noticed the fireflies that glowed and dimmed around us. The night had grown darker and cooler. Aurora remained silent while I gathered my thoughts.

"Maybe we can check it out," I said at last. "See what it's like before making a final decision. Besides, it's not just *our* safety that worries me."

"Whose safety is it?" Aurora asked. She knew what I meant, but I could tell she wanted to hear me say it.

"Theirs," I replied. "Our cubs'. They won't be able to run or hide like we can." I realized that I was staring at my paws, so I raised my eyes to meet Aurora's. "They won't be as strong or smart as you."

"We'll just have to find a good place," she said.

Just then my stomach growled. Aurora smirked, rolling her eyes.

"Er, should I fetch us something to eat?" I asked.

"Let's both go," she said. "It'll be faster."

"I'll be quick," I promised.

"No," she insisted. "I'm too hungry to wait."

"But, it's tradition," I said. "I know you're capable of catching your own supper, but someday you won't be. I have to show that I can provide for us."

"You've proved yourself, dear," she insisted. "Let tradition take a night off. Besides, there will be plenty of it tomorrow. Right now, I'm not about to lie here hungry and bored when there are warm meals to snatch up."

I said nothing, nodding my acquiescence. Aurora sniffed the air and walked off. I waited till she was out of sight and then got down to business myself. Once my head had cleared from the annoyance I felt at Aurora's dismissiveness, I explored and located several potential targets. I settled on a field mouse.

Once I had tracked and caught the tiny creature, I gnashed it in my jaws a few times just for fun, savoring the warm flesh. Mice are usually not alone, so I gulped down what I could, careful of the bone fragments, and then turned my attention to catching another. At the physical release of killing, my heart rate and breathing steadied. With the second morsel warm in my muzzle, I trotted back to the clearing.

Aurora was waiting. She held her own fresh kill between her forepaws. The distinct, earthy scent of mole filled the air. I dropped my mouse to the ground a few feet from her. "Was it hard not to eat that on the way here?" she asked, clearly amused.

"What makes you say that?" I replied, deciding not to mention the mouse I had already consumed.

"The drool pouring from your muzzle, dear. Anyway, thanks for being flexible for me."

"Only because I love you," I said and began to tear into my prey's chewy hide.

Since we had both caught something, there was no need to take turns. Unlike wolves, foxes do not hold to a strict hierarchy in dietary matters. If anything, the vixen and cubs will eat first, essentially a reversal of the lupine custom. Wolves are our cousins, but in many cases their ways are far different from our own.

I finished my meal quickly and lounged beside Aurora. I sighed and closed my eyes, enjoying the slobbering, gulping sounds as she continued to feast. They were sounds of life, of abundance and health, and they heightened the pleasure of my own full belly.

After a few moments, everything stopped. I heard Aurora lick her lips, and then she jabbed her wet nose into my shoulder. "Don't fall asleep!" she said.

"I'm not sleeping," I muttered lazily, my eyes still shut. "Just enjoying the moment."

"Well, I'm all done," she said.

"Shh," I whispered. "It's okay, dear. Just lie here with me."

Leaves rustled as Aurora lay her head on the ground, brushing against my paw. Without opening my eyes, I pressed gently against her warm side and draped my brush across hers. I don't know how long we lay there, possibly a half hour.

"Nimbus," Aurora asked, "are you awake?"

"Yes," I mumbled. "I'm awake."

"Nimbus," asked Aurora, shifting at my side, "how many stars do you think there are?"

"Well," I began, blinking and lifting my head. "You see." She shot me a toothy smirk. "Okay, okay. You're very clever."

"Well, what would you like to do, then?"

"Just be here with you," I muttered, lowering my head and closing my eyes.

"That's sweet," she said, "but I want to *do* something."

"What would you like to do?"

"I'll trade you songs," she suggested. Trading songs— or stories—was a little custom of ours, not something we did every time we met, but often enough. We would take turns singing a tune we had learned from our parents or, rarely, one we had made up ourselves. We discovered that the older, more traditional songs were known to both of us, though sometimes with slight differences. Aurora seemed to know far more songs than I did, so she sang more. I didn't really enjoy singing in front of her anyway. I felt my talent lay in storytelling.

"I'm out of songs," I admitted, opening my eyes. "You've heard them all."

Aurora's expression told me that she still wanted me to sing. "Are you *sure* there isn't one single fresh song somewhere in that rugged head of yours?"

"I'm sure," I affirmed. "But do you have a request?"

Aurora thought for a moment. "Why don't you sing me that lullaby again?"

I knew which one she meant, and my ears flushed as I recalled the first time I had sung it for her. "Well, if you like, but it's a little embarrassing."

"Don't be so nervous!" she chided. "Just pretend you're singing it to our cubs."

"Okay," I conceded, sitting up. I growled a bit to clear my throat. After a brief hesitation, I parted my muzzle. My voice, breathy and wavering at first, grew steadier and richer as I sang:

> *Lo the moon waxes, high in the sky.*
> *See its light growing, full by and by.*
> *And, the stars' chorus sings with us, too,*
> *Smiling and dancing for me and for you.*
> *You are my dear one! No reason to cry,*
> *For I'll watch without waning till morning is nigh.*

Aurora's golden eyes had been fixed on the thin crescent moon as I sang. Now she turned and faced me. I shifted my weight, suddenly feeling awkward in the silence.

"Beautiful," she said.

The icy wind rustled my whiskers, which then twitched of their own accord. "Thanks," I said, "but I'm sure you have something even more beautiful for me."

"Any requests?"

"You decide."

Aurora paused a moment. "You sang about the moon. Even though it's night, I will sing about the sun. This is one I don't think you've heard."

She sat upright, back straight, and tilted her head upward. Her breast expanded with a sharp intake of breath. The tune cascaded from her muzzle like a clear summer waterfall:

*I saw my love! I saw the rising sun,*
*Whose rays pour down and warm us from above.*
*The fi-ire burns! It blazes as the seasons run*
*And ever turns the dark of night to light.*
*No merit earns, no skill or art devises it,*
*But in its sight all creatures learn to love what lies beyond.*

"Almost as sweet as you are," I muttered dreamily when the last syllable had faded. "But, what does it mean?"

"I'm not entirely sure," she replied. "I asked my mother the same thing when she taught it to me. She only said that this song is very old."

"I'll take it to heart," I said, humming the melody under my breath. "Maybe you're the sun."

"If I'm the sun, then I'm the one that spoils the good hunting."

"No, no," I said. "I prefer night for hunting, too, of course, but the sun is what gives life. It's what makes the nighttime fruitful."

"That's true," she mused. "Although, the night dazzles in its own way."

"Besides," I continued, "I like to see your rosy fur in the light."

"I prefer your eyes in the dark." She grinned, and her teeth flashed in the faint moonlight.

Pleasant warmth rushed to my ears. I glanced down. "Thanks," I said, "but, speaking of dark, we are running out of it tonight."

"Should we talk about tomorrow, then?"

"Yes, I think so. Are you still ready?"

"I'm ready," she affirmed, "but you have to make good on your offer to look at the city."

"Well," I said, "what if we make our way there over the next few days and see if there's territory available near the outskirts?"

"That would be fine," Aurora agreed, "as a starting point and maybe as a backup, but I don't want to stop there."

"I promise that we can give the city real consideration," I said, "but let's get through the process of leaving home first."

"Of course."

Each autumn, newly mature foxes pair up and leave home. It is a firm rule that male foxes must leave, even those who have not found a mate. Occasionally, however, a female will remain with her parents and help raise their next litter. That was what my sister Amber would most likely do. Being undersized and sickly her whole life, she had not secured a mate. My brother and other sister had already left home, so I would be the last to wed.

Now a fox's wedding is a solemn affair—solemn and therefore joyous—but simple. It has its own kind of glory, drawn from careful movement and implication rather than showiness. Aurora and I would meet here in our usual place. We would approach one another with deliberate, prescribed steps, a ritual holding the weight both of instinct and tradition. Only our vows would break the silence, spoken and accepted by each other alone. And, then, we would chase and dance. That part could not be planned out, only prepared for. First the serious, verbal articulation of our promises, and then the unguarded, spontaneous dance. Both were forms of candor. Both were necessary. But tomorrow we would not return to our childhood homes. Instead, we would venture out to find territory of our own, together and for life.

"Shall we meet here at midnight?" she asked, interrupting my thoughts.

"Do you think that's too late?" I countered. "Will we have time to cover much distance? Don't forget that we'll still need to eat something."

"A *little* earlier, then, if you like, but not too much. I want the timing to be perfect."

I agreed, and we finalized our plans without fuss. Soon we were both weary and ready for a last slumber in our family dens. I rose and sniffed the air with caution. All felt safe and clear around us. The dawn was not far off, its first rays just minutes away. I wished my mate farewell.

"By the way," Aurora called as I left the clearing, "I'll have a surprise for you!"

I awoke too early the next evening and paced around the entrance to my family's den. I hunted insects, catching only a few, since the cold had already driven most below the freezing surface or into the hearts of trees. It was just as well. I didn't want to spoil my appetite for our meal later, when I would hunt and Aurora and I would feast for the first time as a life-bonded pair. In any case, I wasn't truly hungry yet, just restless.

Amber suggested that I could do with a proper grooming before the ceremony. I protested, but not much. She was right, and it felt good to let my sister help clean me one last time. We talked about how we used to play and about growing up together. I asked her how she would like staying at home another year, and she told me that she looked forward to teaching our parents' next litter. I told her I would miss her lessons. She was the smartest of our litter and enjoyed sharing her knowledge.

Saying farewell to my parents was a strange experience. It was not formal, not exactly, and the finality was hard to grasp. My parents had seen children disperse before, of course, in previous years' litters. Nature demanded it. But, when it was time for me to go, I could not help feeling the pain of leaving the family I was born into in favor of the life I had chosen for myself.

In the final analysis, foxes are territorial creatures. We are made to break the ties we are born with and form new ones, to go out and claim our own land and make our own life. Maybe this was what leaving my family behind masked—or protected—the true fragility of those unchosen bonds. Instead of future competition over space or food, in place of jealousies and rivalries, my parents, siblings, and I could all retain a pure memory. Absence protected love that might not be strong enough for a continued presence. The annual departure of the newly grown cubs crystallized each family's memories at their best. I didn't say it out loud, but I felt sorry for vixens like Amber, who stayed home rather than make their own life.

This raised the further question. How would I feel when my own sons and daughters one day ventured off on their own? I would then experience the dispersal's other side, the other side of the separation that kept love wholesome. Litters would come and go while Aurora and I remained united through the seasons. Life would flow around us, like the waters of a stream that part and mingle again when rushing past an unmoved stone, or like some vine twisting toward the sun at the base of an ageless tree.

Finally, I trotted to our clearing. My fur crackled with electricity in the dry air. I couldn't sit still. There was no moon to watch this evening, but my body told me that midnight had come. My stomach churned. I was still alone amid the naked trees, looking east, waiting for those golden eyes to appear.

But they never did.

CHAPTER

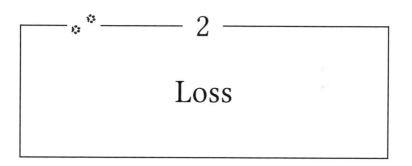

2

Loss

I felt feverish, despite the cold, and realized how hard I had been pacing. I had to decide. Should I stay and wait in the clearing where Aurora expected me, or should I try to find her? Perhaps she was fussing about her fur or some other detail. Would she arrive later and worry that I had left the clearing, or was she in danger and crying out for my help?

"A cautious fox beats a clever fox," I muttered, echoing one of my father's aphorisms. A moment of consideration now could obviate the need for ingenuity later. I tried to slow my breathing and let my heart quiet down. The adrenaline building in my system made it difficult, but I needed to think clearly. It had to be at least two hours past midnight. No doubt that something was wrong. I had to find her.

And so I headed through the eastern woods. I detected Aurora's scent from the previous night and followed it beneath the canopy of spindly limbs, sometimes doubling back to regain the trail. Thankfully, I never lost it altogether as I made my way over the knotty roots and brush. Other scents and sounds disappeared as I concentrated on my mate alone.

Eventually, I exited the forest, reaching Aurora's familial territory. I had been here before, but only once or twice. Truth be told, the proximity of the human farm unnerved me, not only because of the humans themselves but because of the artificial rows meant for vegetation and the large domesticated animals, like giants but dumb and dulled by some human spell. At the same time, I had to admit that these very features, as unsettling as they were, provided a predictable supply of resources. Aurora's family lived on it, and so I understood Aurora's point that where humans are there is food and appreciated her interest in the city a little more.

Daylight was a few hours off, so I was not certain where to find Aurora's family. Perhaps they would be sleeping in their den already, or maybe they would still be out on the nightly hunt. The land was so open that the wind scattered their scents, leaving any trail of her parents and siblings tangled and confusing.

As a matter of etiquette, I had never been to Aurora's family den. Foxes generally respect one another's territory, and although Aurora was destined to be my mate, her parents' land was not mine. My present errand marked an obvious exception.

Fear rushed through my entire body as I ran across the broad field, exposed. The earth was dark and hard beneath my paws. Although filled with a grid of straight-rowed crops a few months ago, it was bare and open. I sprinted as quickly as I could, allowing myself to lose all scents. My only goal was to get out of the open. I took some comfort in the fact that it was quiet. From my little experience with humans, I knew that they were noisy. Besides, I told myself, Aurora's family used this land. It had to be safe. Or else, they were exceptionally naive.

The frigid air stung my lungs, my breath darting out before me like a cloud. At last, I came to a trench on the far side of the field and dived in. Pausing, I let my brain sort out the hodgepodge of smells assaulting me. Two of the scents belonged to foxes. Neither was Aurora. One of them was a male, three or four years old. I followed it.

I traced the scent along the trench, eventually hopping out and circling around a small grove of apple trees, never completely losing sight of the farm. At last, I came to the den. It was set in a small hillside perpendicular to the field I had first run across. I looked up at it, the small entrance barely visible through the grass. Some bones and feathers were strewn quite casually at the foot of the hill, marking out the den for anyone who cared to look. I could hardly believe such negligence. My own family took great pains to keep the den entrance free from signs of habitation. Aurora had told me that humans kept large predators away. Clearly her family counted on it. But what if they were wrong? What if some creature had gotten to her after all?

I shuddered and approached the den. My nose told me it was occupied. The older male fox was there, as were a female of his age and another of my generation. All traces of Aurora were a day old. Stopping at the entrance, I sniffed the air. There was no wind at the moment, so those inside, if they were still awake, knew of my presence. The male poked his head out, blinking. Dawn's first rays were striking the hillside. He took a careful look at me and then emerged. His deep burgundy coat highlighted a black streak encircling his white-tipped brush. He was bigger than any fox I had seen, with angular features. He looked strong.

"What can I do for you?" he asked.

"I'm Nimbus," I answered. "I'm looking for Aurora."

The older fox relaxed his stance. "I see. So you're Aurora's mate? I thought the two of you were dispersing today." He paused. "You don't know where she is?"

"Sir, she never arrived last night. It has me worried."

He raised his snout to the wind then trotted down the hill till we were nearly level. "We had better go."

"Go where?" I asked.

He brushed past me. "Did she leave our territory?" he called, picking up the pace.

"I don't know," I replied, running after him. "Where are we going?"

"Aurora told me last night that she had some business by the farmer's shed. I don't like the young ones going there. She insisted that she is grown, and she's mostly right. I can't dispute that. She wouldn't tell me why, but she had it in her head to get there before your wedding."

We ran nearer and nearer to the farm. The residual scent of humans and the smell of horses, cows, and poultry overwhelmed me. My brain screamed at me to turn and flee, but I pressed on. Even Aurora's father gave off a scent of fear. We were near a complex of buildings, what I presumed was the barn and a few others. I could sense dogs, which my mother had taught me were among our most dangerous enemies, particularly those whom the humans kept as servants and pets. If the shed was in this place, I understood why Aurora's father did not want her going there. Skulking and hunting around the periphery of the humans' property, eat-

ing the vermin and enjoying the lavish excess of human beings, is one thing, but invading their settlement is another.

The older fox stopped. His ears stood erect, spread out
and trembling like broad leaves in the wind. I fell in behind
him and kept still.

"She was here," he said.

My nose told me he was right. Aurora had been there
some time last night. No signs of distress. It was still unclear
to me why she would have ventured so close to the humans'
dwelling, with their strange lights and noisy animals, not to
mention the dogs. Aurora was brave, even brash. I hoped
her courage had not become recklessness.

"Follow me to the shed," whispered her father.

We stood, creeping single file. I followed so closely that
his tail brushed my snout as we rounded a corner and penetrated further into the complex of buildings. The scents
had become overpowering, many unknown and pungent.
In another context, I would have found it exhilarating, even
intoxicating. Instead, the panoply of human smells elicited
only a throbbing dread in my breast.

We came to a small, wooden building. It was gray and
stank of mildew. But this was nothing compared to the terror hanging in the air. Aurora had been here, and something
horrendous had happened. The lingering traces of her panic
seized me, invading my body and implanting themselves in
my brain. Aurora had frozen in fear and felt the crushing,
paralyzing embrace that had seen the demise of a thousand
foxes.

For a moment, I saw through her eyes and heard through
her ears. A man's voice roared. A dog barked. Everything
went bright and then dark. My paws gave out, and I collapsed in the dust, one with her in her last moment.

Aurora's father said nothing. He seemed not to react.

In truth, I had forgotten him. As the moments passed and I returned to myself his silence roused me. How could he stand stoic and unfaltering like a tree or large stone that weathers many seasons inert and unmarred? It bothered me. I struggled to get back to my feet.

"Nimbus," he hissed. "Nimbus, listen to me—"

I couldn't take it anymore. "Aurora!" I yelped, jumping up, abandoning stealth and caution. "Aurora!" My voice carried and echoed among the buildings.

No reply.

Frantically, I darted through the deadly area, sniffing and casting my eyes wildly around. I heard a thousand sounds, distant and near, but no response. I saw nothing, found nothing. Every moment I expected to rush upon her disfigured, bleeding body and to know for sure that my sun had been darkened at its very rising. She burned and made my soul to burn, and I would find her cold and dead. I expected this, I feared this, but I did not see it.

I don't know how long I searched, but I covered the same ground many times, shooting in and out among the buildings, heedless of all risk. Only once I had forced myself to slow and focus on the far side of the shed did I realize that for several minutes a strange, expanding scent had been stinging my nostrils.

At that time, I knew it only by instinct as a nameless trace of man's art. It smacked of artificiality, a sharp aroma far different from anything nature produced. The course of nature, to be sure, is filled with death and dying, with illness, decay, and slaughter—but not like this. This acrid scent was the lingering specter of an art that only man had devised or could devise. Much later, I would learn that it was burnt gunpowder.

"Nimbus!" Aurora's father brushed against me, jolting

me back into the present moment. "Nimbus, listen. Aurora is not here. Do you notice that? Yes, something horrible has happened. A gun has fired. But she is not here."

I must have looked a fool, staring as I did while my still-intoxicated mind pieced this together. "She's not here," I said.

"She's not here," he repeated, stern eyes fixed on my own. "Her body is not here."

My mind struggled to confront the possible explanations. Spiced musk mingled with gunpowder choked my nostrils like a cloud, and yet my Aurora could be alive. She may have run off and hidden herself. Again, she could be dead. Not finding her body was no guarantee the humans had not killed her after all. Who knows what human beings did with their victims? Perhaps they devoured them bones and all. Humans were perverse. At times, I knew, they left their prey by the side of the great road, which their terrible, noisy, smoking machines patrolled all day and night. Whether they meant these twisted corpses as a display of power, no one knew. I had even heard that they sometimes liked to drape themselves in the skins of animals they had slain. In a flash, in my mind's eye, I saw Aurora's body, iron hooks tearing her beautiful, rosy pelt as it hung over a pool of dried blood. I felt the claws in my belly, and I wanted to rip my own skin off just to get away.

"We have to look for her," I said, coming to my senses. "Who knows where she could be?"

"I fear," said her father, "that you may not want to see what you find." He pressed his muzzle to the ground, sniffing the dirt. "See," he said, "traces of fur."

I lowered my head beside his, inhaling deeply. "And blood," I added. Not only could I smell it, but I could see drops of Aurora's blood spotting the ground and the shed's gray panels. How had I missed it before?

"In any case," said the older fox, "we can't stay here. We've made too much of a ruckus. Every moment we are in mortal danger, just as she was."

He was right. The risk was so obvious. Why would Aurora take it? Why had she come here at all? Perhaps one of the dogs had attacked her out in the field and she had run this way to escape. But, no, her scent trail had shown no traces of fear until this point. Whatever had befallen her had been sudden and had happened only after she was well within the humans' complex.

"Did you hear anything last night?" I asked.

"Possibly," Aurora's father answered. He was standing with his back against the shed, his ears perked up. "I may not have noticed. The humans are noisy, and we are used to ignoring them from a safe distance."

Just as I was about to raise my head and agree that it was time to move on, my eye caught a flash of white and brilliant yellow behind the shed. Flowers. A patch of autumn daisies. Given the recent frosts, they must have been the last of the season, but there they were, just barely alive.

No need to ponder. I knew Aurora's motive at once. She had come here, had risked her life on the eve of our wedding because of that stupid dream. I had told her about the daisies. I had told her I liked how they smelled on her. I could see, examining the earth, that some of the flowers were matted down, stems bent and petals torn. She had tried to gain their scent. She had done this for my sake, to satisfy some passing fancy of mine.

"The daisies," I mumbled. "She rolled in the daisies."

"What?" Aurora's father asked, perplexed. Then he shook his head. "No matter. You can explain later. Right now, we have to go. It is already daylight."

Besides the guilt—the guilt that from that moment would define my future, though I did not know it yet—I could not begin to explain the daisies to him. He was right. There was no time for that, no time to make a silly dream shared between me and Aurora understandable to anyone else. I already knew myself a fool, a shameful fool, a cub with cub's dreams. I looked to Aurora's father. The strong, older fox's yellow eyes were fixed on me. We could not stay another instant. By any fair estimation, we had already wasted a dozen foxes' good fortune.

Saying nothing, I ran, not yet at top speed but quickly. Aurora's father followed. We headed away from the human buildings, winding and dodging in case we were in our enemies' sight, till we emerged, at last, on the opposite side. A rooster crowed. We were far from the den. Very far. I could even hear the faint roar of traffic, the din of those marauding vehicles that rush to and fro down the great road, never veering from their fixed path and for that reason fearsome. A wolf or a dog, even a man, pursues its prey, like any living being, out of its own appetites. These creatures, these slavish vehicles of metal, were something else. They gave off no scent of desire or of fear.

I had seen traffic only once before, not here but on the western side of the woods, just out of my parents' territory when I had ventured too close to the road with my siblings. Our curiosity had earned us a sharp nip on the rump from our mother when she found us, and I had not been back since.

Aurora's father and I ran toward the highway. The roar of a passing vehicle punctuated the silence. By unspoken understanding we slowed till we were ascending the patchy bank leading up to the road itself. Loose dirt crumbled and rolled downward beneath my paws as we climbed. We nearly halted, affording me the chance to catch a trace of Aurora's scent again. Despite the stench of fear, her trail gave me hope. If she had made it across the highway, she might be safe.

All along, even as we raced, I had attempted to hold to her general direction, knowing that she had run away from the shed and not back toward her parents' den. I was proud of her. Even in her panic, my sweet vixen had retained the clarity of mind and the resolve to lead the danger away from her family and take the risk on herself.

I smelled, then, that Aurora had run to the same embankment, toward the same menacing sound of traffic, and seemingly had crossed. Aurora's father sensed it, too. We had to halt, prone, bellies pressed to the earth, while the deafening vehicles rushed mere yards from our noses. I lowered my ears flat against my head as tightly as I could. At least, it seemed, we had not been pursued.

"We have to cross!" I called, shouting, even though we were side by side.

"It's dangerous!" he cried. "Even if my daughter is alive, we may not be!"

"We have to!"

As Aurora's father and I waited by the roadside, trying to work up the nerve and looking for an opportune moment to cross, my stomach churned. I suddenly realized how hungry I had been. The excitement and the pain had distracted me but left me weaker than ever. I was spent.

"Go!" Aurora's father yelled, bolting onto the great road.

I snapped into action at once, my hind legs pushing off from the earth, kicking up dirt and launching me over the edge, up and onto the pavement. For a split second, I scrambled, unaccustomed to the hard, black surface beneath me.

The pads of my paws gripped it easily, and I ran at top speed, heart seizing within my chest.

Before I knew what had happened, I was diving from the opposite side, falling and tumbling down an earthen bank like the one I had climbed. Aurora's father had landed first. I rolled head-first into his side, enmeshing my face in his shaggy fur. He seemed as disoriented as I, and for a moment I felt that we were equals.

I said that the embankment on both sides of the road was the same. This was true as far as it went, but on the southern side the embankment rolled directly into the pond bordering the highway. If the larger fox had not landed first and stopped my tumble, I would have slid right onto the icy surface. The muck below us, itself in the process of freezing, was as yet soft enough that we sank into it just a little. It stank of asphalt and decay.

In the midst of that stench, I caught a trace of my beloved. She had made it across the road! My heart surged with hope only to plummet. The ice covering the pond was broken. A hole two—no three—yards out revealed the dark water beneath. From the bank, I could just make out scraping, scrambling claw marks etched into the frozen surface.

"Aurora!" I called. "Aurora!"

Nothing.

Wounded and drenched in icy water, if she had climbed back out of the pond, Aurora wouldn't have made it far. There were no signs that the humans had pursued her across the road. If she was alive, she would be nearby. She was nowhere to be seen.

"Please, no," I choked. "It isn't true."

"It seems to be," said Aurora's father, whose presence I had again forgotten. "She must have leaped across the road and slid onto the ice."

I wanted to curse at him for making such an obvious statement, but I couldn't speak. It was clear that Aurora's resourcefulness and daring had undone her. I imagined her leaping clear from the great road, striking the embankment, crumpling, and sliding through the muck and across the ice. She had clawed and scratched, trying to get back to the shore, but the ice was too thin. It had cracked and consumed her breathless body. Perhaps she had climbed out and onto the surface again once, twice, or a dozen times. It didn't matter. In the end, exhaustion, cold, and loss of blood had all been too much. The black water had claimed her.

For a long time, I whimpered and paced along the perimeter of the pond, hoping to find a scent trail. No luck. In frustration I swatted the ice. How easily it cracked!

Eventually, I realized that my stomach was growling again. I felt faint, but I had no desire to eat. I deserved to starve. I wanted to starve. I imagined myself fasting in penance, keeping vigil till the end. I would feel my flesh wasting, clinging to my fragile bones. A tribute to my sweet vixen.

That fantasy was interrupted by large muzzle jabbing my neck. "Nimbus!" Aurora's father called.

I growled.

"Nimbus," he repeated, "please listen to me for a moment."

"I am not some cub!" I cried and bared my teeth, casting my ears back, flat against my head.

"Please," he replied. The softness of his voice startled me. "I have lost several children. I have lost a mate—my first mate. Hear what I have to say and then I'll leave you alone."

I wanted to attack him, to throttle him for his callousness. He may have lost a daughter, but he didn't know about the daisies. A chasm divides guilt from innocence. He could never understand. Whether I intended it or not, she had died because of me. And for what? A trifle? Still, I did not attack him. I did not hurl myself at him like I wanted. In my weakened state, he could easily have killed me or dealt me some crippling blow. Even at peak condition, I was probably no match for him. Besides, he wasn't my enemy, and if he was about to leave me to my grief, all the better.

"Dear young fox," he said, sitting at my side. "I am truly sorry. Believe that my heart breaks, too. I do not show my pain as you do because I am too old. I have lost the luxury of young grief. I have a mate and children. For their sake, I must safely cross this road once again. By now, they have awoken to my absence and are afraid for me. They will be hungry again. They will be in danger again. Losing myself right now would not bring back my daughter—a daughter I loved—it would only hurt my family."

I sat, remaining motionless at his side. "That's well and good," I retorted, "but I have nothing. I have no one now. No one needs me."

"Not yet," he said. "Give it time."

I began to protest.

"Nimbus," he interrupted. "I am not telling you to forget Aurora and move on, not at all, especially not at this very moment. What I am saying is don't end your life before it has begun. Don't despair at the beginning. You will have a thousand chances to do good, but you forfeit them all by one choice for evil. My Aurora loved you because you are good. She would not have chosen a bad fox. For her sake, please give yourself time. Don't do anything hasty."

"Like what?" I asked.

"Like throwing yourself into the pond or onto the road. Or, like wasting away and dying of starvation or cold."

I said nothing. I was exhausted, ready to collapse into the mire. My stomach pained me once more, urging me to gratify my instinct for self-preservation. I had to eat. With my beloved dead, satisfying my own appetite seemed ignoble. But Aurora's father was right about one thing: Only the living have a future. Only the living can choose.

*A careful fox beats a clever fox.* Some time to think, to plan, to discern what to do next might be forgivable.

"Let me bring you something to eat," said the older fox. "You look famished. It's okay to take care of yourself right now. You still have needs."

I couldn't argue. In any case, I wanted to be alone for a while. I wanted to lie in the half-frozen mud by myself and let my mind go blank.

Some time later, Aurora's father returned, bringing me a whole chipmunk. He dropped the carcass in front of me. It thudded against the hardening muck. I murmured a word of thanks and tore into it, nearly choking in my greed.

Satisfied, at last, I felt a little better but still worn out, idly studying the tiny bones before me. I thought about searching the full perimeter of the pond, but I knew this would be useless. It was too broad, and the ice was broken only in one place.

"Nimbus," said Aurora's father, "I have to go home. My family will be worried."

"I understand," I said. "Will you tell them?"

He sighed. "No," he said. "Not everything. You and I are males. It's our lot to protect those we love, to shelter them, to carry secret burdens. What good would it do my family to spread my grief to them? I will have to explain my long absence and any strange scents clinging to me, but I don't have to tell them that Aurora drowned in the pond. All I will share is that she went missing, that you and I were looking for her, and that when our search led us across the road, I let you go on by yourself."

He rose and began to climb up the steep embankment toward the road cautiously. Then, he paused and turned, fixing his tired eyes on me. "But I don't want to abandon you altogether. When you are ready, please promise that you'll come see me again. I will be waiting each day for the next week or so across the field on the south side of the farm. I like to go there often, so my family will not suspect. I know this region pretty well, and I will help you however I can."

"Okay," I said. "I will. I promise. Thank you."

I lost sight of him as he reached the peak of the embankment, but I could hear him cross the great road in safety. He yipped three times from the other side, and I did not hear him again. I was alone. All I could do, all I wanted to do, was rest and think, to let the events of the past night and day sink in fully. Only then would I be able to act with full deliberation. I owed Aurora that much. And so, I rose to my aching feet, fur soiled and clumpy with dirt, and looked for a place to sleep.

CHAPTER

3

# How We Met

This is how Aurora and I first met.

There were four in my litter, two males and two females. When our play-fighting inevitably ended in tears, my mother, a firm, no-nonsense kind of vixen, would grab the latest offender by the scruff of the neck and separate him or her from the victim. I was rarely the offender, more often the victim, and the one of us least willing to upset my mother.

My brother was the strongest of our litter, and he knew it. We all knew it. The only way to beat him was either to sneak up on him, which I thought was cowardly, or to trick him. We had developed—or I should say my sister Amber had developed—just such a deception. She explained it to my other sister and me, and we committed it to memory, even drilling each other on the details.

The pretense was a contest to see who was brave enough to run into the woods the farthest and stay there the longest. We would all dash in together. Then, we would double back one by one, fooling my brother into running on alone. Amber had devised the perfect premise, so we knew he would agree to the contest and would be likely to get caught up in it. None of us had been in the woods at that point in our life, so we were all dying of curiosity.

Our parents were only beginning to let us leave the den unsupervised, and only if we stayed together. They preferred us to keep within sight or close to it, and they certainly had forbidden leaving our territory and going beyond the field. So, the small forest bordering our land enjoyed not only the mystique of the unknown but also the thrill of rule-breaking.

So there we were: four gawky fox cubs lined up, waiting for Amber to signal us. It was a bright, hot early-summer afternoon, and we had sneaked away, leaving our parents napping in the den. My sisters could barely keep our mischief to themselves, proud of its cleverness and ready to give us away at any moment through a misplaced comment or unsubtle glance. I took the matter more seriously, partly because I had a key role in the plan, since I was to dash farther than the others before doubling back, and partly because I was determined to get the best of my brother for once.

Amber yipped sharply, and we took off. My brother launched himself into lead position, but I was not far behind, paws scrambling through the field's tall grass. A thick row of trees loomed before us. As we reached the edge of the woods, I channeled my fear into exhilaration and bounded forward like never before. I dived and darted over spindly roots and fallen limbs, crashing through the leafy under-growth.

I was so engrossed in my task, maintaining speed while avoiding obstacles, my nostrils overwhelmed by fresh scents, eyes adjusting to the shady forest light, that I forgot the plan! By the time I remembered that I was supposed to double back, the others were long gone. I slowed, halted, and found myself alone. All of a sudden, the woods were enormous, no longer a thrilling, linear obstacle course, but a tangled spider's web of growth and dappled light.

A glance to any side revealed a dozen paths and a hundred worthy hiding places. I could go anywhere. Two things struck me then. First, if I could go anywhere, I could also get lost, and maybe was already. Second, if I could hide, so could anything else.

Slowly circling, I trembled. Just what lived in these woods anyway? I turned to retrace my steps, but I had lost my path. What if I hadn't run in as straight a line as I had thought? Strange scents overwhelmed my nostrils, too many to filter out. If I could not lock on to my own scent and follow it to safety, all was lost. Whatever evil surely ruled these woods was soon to strike and claim me forever.

A surprise impact from the side, and I went rolling, tripping and tumbling over roots and brush, unable to regain my footing. I gasped, wanting to cry out, but the monster pounced again and seized my throat! Narrow but strong jaws gripped me. I lay frozen, flat on my back, except for my black-socked paws, which flailed in the air. This forest creature's body crushed my unprotected underbelly. I sputtered for breath. Fangs gripped my throat, but they did not tear it. I was not bleeding. No claws slashed me.

It was a fox—a female, not even an adolescent. She leaped to the side, crouching, her tail waving. She gave a few mirthful yips, oblivious to the deadly forest surrounding us, as she bounced and danced around me. I remained on my back, gobsmacked, my creamy underside exposed, legs sprawled out and kicking against the air.

"I got you!" the stranger cried, flashing a toothy grin.

"What?" I squeaked, forcing myself to roll onto my feet. "Who, I mean. Who are you?"

She stopped bouncing, and her expression fell. "I'm sorry," she said. "You're shaking. I didn't mean to scare you." She paused. "Well, I mean, I *did* mean to scare you, but not that bad."

My ears burned. I wanted to growl, to yell and tackle her to the ground in retribution. Instead, I brushed it off. "I wasn't scared," I lied, trying to keep my voice level. "Only startled for a moment, since I've never been in these woods before."

"Well, there's nothing to worry about," the young fox said. "My name's Aurora. I live close to here, and I play in these woods all the time."

"I'm Nimbus."

"Nimbus," she repeated. "I like it! Where do you live?"

"Well, to be honest," I said, "I'm not sure where it is in relation to here. The western side."

"You ran into this clearing from over there by that overgrown shrub," she said, gesturing with her muzzle. "Then you sniffed around and wandered in and out a few times."

"You were spying on me?"

"Not exactly." She paused. "You did make quite a ruckus, after all. It drew my attention."

"And you sneaked up on me!" I protested.

"I couldn't resist," she said, hopping to the side. "Come on, let me show you around!"

I don't know how long Aurora and I played after that, tumbling and chasing each other through endless hidden passages. When finally I explained that I really had to be going, Aurora said she would escort me to the edge of the woods, joking that she didn't want me to get lost again.

Soon we were engrossed in conversation. We discussed pouncing, debated which insects were tastiest, and competed for worst sibling story. She shared reports from her wide explorations with me, and I told her a ghost story that Amber had made up once. Aurora listened patiently, but I got more scared telling it than she did hearing it.

At the tale's climax, however, we both froze, our black-tipped ears pricked up. Something big had rustled the foliage nearby. Trying to keep my head still, I glanced furtively toward the sound. Nothing.

Aurora hopped up, ready to investigate. Just then a large figure burst through the foliage, barreling toward us. My mother. I had never seen her like this!

"Nimbus!" she growled, ears flat, her snarl flashing an arsenal of fangs. She trained her piercing, emerald eyes on me.

"Nimbus," she barked again, "what were you thinking?"

"I- I-," I stammered, unable to respond. Backing into Aurora, I slumped to the ground and wailed like a newborn.

My mother's expression softened. She sat and sighed. The savagery in her eyes gave way to concern. "Oh, Nimbus," she said, "I was so worried about you."

With great effort, I squeaked out an apology.

"You know you're not supposed to go off so far by yourself, especially not here where anything could have happened. There are coyotes and maybe bears. Even those human children like to play here. Can't you smell them? The older ones hunt in these woods."

My mother's disappointment stung more than her wrath. I had no excuse. Even if I could have begun to explain the trick we had been playing on my brother, that plan suddenly seemed immature and foolish. Evidently, my siblings had not run off at all. I alone had been so caught up, so consumed with trying to outdo my brother that I had ended up lost, and then I had spent the whole afternoon playing instead of thinking of my family. What defense did I have?

Aurora stepped in front of me. "Ma'am," she said, "please don't be upset with Nimbus. He was only helping me find the way out of here."

"Who are you? Where are your parents?" my mother asked, acknowledging Aurora's presence for the first time.

Aurora introduced herself and added, "My parents are at home, on the eastern side of the woods."

"By the farm?" my mother asked, scoffing. "And your parents let you wander into the woods?" I recognized the irony in the latter charge, but I kept my muzzle shut.

"Yes, ma'am. I come here by myself often, but just now Nimbus and I were trying to find the right scent trail to get back home."

"Well," said my mother, shooting me a look. "We'd better all get back home, then."

My mother and I began to walk Aurora to the eastern side of the woods. Aurora protested that she could go alone, but my mother insisted on accompanying her. The shadows, darker than before, multiplied the forest's manifold hiding places, but our afternoon of play had cured me of all fear. Myriad scents and sounds surrounded me, no longer threats but so many opportunities for adventure, and I wanted to investigate each one in turn. No spirit or creature could harm me, if only I could get back here and explore freely. Aurora and I kept quiet. My mother, likewise, was all busi-

ness, maintaining a steady trot eastward. I glanced surrep-
titiously to Aurora and caught her studying me before she
looked away.

We reached the edge of the woods. It was nearly twilight. Normally, I would have been getting ready for a night
of hunting practice, but I had stayed up all day. My exhaustion caught up with me all at once when we stopped, and
even the unfamiliar landscape before me could not hold my
interest for long. I had never seen farmland before. The
rows upon rows of perfectly linear crops were curious but
off-putting. Some other day I would have to come back here
with Aurora, if it was safe. My mother looked haggard as
well. Her fur was ruffled and her eyes somewhat glassy.

"Mom," I asked, "can I please have a moment to say
goodbye to Aurora?"

The vixen sighed. "Okay. Just a moment. Then we have
to go." She stepped into the woods.

I turned to Aurora. "Thanks," I said and then whispered,
"I can't believe you lied to my mom!"

"I didn't lie," said Aurora. "Not technically. I just em-
phasized a small part of the truth. It's true that we were
trying to find a way home. I just didn't specify that it was
for you, not me."

"Whatever you call it," I said, "it was smart." I didn't
add that I never would have had the guts to bend the truth
myself. If my mother had asked me directly, I would have
folded instantly.

"Thanks," Aurora said casually. She looked clever with
her narrow muzzle and keen golden eyes.

"So," I added, "could I see you again?"

"No problem," she replied. "I had fun. And we have to
get together again because I still need to hear the end of that
ghost story."

"I'll try to get my mom to let me visit you in the woods some time."

"Do you think she will?"

"Hard to say," I said. "I'll have to lie low for a little while."

"Well," said Aurora. "I'll be waiting around for you."

"Sounds good!" I affirmed. I wished her farewell and turned back to my impatient mother.

The two weeks that followed were torture. I forced myself to be as obedient and pleasant as possible, all the while worried that Aurora would forget me. Finally, my father reminded my mother that her children had to meet their future mates *somewhere*, and they allowed me to go back to the woods.

In reality, most of my siblings had regularly been sneaking off, not to mention chatting with every fox that crossed through our territory or skirted its borders. We were not the only maturing cubs whom nature was urging out and away from home. But for me curiosity about the wider world was nothing compared to my growing interest in that young vixen who had tackled me in the woods.

CHAPTER

4

# The Wild

I broke my promise to return to Aurora's father. For three days I remained near the pond. I had cleared out a little hole amid some brush on its southern edge. It was no den, but it was enough. The screams of highway vehicles were faint, but they occasionally troubled my sleep, sweeping like banshees across the landscape.

Jumbled memories and images penetrated my dreams. One moment Aurora was coaching me in pouncing while I studied her sharp muzzle and intense gaze instead of the footwork I was supposed to be observing. But, when I looked again, I saw only my mother's graying face as she sighed in our dark den. Sometimes, I disappeared or stretched and twisted into human form before Aurora's gaping eyes. One time I jolted awake with the taste of gunpowder in my mouth and had to lick the ice till I got rid of it.

I also indulged in some pleasant fantasies, wheeling through the seasons with Aurora at my side, first leaves, then snow, then the happy blossoms of spring floating all around us, till the sharp pain in my empty stomach would force me to shake myself and go dig up a few insects or roots.

From time to time, I thought of death. I considered throwing myself onto the highway or breaking through the ice to drown. But by the third day I knew that I would never do it. My exhausted, scrawny body was pitiable, but it lived and wanted to go on living. What is a living creature but eating, sleeping, and breathing? These things I did, despite myself. I, too, was a slave to self-preservation, afraid to die.

I couldn't stay where I was any longer. Although this was no fox's territory, scent markings indicated that coyotes roamed the land I currently occupied. They are ugly, deceitful creatures. They hunt in packs like wolves but pretend not to. In my disheveled state, I would be no match for them.

Although nature dictates that male foxes must leave home their first year, my parents' charity would probably have tolerated me for a few days in the circumstances. But I had no desire to return home a failure only to leave again soon after.

In my sober moments, I tried to convince myself that I was innocent. Rationally, I knew that Aurora's death wasn't my fault. But knowing that there was nothing I could have done only made me feel worse. How could the fact that I made no difference in whether my mate lived or died be comforting? *I'd rather feel guilty*, I thought.

Instead, I got angry. I learned then, for the first time,

that anger can be cold. Hot rage I had felt often in smaller matters: a sibling's lie, a parent's unfairness, petty injuries and failures. A growing wrath chilled my veins, and soon fire and ice vied within my breast. It was the humans who had the power. It was their gun, their dogs, their great road that had taken Aurora. An ember burned, sputtering for retribution. It seared, branding me with contempt for the human race. And yet, the frost also spread, radiating out like so many fractal shards across a freezing pond.

*What can you do?* the cold whispered. *Even if you spoiled some crops and slaughtered a few livestock, the humans would never know it was you. Fox vendettas mean nothing to them. Nothing matters anymore.* And the refrain echoed in my skull, *Nothing matters.*

This held a seed of truth. It wasn't time for revenge. With winter's arrival, farm activity would be at a minimum. Besides, going back to the farm meant running into Aurora's family, which was another hassle I wanted to avoid.

But I wouldn't give up on revenge so easily. My immediate needs were shelter and food. Once those were secured, I decided that I should study humans as much as possible. What if there were a way to get back at them after all? If not this season, then the next, or whenever I was ready. I had all the time in the world—if I could survive.

I shook myself till my head smarted. I couldn't brood around anymore. It was time to act. I would head west toward the human city. There, on the outskirts perhaps, I could establish a comfortable den and get close enough to the humans to observe them. As a bonus, it would make the winter easier. *Where there are humans, there is food.*

Having never been to the city, I didn't know how long the journey would take. I guessed it would be at least three days. From my home, I could barely see the city's lights and then only from a hilltop on a clear night. I had no sense of its true scale. Everything I knew was based on stories. The great highway penetrated straight into the city's heart. I planned to follow it. But first, I needed the nourishment and rest that only a full belly affords.

And so, I stalked a small hare, less than one year old. My prey crept through a grove of wild pear trees bordering the open, hilly space southwest of the pond. Moonlight filtered through their branching limbs. From time to time, the hare paused to nibble whatever green remained amid the fallen leaves carpeting the earth. Behind a trunk I crouched, lowering my reflective eyes in the shade. A cold northern breeze hid my scent. Another step.

The hare paused, stretching its lithe body upright till it stood on its hind legs. The creature tucked its forepaws against its creamy breast, splaying long, umber ears from side to side. I stood motionless, holding my breath. Silence. Almost imperceptibly, a chestnut eye twitched.

In that instant, I leaped, whipping around the tree trunk and hurling myself straight for my prize. I thrust my black-socked paws forward as a single point. My gaunt frame followed, flying toward my target. The hare, too, had sprung into action, bounding away. I had a slight head start, since it had dropped to the ground before pushing off with its powerful haunches.

My prey streamed through the air like a jet of water, its russet length curling and sprawling with every leap. The close confines of the grove gave my own short, bounding pounces an advantage. Even in my weak state, I gained on it.

Hot panic flooded my nostrils. I sprang after the hare as it escaped the trees and leaped for the rolling landscape beyond. No time. I enlisted the strength of every cell in my body, sprinting, throwing myself down the first large hill. In the air, I thrust my muzzle and paws forward, like an arrow, sailing above my prey and outstripping it by mere inches. The still-rising moon's silver light cast a shadowy cradle between two great hills. The hare's body thumped against the grassy earth as it landed in that dark valley.

A second later, I crashed down upon it. I had intended to trap the hare between my paws but had overshot the mark. It squirmed beneath my rib cage, and, without thinking, I thrust my muzzle back for a strike, curling my own body around to hold it in place. I seized a muscular leg in my jaws and clamped down, crushing the bone. My fangs struggled to pierce the hare's tough skin and sinewy flesh. Rapid squeals filled my ears. In ecstasy, I whipped my head back and forth, thrashing the hare's body against the cold earth until the bleating stopped.

When I saw that the hare could not run, I released my grip and studied my prize. Its quivering form lay twisted before me, the intoxicating scent of blood flooding my nostrils. I sat there, panting, ears erect. My tongue lolled from the side of my muzzle. My breath produced a gray cloud visible against the starry sky. I felt good for the first time in days, proud that I had caught my prey and ready to feast.

With relish, I tore into my meal. Hot blood stained my muzzle while I gulped down flesh and organs as quickly as my teeth could pierce them. Greedy beyond satisfaction, I licked and gnawed the loose skin and bones that remained, sucking every microbe of nourishment from my victim. When at last I felt I had exhausted the corpse, I threw my head back and yipped my triumph to the open night.

And then my own blood chilled. I inhaled sharply, skin pulling tight against my ribs. My eyes widened, and my ears shot straight up. Footfalls echoed through the hills. Brush stiff, I made a quick circle. The stench of coyote radiated through the cool air. I cursed my foolhardiness.

A figure crested the southern hill. The moon lit up the silver streaks in her tawny fur. Instinctively, I lowered my belly to the earth, hiding in the shady valley. I had heard once that coyotes were not native to this land, that they had migrated from far away and interbred with wolves in generations past. This coyote was smaller than a wolf but larger than any fox. Her yellow-green eyes glinted as she surveyed the land below.

Her eyes flashed over me, and I took a chance.

"Good evening!" I called, leaping to my feet. "I've just had a hare for supper. There's a little left if you'd like it." This was not exactly true, since I had picked over the hare's carcass, leaving only its ragged pelt and bones.

"And who," the coyote growled, "are you?" The words stretched and rolled through her gritted teeth.

My legs trembled. A moment ago, they had powered me through a series of bounding dives in pursuit of my meal, but they had become swaying reeds. I had burned too much strength. I had no reserves, only a temporary burst of adrenaline. I needed time to recover from the hunt and draw energy from my fresh meal. It was pointless to run or attack in my present state. The she-coyote, sleek and commanding in her stance, could overpower me with ease. I had to buy time.

"My name is Nimbus," I said, trying to quell the tremor in my voice. She had not broken her glare. I continued to play dumb. "Is something wrong?"

"You're the fox cub who's been freeloading in our hunting grounds the last few days, then." The she-coyote peered down at me from the hill's peak, a distance of perhaps thirty yards. From her current position, she could cut me off at any direction of escape. Even if I doubled back and climbed the hill behind me, the speed she gained from a downward rush would negate my head start. I hoped she could not see too clearly into the valley. With any luck, I smelled young and strong.

"I am a fox, as you can tell," I replied, "and I don't mean to correct you, but, even though I'm young, I'm full-grown." My voice was calmer, more casual, though it took all my effort. "Anyway, I'm terribly sorry. I didn't know I was trespassing, and I'd gladly-"

"Liar." The icy word cut me short. "You knew quite well this land belongs to us. No creature with a nose and a brain has any excuse for trespassing, much less lounging for days and taking what it pleases." The sounds built up one by one deep within her throat, bubbling over and tumbling out through a snarl.

Without thinking, I stepped back, my brush beginning to curl beneath my hind legs. I froze again. I had to retain control, to project an image of strength. My only hope was to convince my interlocutor that I could at least deal a grievous injury or two before she slew me and, in the meantime, recover enough strength to flee.

I gathered myself and stood up straight, pressing my chest forward. "Well, now," I said flatly. "There's no need to be rude. I apologize, and if you'd like me to move on, I was just about to do so. I'll be no trouble to you anymore."

The she-coyote glared down at me from her post. I took heart from the fact that she had not come any closer. This signaled that she was thinking twice about a fight. That uncertainty was all I needed to continue selling her on the idea of a peaceful retreat—only I couldn't let it look like a retreat.

"In fact," I added, scratching my ear with a hind leg, "I really *must* be going. The moon is already sinking in the sky, and I have a lot of ground to cover before daybreak."

I turned to leave. Footsteps shuffled through the grass, not on the hill, where the she-coyote still stood, but from my side. It was a male, even larger than the female and just ten yards away. Black and gray streaks ran through his tan coat. A younger female stood beside him. They were a mated pair and daughter. I pivoted, trying to keep all three in my sight.

"You were right about one thing," the she-coyote growled, descending. "You'll be no trouble to us anymore."

"Back off!" I hissed, baring my teeth. I thrust my ears back and flattened my front end nearly to the earth. My fur stiff, I swept my gaze across the three coyotes, snarling and barking.

The male faltered, stepping back. His daughter watched at his side with her hazel eyes wide. I smelled fear on her, but not much. The older pair were not afraid, but they were studying me with prudence.

"Look at that patchy coat clinging to his ribs," cried the male, stepping forward. "He's just a scrawny pup!"

"Probably the runt," scoffed his mate, approaching by a few paces. All three stood within my field of vision.

"Why not find out?" I spat, leaping forward. The daughter pressed into her father's side. I held his gaze, noticing a long-healed scar above his eye. He didn't move.

I drew a sharp breath and steeled myself. From my crouched position, I sprang in a modified pounce—the kind Aurora had taught me. Time slowed as I leaped into the air. I arched my back, uncoiling it at the peak for extra thrust.

When at last my paws collided with the cold, grassy earth, I converted my landing into an all-out sprint. I ran straight through the midst of the three coyotes. The male crooked his head, brushing past his daughter, and snapped at my right side, grazing my rusty fur. The clash of his empty jaws reverberated through the valley.

The she-coyote jumped toward me, kicking hard against the ground. Their daughter was the last to react. She fell in behind her parents as they pursued me. I bound through the large, rolling hills, stretching my legs to their limit with each stride. I could hear the coyotes lunging and snapping at my brush. No way to know how much of a head start I had.

Minutes into my sprint, loping and darting amid the hills, fatigue began to sap the power from my haunches. I couldn't keep this up. The days of fasting and troubled sleep had taken their toll. The young coyote, I was sure, could have overtaken me already. She was holding back. Whether she feared besting her parents or had some other motive, I couldn't tell. No time to dwell on it. Could I use her reluctance to my benefit? I couldn't afford to be slow-witted, and no advantage, however slim, could go to waste.

My heart thundered hard in my chest, struggling to push blood to my weary limbs. My paws landed heavier and heavier with each stride. Frustrated snarls sounded in my ears. I dared not glance back.

I could double back toward the pond. The brush and thickets surrounding it might provide cover. A hole or channel just large enough for a fox would be too narrow for a coyote. The daughter was about my size, but I could play to her hesitance and, perhaps, pit the parents against the child or at least make myself too much of a nuisance to bother with.

It was a good plan, except that I had come too far. My straining muscles told me I would falter, crumbling to the ground for one helpless instant before these wild dogs' razor teeth pierced my hide and ravaged me for sport. I would never make it to the pond.

"Now steer him where you want him to go!" the male's gruff voice called between heaving breaths.

I should have drawn hope from the fact that he had fallen back, at least several yards behind me, but his words had robbed me of that small consolation. It was a hunting lesson! The pair were teaching their daughter how to pursue and slay large game. I was only alive, only torturing myself with each aching stride, because they wanted me alive. They wanted to chase me. An efficient catch and kill would be mercy compared to what awaited me. They would catch and release me again and again, till exhaustion crippled me beyond even standing. And then the young coyote would practice slashing and tearing my flesh, repeating and refining her technique while I begged for death.

A nip at my right flank! The daughter was at my side. She struck again but fell behind, struggling to herd me south. I resisted. That open landscape would be my grave. I needed cover, obstacles, anything to obstruct my pursuers. Perhaps I could separate the pair from their daughter. If I could escape her, I could escape them. I veered north, forcing a long parabolic course. Beneath the violent panting at my backside, I heard the punctuated roar of traffic in the distance.

Straining, I wove around the base of a steep hill and ascended its far side. The frosty air stung my lungs. I heaved, my thin muscles burning as I forced my way up. The male's bark sounded in my ear. Saliva glistened, trailing from his muzzle as he ran beside me. His pale-yellow eye caught mine. The coyotes had cut the corner, running straight up the hill. The female and their daughter were cresting it before my eyes.

I dug my hind paws hard into the earth, my claws scraping through the soil. Had I reached greater speed before, the momentum would have flipped me over face first. Instead, I came to a hard stop and thrust myself into a back flip. I tumbled backward down the hill, trying in desperation to tuck in my head and my brush beneath my paws. My snout struck the ground several times. I sniffed, choking on the blood streaming from my nostrils.

When at last I halted at the hill's base, I wanted to lie there, to collapse in a bruised heap. Instead, I pulled myself up, clinging to my single chance. I forced my exhausted body to a brisk trot. I ran north, weaving till at last I emerged from the hills and reached a level plain.

"Strike his legs!" the she-coyote roared in frustration far behind me.

The young coyote bolted toward me, alone, approaching at a sharp angle from my right. She panted, her pace slower than before but still faster than my own. With every bounding stride, she overtook me a little more, but I was nearly at my goal. Before me loomed the steep embankment of the highway's southern side.

I heaved myself onto that artificial hill, snorting and sputtering. My belly thudded against the packed earth, and I scrambled, digging my claws into the soil and kicking. I climbed, struggling for vertical momentum till in the last moment I reached the top and froze, paralyzed by the great road's spell. It lay stretched out beyond measure to my left and right. A car roared past. The wind rushing in its wake struck me all at once like a wall. My brush bristled. I clung to the earth, ears aching.

Suddenly a stabbing pain seized me. I fell to the ground, yelping. The zoom of another vehicle drowned out the cry. I wrenched my head back and saw the young female digging her fangs into my hind leg. Her greedy yellow eyes met mine. She growled, and I kicked hard at her face. Jolted, she relaxed her jaw, and in that moment, I tore my leg away and heaved myself onto the highway.

I staggered, my leg torn and burning. Dragging my disabled limb across the rough, unyielding asphalt, I hobbled toward the other side. I had nearly reached the middle when the young coyote leaped onto the road behind me. She crouched, ready to tackle me, when blinding lights froze us both. A roaring car tore the space between us. My palpitating heart nearly burst, and I reeled, fur on end, bracing for the heavy gust that followed.

To make matters worse, in that same instant the two older coyotes crested the embankment to my left. They barked something to their daughter, but my ears were ringing, and I could not discern the words. They paced along the road's shoulder as I pressed on, dragging my crippled body toward the other side.

Delay meant death. The road tempted me to pause, to peer down its impossible length, searching along that manmade corridor. But that moment's study, that brief, curious glance, is when danger strikes. The only way to escape death was to ignore it.

The young coyote circled around to my front, standing fierce and proud against the black sky. She growled, menacing revenge. This was madness. Each second on the road betokened death for us both. From the roadside, her parents snarled unintelligible instructions. If she understood, she didn't heed them. I met her eyes and saw in them that she would never quit. She would follow me to the end, desperate to prove herself.

A car zoomed behind us, a screaming specter drowning out all other sounds. I ran. I ran through the pain in my bleeding leg, not to the other side but straight down the middle of the road, headlong into the lights.

The young coyote faltered. Her eyes widened. She took a single step, turned back and then shook herself. I could no longer see her, still running as best I could along the great highway. I reeled as a car rushed past in the opposite direction. From the shoulder, the pair gasped and called out.

Their progeny nipped at my brush. Her jaws snapped shut, empty. Again. Again, and this time she caught hold of the creamy tip of my tail. I yipped, falling to the pavement. Another vehicle sped toward us. Blades of light cut through the night's darkness. A horn blared. I shut my eyes, expecting the end.

The car swerved. Its brakes screeched, and the smell of hot rubber stung my nostrils. A panicked scream and weighty thud. I cowered, helpless like a cub, and balked when I realized that I was alive and that I was free. I glanced at the vehicle, stationary on the shoulder. It had struck the two coyotes, throwing their bodies down the southern embankment.

The daughter ran, not directly to her parents but away from the road, circling and skulking from a distance. A man stepped from the car, slamming the door and shouting. Even with adrenaline flooding my body, his act of exiting the car confused me. I had never seen a human get in or out of a vehicle before. It was a human mystery, but I had no time to puzzle over it.

Coming to my senses, I limped from the roadway and descended the northern embankment, panting. I had to get as far as possible and hope that the daughter didn't pursue me.

Dawn was not far off by the time I collapsed in a thicket to inspect my hind leg. The bleeding had stopped. I licked the wound gingerly. It was painful but not deep. No broken bones. As the calm, cold day began I slept in safety.

CHAPTER

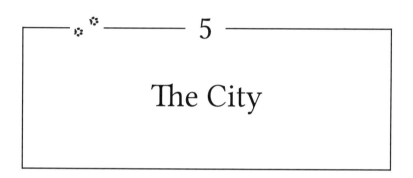

5

# The City

I rested a full day. My body begged for more, but I was not about to dally again in strange territory, not till I reached the city. Besides, to eat I had to hunt. To hunt I had to move. Edible plants and insects dwindled. Cold winds raked spindly fingers through the landscape, snatching up small game and leaving hunger in their wake. The full scarcity of winter was on its way.

Foxes are bonded to the seasons. Vixens come into estrus once a year in early winter. Spring smiles on the birth of cubs, who mature through the hot summer and prepare for their own dispersal and pairing up in the fall. The ever-turning cycle bears us with it, each fox recapitulating the annual pattern of birth and death.

This year I would have no mate, no cubs. I felt at the moment that I would never take a mate, would never want a vixen other than Aurora, and I resented a tickling, haunting thought that someday I might wish otherwise.

To love is to bind oneself, to promise beyond one's means. I did not know who I would be in a year or two years or three, but I knew who I was, or at least who I was not. I was not like those vagrants, those bachelors who never settle but seduce one vixen after another only to abandon them. I was a fox of integrity.

But the practical part of my mind—usually Aurora's strength more than my own—nagged me, telling me I had never said my vows. I had turned those promises over in my mind many nights in preparation for our wedding. I would have sworn loyalty, protection, honor, and all the needed virtues. I would have spoken those solemn words and meant them, but the chance had been stolen from me. Aurora was gone and with her any claim she had on me. Technically, I was free to seek another vixen. My stomach turned, and I pushed the traitorous thought from my mind. I wanted no one else.

No matter. There was no time. The wind blew colder each passing day. The last lingering leaves tumbled from their perches. My only goal was the city.

The journey took nearly a week. When I arrived at the first suburbs, my hind leg was still sore but mending. The skin had scabbed. No signs of infection, though I struggled to see the wound through my thickening coat.

At first, I mistook the suburbs for the city itself. The end-less structures, repeating along a labyrinthine web of roads fascinated me. I had never suspected that roads would intersect each other so much. I came to realize that the great highway was an exception, not the norm. My childhood glimpses of the city's silhouette had not prepared me for the sprawling maze of buildings bubbling out across the landscape from every side. One could wander among them and still look up with widened eyes to even further heights.

I skulked at a distance from the human dwellings for two more days before approaching. The whole complex was an indecipherable and contradictory amalgam of scents. Raccoons, deer, and foxes permeated the landscape. I even detected the unwelcome odor of coyotes, though as far as I could tell they never entered into the suburban area itself but only patrolled its edges. Most of all, the air was thick with dogs, not wild dogs but those the humans keep as pets. Given the crisscrossing, confused jumble of scent-markings, I marveled that continuous war did not engulf the whole territory. Somehow, natural enemies coexisted.

The humans, too, held me spellbound. I took great care to hide from them. The bushes were bare, so I had taken to sleeping each day under a porch on the remotest outskirts of the suburbs. Many such locations had been claimed by other animals. The family that owned this house had no dogs, nor did their immediate neighbors. Even with this element of safety, I woke in near panic several times the first week or two in my new residence.

From that vantage, I tracked the humans. Scents drifted through the lattice. If I pressed against it, I could see out a little. I grew to trust the environment enough to sleep through the day, but I still liked to spend some time awake before the twilight for my observations.

In addition to their garish, piebald features, the humans had unnatural habits. I had already known, of course, that they walk on two legs, slowly, and that they drape themselves in strange, woven fibers. I learned that wherever there was more than one there was bound to be chatter. I concluded that they had a language and could understand one another. Many times I watched them enter and exit vehicles, as I had seen when the coyotes were struck. They had a strange way of insulating themselves from nature. Their world was armored by concrete and metal. The suburbs were a protective shell encrusting them like some giant tortoise.

As far as I could tell two humans lived above me, a male and a female. Their movements were slow and limited. They emerged from the house at the same times each day. In the morning, the man walked down to the street and back for unknown reasons. In the afternoon, the woman walked around the neighborhood for approximately twenty minutes. The couple did not race down the sidewalks each day or chase one another like the children I had seen playing in the neighborhood. I gathered that they were older, but I had difficulty telling human ages. I varied the times I stayed awake for observation till I was certain of their daily routine.

I took care not to grow sloppy. This demanded steely focus, since the human world enjoyed a veneer of innocence. Some predators camouflage themselves or mimic weaker prey to lure in careless victims. Even a fox might play dead in hope of pouncing on a crow or raven come to scavenge. Humans were just as deceptive but more lethal.

"A cautious fox beats a clever fox," I reminded myself more than once on my daily rounds.

Even the elderly couple was not harmless. All humans were killers. That much I had known before. I had tried to warn Aurora! But my recent investigations had also corrected a false impression. Previously, I had considered human beings to be far unlike normal animals and, therefore, especially dangerous. The reality was far worse. Human beings had no conspiracy against other creatures. They only sought their own interests, like any of us. The difference was their unique power, as the deformed and twisted suburban landscape bore witness. Predators stalked and killed prey and were, therefore, deadly, but man was worse. Men didn't kill other animals because they thought of them as prey but because they did not think of them at all. Humanity had no prey, only casualties.

Despite the progress of my study, humans remained a paradox. I wanted to understand their aims, their ambitions. They seemed to operate within a structure of their own. Other species were born into a system, a web of instincts and customs that sometimes supported and sometimes impeded their interests. A low-ranking wolf might forgo mating for the good of his pack, or a trapped fox might sacrifice a limb to bring food to his cubs when, left to himself, he would rather die than be crippled. I could not decide whether humans were beholden to a system, a cycle of nature, like other creatures, or had established their own. They appeared to live in tension and contradiction.

Each night or day, depending on how I had arranged my patrol, I returned to the safety of the porch to devour whatever morsel I had picked up and to plan and rest before my next excursion. Sometimes I went out several times in a day, sleeping for a few hours between outings. Like many predators, I retained the ability to wake myself at set intervals.

Aurora still graced my dreams—or haunted them. Her ghost did not steal my rest as it had weeks before. Instead, I began to cherish a kind of warm familiarity with her memory. The dreams were thick, every image and scent—a golden-eyed glance or pungent hot-summer moss—leaving a syrupy impression as it dripped through my imagination. But I always awoke alone beneath the porch in cold darkness.

Waking one day in late afternoon, I shook my head and tried to clear my mind of those residual phantasms. My senses felt dull, plugged up. I blamed it on the shortening days and my erratic sleep schedule. Already, shadows stretched long and slender across the yard as the sun sank below the horizon. Powdery flakes were falling, silent and light. The thinnest dusty layer covered the earth.

I went out to hunt. Standard fare, vermin like mice and rats, inhabited the neighborhood, though they were harder and harder to find each day. Squirrels were too much work for the present, spending most of their time nested high in the trees dotting the suburban landscape. The earth was cold, so digging for earthworms or larvae was more tedious than ever. Once, I had come across a toppled garbage can behind a nearby house and feasted so much that I couldn't complete my patrol. Ever since, I eyed the cans whenever I went out at night, hoping to find something tasty before the raccoons got to them. I had to be careful because the humans tended the cans with regularity, filling them, emptying them, and arranging them according to some mysterious rule

On that particular evening, despite feeling unusually tired, I decided it was time to explore the city proper. I knew the suburban climate well enough to avoid its dangers. The cats were mostly an annoyance, not a threat, and the humans restricted the dogs by tethers, fences, and whatever inscrutable threat kept them obedient. Once I realized how powerless most dogs were to chase me past the boundaries their human masters had defined, I trotted where I wished.

The coyotes who lived near the suburbs, as I said, never came far into human territory. As for other foxes, although I scented them from time to time, I had yet to meet one in person. I inferred that the strange peace among enemies that reigned here meant no territorial disputes. Everyone shared the area, as if the artificial human environment trumped our natural code of behavior. For that reason, I was considering a move into the deeper city where I hoped to survive entirely by foraging. It almost amused me to think how in some ironic way I was living out Aurora's plan.

I loped along the snowy grass parallel to a main road. Streetlights played with my night vision—one of the annoyances of city life—and blocked out the stars. I held my brush, fully thickened for the winter, stiff behind me to avoid dragging in the dusty snow. I was farther and deeper into the city than I had ever been. Actually, the suburbs still surrounded me, their repeating cul-de-sacs more numerous than I had imagined. Hunger gnawed my belly. At times on my excursions, I would find some dead creature in the road and enjoy a few effortless bites of meat, but the present night had brought no such luck.

With every stride, I inhaled the brisk air, my own breath visible in the bright lights. The buildings grew tighter, the vehicles more frequent, as I trotted toward the city's heart. Soon massive structures loomed over me, eclipsing the black sky. Parked cars lined the narrow streets. Alleys jutted out from every side. My heart pounded.

I would have turned back, returning to the familiar safety of the suburbs, if not for the fog of aromas that enveloped me. The lots and alleyways were thick with rubbish. Every manner of human refuse and more food than I could imagine, including meat, beckoned me. I stopped and raised my nostrils to the air, inhaling deeply and letting my brain sort through the array of delicious smells.

Warmth embraced me. Saliva rolled down my muzzle. I savored the intoxication. All around me falling snow glinted in the streetlights before hitting the pavement. Black slush clogged the gutters. Cars passed, their headlights sweeping across the many-windowed buildings, but I was too dizzy to be afraid.

"What the hell are you doing?" came a coarse bark not three feet away.

I jumped, scattering snow dust from my fur. Against the brick wall beside me sat a fox, clearly amused. He looked older, but his striking argent coloration was not due to age. Shooting streaks of dark ash flecked his sparkling gray coat. His ears and socks were deep black as was his thick brush, except for its milk-white tip, which seemed all the brighter by comparison. Rolls of fat hung loosely beneath his fur.

"I'm new here," I said, heart pounding.

"Even the infant rats can see that," howled the silver fox, "and they're blind!"

My ears burned. I scowled at the stranger, nearly snarling. "Well," I said, reminding myself that I didn't want to risk a needless fight, "there's no call for sneaking up on someone who's just sorting out the area."

"I'd hardly call it 'sneaking up,'" he replied. "You were frozen there for at least five minutes. The way your tongue was hanging out, I thought maybe you had died standing up!"

A car shot past us, and I realized for the first time how exposed I was. I took a few uneasy steps away from the road and into the shadows, giving the other fox a wide berth.

"You were watching me?" I asked.

"Call it what you want. I like to keep track of new foxes in the city."

"Is this your territory?"

"In a way. We don't keep strict lines here, but we try to keep out of each other's fur."

"Isn't that the same thing?"

"It's more of an informal arrangement." He scratched behind his ear with a hind paw. I noticed that one of his claws was badly broken. If it hurt, he ignored it.

"I see," I replied flatly.

"No need to be so serious," the silver fox scoffed. "You're obviously from the country. We city animals know how to have fun, you know? You can forget all the formality of life in the wild. I remember it, too. Believe me, once you realize you don't need all that rigmarole, all that rigidity, you'll have fun, too."

"Fun?" I asked.

"Fun," repeated the older fox with mock pedantry. "Don't worry, you'll learn the definition—if you study hard."

I opened my muzzle but hesitated. My head spun. Here we were in the city proper. Concrete, steel, and glass monoliths towered on every side. Myriad dangers, human dangers no other animal could grasp, lurked in each artificial crevice. Yet, this strangely colored old fox, who also happened to be the fattest I had ever seen, was lecturing me on fun. I couldn't decide whether he was angry or just careless. Was he perhaps a victim of that terrible foaming disease my mother had warned me about, which robs creatures of their sanity and, in the end, of all bodily control? I took a step back.

"Oh, lighten up!" The fox threw his head back and roared with reckless mirth, like a wolf baying at the moon.

I watched the spectacle in silence. "So, what's your name, kid?"

"Uh, Nimbus," I said.

"You don't sound like you're sure of that," he quipped.

My blood ran hotter. "What's *your* name?" I snapped.

"Silver," he said. "Would you believe it? My parents were pretty damn creative, huh?"

Silver seemed oblivious to my frustration. Or else, he seemed to enjoy it as much as he enjoyed my bafflement. I decided that the usual etiquette was unnecessary, since it would be impossible to offend him. "What kind of fox are you?"

"A successful one!" he cackled.

"No, I mean I've never seen a fox with your colors before."

"I know what you meant," he chided. "It's a joke! Anyway, I'm just a fox—a particularly fine specimen to be sure—but just a fox. My father looked like me, and my mother, well, she looked like you." He roared again at his own joke. "Anyway," he said, calming down, "you should have seen my litter mates. You've got me, silver, two reds, and one sort of mix. We call that a 'cross fox,' but it doesn't happen too often. There must have been something in the water when my mother was pregnant." Silver trained his jasper eyes directly on me. They glowed like fireflies from out of his black-masked face. "You've really not been out much, have you? Not even full-grown, so this is your first winter, I'll bet?"

There was no point denying it. "So what?" I grumbled.

Silver stepped toward me and ran his dark muzzle all around my body, sniffing. Despite the abuse, I held my stance, refusing to let my shoulders fall or my brush curl beneath my legs.

"Are you well?" he asked at last. "Something about your scent is off. What brings you here? You're obviously unattached. Looking to live it up as a bachelor?"

The question and its tone turned my stomach sour. The heat welling within me overtook me. "How dare you!" I hissed then barked in anger and dashed away.

I felt dizzy but ran through it. I had to get away from this vulgar creature. I couldn't stand him a second longer. The falling snow became a haze around me, glittering in the streetlights and clouding my sight of the buildings. A car flew past, its horn blaring. A cold rush of air trailed in its wake. I turned to my right, trying to find my way off the street. Soon I was running along the sidewalk, row after row of dark, looming buildings to my right, the street with occasional passing cars to my left.

"Hey, c'mon!" Silver called, running after me.

I changed course, diving down an alleyway. Snow-covered debris littered the path. Heaving, Silver still pursued me. I weaved around piled bags of garbage and metal bins until a chain-link fence blocked my way. I sniffed at its base, looking for a hole or a way to tunnel under it.

"What's your problem?" Silver gasped, sliding to a halt behind me. He panted for a few moments while I continued to search the fence. No luck. "You are unattached, right? You smell single, anyway. No need to be upset about it."

I whirled around, baring my teeth. "She died, all right? She was shot, and she bled, and she ran, and she fell through the ice and died. I'm not single by choice, and I'm not like you. I'm certainly not looking to 'live it up.' Whatever that means."

"Fine, fine," Silver panted. "I didn't know."

"No," I growled, eyes narrowing, "you *didn't* know. And you didn't ask. And I didn't plan on sharing that with a stranger tonight."

"Look, I'm sorry. Okay? But you don't know me, either. And you made assumptions just like I did." He paused. "She was young, like you?"

"Too young." I gasped. My veins still burned. Boiling blood clouded my brain more and more each second, but something else welled within me. A pressure, rising, pulsing and pushing its way through my breast. I wanted to scream, to wail before I burst. I opened my muzzle again, hoping for release, but nothing came. The pain still strained against my ribs. My legs turned to straw, and I collapsed on the snow. I moaned and sobbed till my throat was on the verge of bleeding, and then I lay mute, shuddering in the street.

Throughout my display, Silver paced around me. I was aware of him and even detected concern when he called my name, but a great chasm divided us. I couldn't respond even when I wanted to. Time slowed as well, and every tremor pulsed throughout my frame like ripples disturbing an otherwise stagnant pond.

When finally my weary body gave in, and I lay a crumbled, gasping heap in the dirty snow, Silver pressed his muzzle repeatedly into my shoulder. "Nimbus! Nimbus! You're awake? Can you understand me?"

From somewhere far off, his barking reached my ears and found its way to my brain. "I- I'm okay," I squeaked.

"You're sure as hell not okay. You had a seizure... or something. To be quite honest with you, I've never seen anything like it. Like death throes, except you haven't died yet."

"I'm thirsty," I whispered. My lungs and throat burned like I had never felt, but from deeper within I felt an unwonted peace, like I had vomited up at last whatever poison had been eating away my bowels, or at least enough to gain a temporary respite.

"Thirsty? Damn, kid! I thought you were dying. Don't forget you're lying pretty much in the open, too. There's cars coming past this alley, and I guarantee other animals have heard you. You're lucky I'm here."

"I need some water." My head was beginning to clear, but not much. Rolling onto my belly, I lapped at the nearby slush. It felt cold on my tongue and made me realize how warm I actually was.

"I think you've got a fever," said Silver.

*Fever.* The word echoed in my head. It sounded strange, made-up. Had I heard it before? What did it mean? "I've got a fever," I parroted.

Silver pressed his snout to my forehead. His wet nose felt good against my skin. "Yep. Definitely," he affirmed.

"Am I dying?" I asked, raising my head slightly. Even with all my strength, I wavered, struggling to keep my neck erect.

"Maybe." He towered over me, sniffing. His heavy frame bulged in every direction. Then, Silver lowered his head so that his jasper eyes peered directly into mine. "Listen, friend. Normally I wouldn't take in another fox, especially a sick one, but something tells me you'll live. You're probably just adjusting to the city food. Believe me, I thought death was certain after a few weeks of eating garbage. In fact, I begged for it. But once you power through that phase, it's a universe of delights. A real smorgasbord of comfort foods. More about that later. For now, let's get you someplace dry and let you sleep this off."

"Okay," I croaked. Part of me wanted to fight him, but in all truth, I felt as weak as a newborn. Fear overtook anger, and as much as I found the idea of going with Silver repulsive, it was preferable to dying alone in the alley.

"All right, then, let's get you up. My place is a little bit of a hike from here, but we'll take it slow if you need."

He nosed me in the side, and I moaned, forcing myself onto trembling paws. I stood for a moment and then collapsed in a heap.

"Get up!" Silver barked.

"I can't," I groaned.

"Look," he said, "if you can't get up, then I can't help you. You're going to lie here in the mud in agony and maybe die. Is that what you want?"

I hesitated, shaking, working up the strength to try again. Silver turned and began to walk away. When he was halfway down the alleyway, almost out of my sight, I barked, begging him to wait. Somehow, I pushed myself into a standing position and staggered to him. My movements were painfully slow but consistent. Every bone felt brittle like it was on the verge of breaking. Every muscle ached, tight and ready to seize up at any moment. Yet, I managed to reach Silver, who pressed himself against my side, urging me onward.

I don't recall how we made it to Silver's den. When each step is like a thousand, a thousand steps are more than the senses or the mind can reckon. Somehow we arrived at an abandoned building, its windows shattered and entrance barred. Silver coaxed me through a winding back entrance till all at once I realized we were inside and even underground. There, in the basement of that great structure, beneath an old wooden desk and a few broken chairs, I collapsed.

CHAPTER

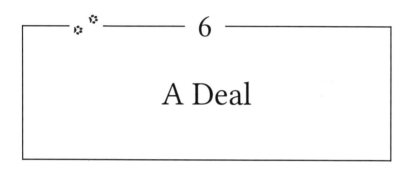

6

A Deal

For several days Silver brought me food, not garbage but rats and smaller vermin. The fresh meat did me good. A few times he tried to bring me mouthfuls of snow, but he moved too slowly and it always melted, leaving a trail of drips up and down the stairs. So, when I got thirsty, I had to pull myself up and slink outside.

Silver's den was the basement of an abandoned building. It was totally underground, accessible by a back staircase leading to an alley. Various furniture littered the room, and an old rug covered a portion of the cold tile floor. The space was dim. Somehow it felt like the human version of a traditional fox den.

In that dry, quiet shelter, my blood cooled and my

strength began to return. When I was healthy enough to go out looking for food on my own, I thanked Silver for his hospitality and informed him that I would soon be ready to leave.

"You don't have to go necessarily," he said.

"What do you mean?" I asked. "This is your home."

"I know it's unusual," said the older fox. "We've been raised to be territorial from our birth. But remember that we're not in the wild. We're in the city, and boundaries don't work the same here."

"Well, you may be right about that," I answered. "You've saved my life, and for that I'm in your debt, but I can't possibly impose on you anymore."

"You wouldn't be imposing on me. Why do you think I saved you? Just out of kindness? No, I've got a business proposition for you."

"Business?"

"Yep." Silver's eyes flashed in that dark basement corner. "Nimbus, let me ask you why you came to the city in the first place."

"I need to understand humans better," I said. "And I figured this would at least be a good place to pass the winter. Although, I didn't count on the food not agreeing with me."

"I told you that your body will adapt. It is already. You're building up an immunity as we speak. But listen to what you said. You said you 'need' to understand humans. That's not just some oddball hobby for you, is it? Why did you *really* come to the city?"

His intensity and the fact that he had probably saved my life made me feel I owed him an explanation whether I wanted to give one or not. "Well," I said, "the night I met you, I told you how my mate died. A man shot her. And, well, I guess I want to get back at him." I looked down, embarrassed to say it out loud. Silver already thought of me as a cub, naive and overly romantic.

"That's what I suspected," he said. "No need to be sensitive about it. Makes perfect sense. And you're in luck. I've lived in this city for four years. I can teach you all about the ways of humanity."

"What's your proposal, then?" I asked, glad that the older fox hadn't laughed at me.

"I'm looking for a protégé."

"A protégé?"

"Of course. Someone to inherit all my acquired skills. I'm not going to live forever, and I'd hate for my life's work to go to waste. Plus, there are some tasks for which I need a partner, a young and agile one like yourself."

"You haven't exactly seen me at my best," I said, "so, I'm flattered, I guess. But, what do you have in mind?"

"Don't sell yourself short. You've got potential. You're getting stronger by the day, and pretty soon you'll be back to normal. You said it yourself. Anyway, I told you there's more food in this city than you can even imagine. That's true. You get used to the garbage so that it doesn't bother you after a while—doesn't make you sick, I mean. At least, not too often. Trouble is that when you get used to eating trash, it's easy to get tired of eating trash. You're constantly surrounded by the smell of better meals, human meals, that you can never quite get to."

Silver had a dreamy look in his eye. I pretended not to notice that he had begun to salivate. "I know what you mean," I said.

"You have no idea," he retorted. "You lived where? Out in the suburbs? I don't suppose you've run into one of their food carts, then."

"No," I said. "I mean, I don't think so."

"You would know if you had. Keep heading into the city center and you will. Sure, some of them close up during the winter, but not all. I know a place where there are dozens of them within a few blocks all year long, rain or shine. You know what a food cart is?"

"No," I admitted sheepishly, "I guess I don't."

"It's just what it sounds like. It's a cache of hot food that humans move around inside a specially made contraption. There are even food *trucks*, if you can believe it. They set up in a certain place each day, and then other humans flock around and come away with the most enchanting meals, like hot dogs, or pretzels, or falafels, or pizza." Silver licked the excess saliva from his lips. "A mouthful of garbage can't satisfy once you've had a feast like that."

"Have you ever had them?" I asked, trying to imagine what "hot dogs" might be. Did humans eat their pets after all?

"From time to time," Silver said. "I've managed to steal a morsel off a park bench here or there. On a few blessed occasions I got the whole thing. I'm talking fatty meat dripping with cheese and grease."

"Wow." My own mouth began to water.

"That's not the half of it," he said. "Once in a while the humans will even give you a scrap or two voluntarily."

"They just give it to you?" I balked. "Why would they do such a thing?"

"Nimbus, this is why you need me to teach you about human beings. They're not like you and me. We'll watch a squirrel or a pigeon before we pounce on it. What other concern do we have with those creatures? But human beings are different. A good number of them just like to watch things, especially living things. They'll feed us just to get a look at us." Silver leaned in close as if confiding a secret.

"But don't let that veneer of benevolence fool you. They'll feed you to keep you around, but they'll lock you up or shoot you just as quick. They've even got a place on the far side of town, on the outskirts, where they keep all different kinds of animals in pens and cages on display all year long. Most of those poor creatures end up crazy. You can imagine the noise and the choking scents of predators and prey all mixed up together while those homely bipeds gawk at you day after day."

"What kind of place is that?" I asked, mouth suddenly dry again.

"They call it an 'animal park.'"

"The same park where they feed you off the bench?" I asked.

"Kid, you've got a lot to learn!" Silver chided. "So, here's my deal. You live here with me, and I train you. I teach you everything I know about humanity—things I've learned over *four years* with lots of danger, lots of trial and error, mind you."

"And in turn?" I asked.

"In turn, you work with me on select missions. I've got an idea for how to hit the carts directly. If you and I can pull it off, we'll have more food than we know what to do with."

I pondered the old fox's offer. I had to admit, his impassioned descriptions had my stomach growling. Even better, they belied how extensive his knowledge of the city and of human beings really was. Learning so much on my own would be a risky task. At least if I teamed up with Silver, I would have some help.

"These food carts mean so much to you?" I asked, still skeptical. "Are they really worth it?"

"Oh, they're worth it! So what do you say? Don't you trust me after I nursed you back to health and everything?"

That was true. He *had* kept me alive in my illness, even at an inconvenience to himself.

"No, no." I shook my head. "I didn't mean it like that. I'm just trying to understand. I mean, if you're talking about stealing directly from a crowd of humans, then I guess my point is, why take the risk when there's plenty of easy pickings all around us?"

"You're right," he replied. "You *don't* understand. The stuff I'm talking about won't just keep you alive. It's *good*. It's so good. Once you try it, you'll know. At least give me that, at least come with me and try a scrap or two. You said yourself that you owe me."

I thought for a moment. "I'll tell you what. Why don't you take me to the city center and show me what you're talking about. Let me get a sense of the situation, taste the food, and see how dangerous it all is. We can make it a sample lesson, if you like."

"Sounds like a good deal for you," he spat.

"Yes," I admitted, "it is. But I'm also taking a risk in going deeper into the city. Plus, I'm trusting you. And, it's not like it's a bad deal for you. You get to convince me fully, on site, win me over for the long term. You don't want an unwilling protégé, after all, or an ignorant one. This way, we can both discuss our agreement from a position of knowledge."

Silver grumbled but accepted my terms. He didn't have much choice. Frankly, neither did I. Whether Silver realized that or not, I didn't know. He was older and in worse shape than I was, at least since I had nearly recovered my full strength, but he was also moody and clever in ways I didn't fully grasp. I decided to stay on his good side.

Two days later Silver agreed that I was healthy enough for the trip. We rose in the late afternoon, and he led me out through the winding exit of our building, up the cold concrete steps, and into the side street that connected to the nearest major intersection. I didn't like going out in the daylight—even the fading daylight of early winter—but Silver insisted it was necessary. The whole point was to get to the city center while the humans were there with their carts.

We slinked single file down the sidewalk, hugging the building as closely as possible. No snow for a few days, so the path was clear. I sniffed the frigid air compulsively, searching for any possible danger.

"Cut that out!" whispered Silver. "What do you expect to smell, anyway? A bear? A mountain lion? You've got to apply your reason more than your instincts here. If you react like you would in the wild, it might get you killed. This is a different world. You have to adapt."

"Sorry," I replied. "Force of habit."

When we arrived at the intersection, Silver halted and then wriggled beneath a large metal waste bin. I crept up behind him and crawled underneath so that we lay side by side in the darkness. From this vantage point, human activity overwhelmed my senses. Cars crowded the streets in all directions. Clouds of choking exhaust hung in the air. Men and women as well as children hurried down the sidewalks. Their steps echoed, their shoes scraped across the pavement, and their chattering, noisy voices filled my ears. My whole body screamed at me to bolt, to run down the nearest side street or alley to safety. I resisted, sure that Silver could hear my heart pounding. He looked undisturbed, patiently surveying the scene before us.

"Look for the patterns," he whispered. "Notice how each

individual has his own trajectory."

"There's so many," I marveled. "It's like a tangled nest or a spider's web."

"You've seen humans before. This is just more of them at once, but it's the same basic idea. Each follows his own course."

"But those courses overlap like crazy!"

Silver grunted. "You have to *look*. Listen to what I'm telling you."

"So what do I look for?"

"See that man reading the newspaper?"

"Newspaper?"

Silver rolled his eyes. "It's a large, folded piece of paper with ink smeared on every side. You find scraps of them in the street all the time. Anyway, see how he's standing right on the corner, right across a good path to the far side?"

"Yes."

"Everyone else is moving in waves across that path, in one direction or the other. He's the only one who's really blocking it."

"Okay," I muttered, doubting the relevance of that information.

"But the thing is that he's reading the paper. He's not guarding the path we picked out. He has no idea we're even here. We could probably walk right in front of him, and he wouldn't even notice us. Or, if he did, he wouldn't have time to do a thing about it. And that's just what we're going to do."

Whatever the process of "reading" was, it absorbed the man's attention. His eyes were stuck fast to the large paper in his hands. I began to grasp Silver's point. "We're going to dash right in front of him?"

"Exactly. We're going to walk briskly, to be sure, but the main point is that we're going to cut straight through all the cross traffic. Yes, we'll probably get noticed, but not by as many as you think. Humans are not known for their keen senses. You'd be surprised what they overlook."

Before I could respond, Silver pushed himself out from under the waste unit and trotted headfirst into the intersection. Instinctively, I pulled myself back, deeper into the darkness, ears flat and head down. I held the position for a moment, then gulped and sprang out after him. The criss-cross traffic of humans and their vehicles made my legs feel thin, like tall grass in a strong wind, but I forced myself to concentrate on Silver's dark brush. He was not far ahead, moving steadily and about to pass by a large wooden stand where dozens of the so-called newspapers hung from the walls.

We hugged the side of the stand, hesitated a moment, and then ran diagonally across the intersection. The din of cars passing every which way stung my ears, but I trained my eyes firmly on Silver and followed him through to the other side. In a moment, it was over and we were huddled safely in the long shadow of an alleyway away from the street.

"How? How did you manage that?" I panted, not from exertion but from shock.

"I told you," Silver chirped, more gleefully than I thought possible for him. "We ran right through the worst of it, kept a straight path, and had no trouble."

"Didn't they notice us?" I balked. "I mean, I know human beings are quite disabled in their sense of smell—I almost pity them, with those ugly, smashed faces of theirs—but are they near-blind as well?"

"Like I said, a few noticed us, no doubt, but at most they

stared, murmured, and nothing more. After a while, you'll be able to pick out their reactions. It's kind of fun. You can even play with them if you like. For now, though, you'd better just follow me. That's what you need to do till we get to the city center."

"How far is it?"

"About ten blocks. You probably don't have a concept of city distance yet, so it will be good for you to experience this. I've even got a little hideaway halfway in case we need to bolt for cover."

"That's smart," I said.

"I've got hiding places throughout this part of the city. Of course, from time to time they need to be defended from intruders, you know, a raccoon or another fox looking to squat on my property. But it's worth it to have them in an emergency."

"I thought you said territory wasn't an issue here."

"That's right. *Territory* isn't an issue. Everything is too packed together to worry about that nonsense. But living spaces and hideaways are another matter. We need those places to be available in case of emergency. Imagine fleeing through the streets with an irate human or two on your tail and there's a nest of opossums in your hiding place! Well, that'd probably be it for you."

I nodded, trying to picture the scenario. Silver took a few minutes to explain the rest of our itinerary. The hard part, crossing the busy intersection, was over. All we had to do was stay close to the buildings, slinking through the shadows as much as possible, and we would arrive at the park at the city's heart. I felt a nervous wave of vigor in my limbs when I imagined what the park might look like and thought of the food carts waiting there. I was ready.

Following Silver through the city was a surreal experience. Time slowed, and each block seemed an exact replica of the one before. The never-ending smell and sound of cars in the street, the towering metal and glass buildings on every side, and dirty sidewalks underfoot, all repeating over and over again, disoriented me. At one point, Silver directed my attention to a side alley, indicating one of his nearby hiding places. I wondered how he could gauge how far we had come. By the time we halted, once again ducking underneath a large metal trash bin, the landscape had finally changed.

Before me stretched what seemed like wilderness, though not as I knew it. There were flat plains of grass, but paved walkways cut through them at harsh angles. There were ponds and streams, but they coursed with unnatural force even when they should have been long frozen. This was the park.

"It's like they've caged up the whole world," I said, nearly breathless with wonder.

"Indeed," replied Silver dryly.

Just then I smelled the first cart. It was parked along one of the walkways some thirty yards from us. I understood Silver's obsession instantly. The aroma of rich, fatty meat—pounds and pounds of it—saturated the air. I could see the steam rising and almost feel the heat radiating from the enclosure storing it. Alone or in pairs, humans approached the cart, always leaving with some paper-wrapped delight in hand. Saliva poured from my muzzle, pooling onto the cold concrete below.

"I've got to have some," I whispered, licking my lips.

"Now you see," replied Silver. "We have to keep a clear mind, or the whole thing will be spoiled. We have to be cold, insensible now when we execute our plan. Later, *later* we will enjoy the fruits of our efforts." He almost purred when he said it.

"Right," I answered, trying to focus, "just tell me what to do."

"Remember, we're going for a sample this time. So, what I'll do is trot across the path and create a diversion. You see that bench with the man and woman on it? I want you to sneak around behind it and grab what you can." He stuck his muzzle out into the open air and sniffed loudly. "They've got two cartons at least—hamburgers I think."

"Where should we meet afterward?"

Silver flashed me a broad grin. "Now you're getting it! Where do *you* think we should meet up after the grab?"

I studied the landscape carefully. Our current hiding place seemed like a good candidate, except that it would be obvious to the humans if we entered from the opposite side. The scattered trees didn't provide enough cover, nor did any of the stones or reeds near the small pond.

"I don't know," I admitted. "There doesn't seem to be a good place in sight."

"Right again," he said approvingly. "That was a trick question. There is nowhere good around here. That's the thing. Once we spring out of hiding. Rather, once *I* spring out of hiding, we'll never escape the humans' attention. The only way out is to flee somewhere else. We outrun these bipeds easily, so we have to play to our strengths."

"What if we double back and meet at your nearest hiding place?"

"Just what I was thinking. Do you remember where it is?"

"I think so," I began. "It's down that alley three—no four—blocks back from where we came. Then..." I faltered, unable to recall the directions clearly.

"Once we're in the alley, I'll show you," he said. "Are you ready? I'll create a diversion. You grab from the bench."

I nodded. In a flash, it was happening. Silver bounded toward the park, leap after leap. His heavy frame shook with each footfall. I found myself, in turn, following a long arc around the bench so that I would appear behind it at the proper time. In front of the humans, Silver's personality changed from night to day. He pranced and frolicked like a cub, hamming it up and drawing so many laughs and gesticulations from the man and woman on the bench that a dozen foxes could have walked up behind them unnoticed. All the while they chattered and pulled small rectangular devices from their pockets. A few bright lights flashed, startling me, but Silver ignored them.

My whole body tensed as I crept up behind the bench. I had never kept still so close to a human being before, not even the elderly couple under whose porch I used to live. Yet, here I was, only a yard behind these people, out in the open, in the middle of the human city, and all by my own choice. Somehow they seemed oblivious, pointing and barking at Silver's antics. My muzzle trembled, saliva still dripping from my lips, as I inched my head closer and closer to my goal. Then, with supreme effort, I shot forward and snatched at one of the white containers.

I ran as fast as I could, but I didn't get more than five yards away before I fumbled my prize. The slick carton fell from my mouth, and what Silver had called a "hamburger" rolled out of it. Steam rose from it in the cold air. I scooped up what I could and took off once more. Carrying the soft prize in my mouth, tasting its juices without devouring it, was agony, but I pushed myself along the hard pavement till the cries of protest from the park faded.

I was back on the main streets. Silver was nowhere in

sight. I stopped, pressing my body against the cold stone building at my side, hiding in the long shadows cast by the setting sun. How many blocks had I run? I looked around. Sniffing did no good, as the hamburger's tantalizing scent overpowered everything else.

Fresh adrenaline coursed through my veins. I paced for a moment and then took off in the same direction. It was hard to remember places based on sight alone, especially amid the uniform city blocks, but I felt that I had at least run in the right cardinal direction. I had hoped the alleyway leading to Silver's nearest hiding place would catch my eye, but it hadn't.

I ran some more. Only once I was sure I had overshot the alley did I double back. The burger tortured me. Enough of its warm, fatty liquid had poured down my throat that I couldn't help dropping the sandwich on the pavement right out in the open and gobbling up a few morsels. That only made it worse, since I knew I couldn't polish off the whole thing. I scooped it up again and backtracked some more.

Finally, I spotted Silver. He was weaving his way from shadow to shadow toward me. At one moment, he ducked behind a trash receptacle. At another, he crouched under the front end of a parked car. When he reached me, he pointed his nose toward the nearest alley and trotted off. I followed close behind in silence.

We arrived at a wooden crate, smashed open and partly covered with garbage. Silver's refuge. It was dark except for a few beams of light streaming through the slats on one side. I dropped the hamburger at the entrance and we both huddled inside. It didn't take long for the stench of garbage to rival that of the food in front of me.

"Damn, Nimbus!" Silver exclaimed jovially. "I figured for sure you would have eaten it by now." He shoulder-checked me playfully. "You'll make a better apprentice than I thought!"

"I wanted to eat it," I admitted, embarrassed by his praise.

"Of course you did. You have a belly in that skinny frame, don't you? I thought you would do it, too. See, this is perfect. Not only did you have the guts to make the grab, but you had the resolve to hold on to it. That's the real challenge, you see. There's plenty of dumb animals who steal from humans. You see a raccoon or a pigeon do it every day. But they don't have the *discipline* to think with their brains and not their stomachs."

"Don't we do this for our stomachs?" I asked.

"Of course! But we don't let our bellies call the shots in the moment. It takes careful planning and execution, and then, *then*, we indulge." He nudged the hamburger toward me. "Speaking of which, the coast is clear, so let's dig in! You've earned it."

We each grabbed a few mouthfuls. Somehow, despite being cooked, slathered with sauces, and pressed between two pieces of bread, the meat tasted as good as it smelled. Before long, it was gone, and I was running my tongue over my fangs to extract every last particle. Truth be told, the whole ordeal had aroused my hunger enough that I could have eaten another whole hamburger by myself. At least with the edge taken off, I had the clarity to reflect on the cost of our recent meal.

"It seems pretty dangerous," I said at last. "I will grant you that this hamburger has got to be the best thing I've ever tasted. There's no denying that. But we took an awful lot of risks to get it."

"Look," said Silver, "I'll level with you. I've been at this four years. Have there been close calls? Yes. But I'm standing here talking to you, aren't I? Trust me, I know the business, and I'm looking to expand for a reason."

"Four years," I repeated. Silver had a point. If he had survived for so long, then it was possible that many of the dangers might be illusory, like how certain harmless snakes mimic the venomous. Or maybe Silver just knew how to minimize and overcome the risks. In either case, he would have to know an awful lot about humans. I could definitely learn from him.

"That's right," he said. "It's my life's work."

"You've made stealing food your life's work?"

Silver snorted. "What else? I don't care for the wild. It's boring. And, I've mated plenty in case you're wondering. Now, don't get me wrong," he added, as if I were in danger of doubting his virility. "I'd slake *that* thirst again if the opportunity arose, but all the vixens within a three-mile radius are too picky or too high-maintenance."

"I just thought," I faltered, caught off guard by the comment, "that something more *meaningful* in life—"

"Meaningful?" Silver interrupted. "Like what?"

"Well, I mean, did you ever have cubs, for instance?"

The old fox scoffed. "How the hell should I know?"

The flippancy of his reply chilled me. I imagined poor, shivering cubs abandoned while their mother searched for food with no mate to provide for her. I felt an urge to say something, to register my horror, but I didn't. I shifted uncomfortably and, after an awkward pause, tried to change the subject.

"Well, what about something creative? Storytelling or songwriting for example. Not every animal has the facility that we foxes do for the arts."

Silver sniffed. "Nimbus, let me break it to you right now. All day long your little mind is doing nothing but crafting schemes. And those schemes are aimed at just one thing: filling your belly and keeping yourself going another day. You can gussy it up however you want. You can repeat platitudes to yourself all day long, but go without food for a few days and tell me how meaningful life is." His jasper eyes glared into mine. "What significance was there when you were lying in the slush begging me to help you? How noble did you feel? If you're getting ungrateful all of a sudden, then maybe we should just go our separate ways after all."

"Well," I said, lowering my eyes, "I am grateful. I don't want you to think I'm not."

"Then don't be such a damn whelp," he snapped, "and do this with me."

"I'm fully grown," I muttered.

"Sure as hell could have fooled me. Wishy-washy. Wandering down the sidewalk like a lost kitten."

I stepped forward and squared my shoulders. "If we're going to do this," I growled, "we're partners."

"Whoa, take it easy, killer," Silver said, backing up in mock fear. "Don't hurt me!"

"I mean it," I said. "You didn't help me out of the goodness of your heart. You're too old and out of shape to get what you want. You need me, so you'd better treat me as an equal."

Silver's eyes narrowed. "I wouldn't overstate my case if I were you. Yes, I need someone a little younger and more, shall we say, *flexible*, but I don't need *you*. You just happened to be in the right place at the right time."

"And how many others are lining up?"

Silver glared at me in silence. "Forget it," he said, ignoring my question. "I do like you for some reason, and you've proved yourself. I think you should accept."

"As partners, then?"

"Yes, yes. Fine!" Silver rolled his eyes. "Now let's get to planning. You've had a taste—just a taste, mind you—of what this is all about. But what we need to do is find a way to hit the carts themselves, and not just once, either." His voice was thick with lusty anticipation. "Nimbus, it's going to be great!"

CHAPTER

— 7 —

# A Skilled Fox

Silver and I got to work. Winter had begun in earnest, but the city was still alive. Despite my insistence on equality, he called most of the shots. Whenever I couldn't take his bossiness anymore and snapped or grumbled at him, he admonished me for my inexperience. I would retort that I was his partner and just as essential. Silver could hardly object. It was obvious how much he relied on me. He had knowledge, but I had youth and speed. Plus, many of his ideas relied on teamwork.

I admired Silver's ability to switch between nocturnal and diurnal schedules. Years of city life had taught him to override the rhythm of nature at will. I did my best to keep up but sometimes found myself dozing when I should have been alert or vice versa.

From time to time, I still dreamed of Aurora. I started to dream about eating, too. In the past, I had dreamed of hunting, but I had begun to dream about food itself. In the country even when I had savored a meal or played with my prey before consuming it, food had remained on the level of necessity like drinking water or relieving oneself. Here stolen meals titillated me as I slept and left me salivating when I awoke. I fantasized about caches stuffed with delicacies. In my nightmares, though, I experienced the dark side of my new life, the creeping paranoia of the human world. Every so often, I shuttered awake, panting and wild-eyed, overcome by the sensation of being trapped, that every escape was under human control. In those moments, I missed the firm, oak roots that cradled the earthen walls of my childhood den. I had often gnawed and scratched at them, eager to upstage my siblings in the depth and intensity of the gashes I could inflict. Here the pavement kept my nails closely filed and never showed the marks.

Still, I had to admit that the safety I had enjoyed as a cub was more tenuous than I had realized at the time. The old den had a few good bolt-holes, to be sure, but some firm earth and a minute's head start is not much protection against a dog or a gun. At one point or another, every safeguard gives out. Danger stretched its jaws in country and city alike. Aurora was proof of that.

My studies kept me too busy and too tired to indulge long in such thoughts, but the emptiness came to me often as I fell into the release of sleep. Then I was alone, even with Silver's warm body heaving nearby. The older fox never gave any sign of dreaming. He slept soundly at the appointed time, whether day or night. I always feared my own fits would wake him, but they never seemed to.

I hated when Silver lost patience with me, which was often. He would pace around the basement cursing about my ignorance and inexperience. At least I could slink away in the large space, but I wanted to impress him, to gain his respect, if such a thing were even possible.

We didn't make another raid directly into the city center for a while. Instead, Silver took me around, showing me how he classified different zones and where his hiding places were. As he had explained before, there were other foxes and certainly many other animals sharing the space. Still, I came to see that Silver had overstated the city's non-territorial spirit. He himself had a keen sense of ownership over his hideaways, and I got the impression that he would have banished or subjugated all other foxes if he could.

Once Silver was satisfied that I had memorized the surrounding region, we started drilling on what he called "strategy and tactics." Despite his slow, sometimes wheezing pace, Silver's mind and senses were sharp. He must have been formidable in his prime.

At times, Silver asked me to run through drills that made little sense, such as tying and untying knots in an old piece of rope. When I begged for an explanation of this excruciating task, he simply took the length of rope in his mouth, slammed his forepaw on one end, and undid the knot faster than I could follow, as if that were justification enough.

By high winter, when the air stung just to breathe it and snow and slush lined the streets more often than not, Silver judged us ready for our first full-scale strike.

"Are you sure?" I asked, pacing along the wall of our basement dwelling.

"We have to do it some time," he replied. "Now's as good as any."

"A full cart?"

"A full cart."

"Now wait a minute," I said, stopping. "I've been pretty docile because I recognize that you have knowledge that I don't. But if hitting a full cart means that I'm going to jump into a crowd of humans, get inside one of those things, and somehow get the food out, while you sit on the sidelines barking orders, you can forget about it."

"What do you think we've been working toward?"

"You mean, what have *I* been working toward," I objected. "Did you forget that we're partners, or did you never really mean that in the first place?"

"You could have quit any time if you were unhappy with our arrangement," he stated flatly. "You've had a warm place to sleep and the best food of your life, haven't you?"

"Well, yes," I admitted. "That's true."

"And," Silver continued, "you've gotten to pursue your little project of studying human behavior, haven't you?"

"Yes."

"So, I've kept my end of the bargain, then?"

I certainly felt more like a servant than an equal, but when Silver laid everything out, I couldn't find any way to justify that feeling. By every metric I could think of, we were both doing as we had agreed. He was meticulous like that, and I knew that unless I could prove my case, he would just call me irrational or immature and carry on. Maybe it was the way he talked to me or looked at me. Maybe I really was immature. "Well," I said, "it's just that I seem to do all the dangerous work, and—"

"You can't have it both ways, Nimbus," Silver interjected. "Either you're serious about getting close to the humans or you aren't." The old fox brushed past me and lay down in a shadowy corner. "Don't waste my time."

The next few days were routine. Silver and I spoke only about the task at hand and went through our daily exercises. While I still felt that he was treating me unfairly and not in line with the spirit of our arrangement, Silver had a point. I had a safe, comfortable place to pass the winter and plenty of food besides. Leaving would mean giving that up and starting over right when the weather was most dangerous. In any case, Silver was especially possessive of the city center, where food carts could be found rain or shine. He assured me that many more would pop up come spring. Until then, leaving Silver would mean going back to scavenging for trash. Still, my doubts about our ability to pillage a cart remained. Silver didn't have the agility or speed to do it, and I couldn't do it on my own.

This got me thinking. What if the solution was not to split up but just the opposite? Why couldn't we recruit more foxes as allies?

I went to Silver and explained my idea. "Look at it as extending our enterprise," I said. We were both seated on the basement rug, resting before some daytime exercises.

"Hmm. Yes, I can see what you're proposing," he replied, "but it would never work. Foxes aren't so gregarious."

"That's exactly what I said to you before agreeing to move in here," I countered. "You told me that in the city things are different. You're right about that. So, there's no reason why we couldn't convince more to join us."

"We'd have to show them what we could offer and decide what their obligations would be in exchange," Silver said. "It may not be so easy."

"*I* joined," I repeated.

"Yes, but you have a particular drive to immerse yourself in the human world. Others don't. We live in the city because we like what the humans can do for us—well, some of it—not because we have any special interest in them. They're tolerable given what they provide, nothing more."

"The food, then," I replied. "Give them a taste. Like you said, it's impossible to go back to eating garbage once you've had real human meal."

"That might work," Silver agreed. "Or maybe there are some foxes out there who are just plain nuts. You know the type: lovers of danger, reckless."

"There are foxes like that," I said, thinking of my brother. "Clever ones, too, not just foolhardy brutes. They might enjoy applying their wits to a challenge."

"The only problem," Silver said, "is that those foxes will tend to be more independent. They'll be even less likely to give up their autonomy for pack membership."

"Maybe," I said, "but we wouldn't really be a pack, I mean, not like the wolves. We're not coming together for the sake of togetherness but only to do something that no fox could do himself. It's all about the goal."

"I see," said Silver. "It's more of a *coalition*."

"Precisely!" I barked. "You can work with the new recruits, while I go out and round up new ones. Once we've got a few, we'll train together, and by the spring, we'll be unstoppable."

Silver's tail waved vigorously. "This could be good! My mind's already racing. Imagine what four or five of us could do. Diversions. Attacks. Retreats. Contingency plans."

"That's right," I affirmed. "You could direct the planning, the overall strategy and coordination. I could be on the ground calling the tactical shots."

"Play to our strengths. I like it. Well, the urban fox population is high enough. The only issue will be getting others interested. There won't be many unattached adults, especially in winter. Obviously we don't want families. They wouldn't be interested anyway."

"How many members should we aim for?" I asked.

Silver shook his head. "I don't think we have any business worrying about that right now. It'll be hard enough to get anyone to begin with. Growing too big won't be a problem for a long time. If they're not crippled, rabid, or obvious losers, we'll be lucky to get them."

"Shouldn't they have to prove themselves like I did?"

"Of course. And they will. After all, this is life and death."

We searched for new members for a month. All intense training was put on hold, and I did only small exercises to stay sharp with the skills I had learned. Silver sought out some foxes whose usual haunts overlapped ours. I went farther and farther abroad, sometimes for days at a time. Whereas in the wild I could have made such trips in a single day, here in the city it took longer, having to sneak through busy streets. Thankfully, I no longer got lost and could find my way back after each excursion. My trips also got easier as winter passed its peak and the snows grew rarer and lighter.

One night, I came across a fox raiding a trash receptacle between two old brick buildings on the far west side. He was the same age as me with typical red and black markings, though his glacier-blue eyes seemed especially intense in the dark alley. I could smell that he was single.

I greeted him politely and introduced myself. When he saw I wasn't a threat, he relaxed and told me his name was Chestnut. I explained about Silver, our endeavors, and the hope of building a team. I expected to be laughed or growled at and sent on my way. Instead, Chestnut's face brightened. "Adventure!" he exclaimed. "We would do what no other foxes have dared."

"Yes," I said, surprised at his enthusiasm, "we would be rather unusual."

Before I could say another word, Chestnut leaped from the lid of the garbage bin, almost striking me on the way down. "I'm very interested," he stated.

"Really?" I asked. "Don't you want to hear the terms?"

"Terms!" scoffed Chestnut. "My whole life has been dictated by terms. Mom says don't go there, so I don't go there. Dad says start a family, so I leave home allegedly to do just that. I'm sick of it."

"Well," I said, "I have to be honest with you. There's definitely a commitment involved with this. You'll want to hear the details before making up your mind."

"Okay, okay," conceded Chestnut. "Give me the details. How many are on your team so far?"

"Just Silver and myself right now," I admitted.

"That's it?"

"So far," I said, somewhat embarrassed.

"Sounds to me like you can't afford to lay down policy, even if you had a clear idea of it. What you need first, Nimbus, is the team. *Then*, we all get together and work this thing out."

"I suppose," I said. "You seem awfully eager, not to mention straightforward, so I hope you don't mind my asking why you're interested. So far, all other foxes have turned us down."

"You're doing a new thing," he said. "Something new. That's what I'm looking for. Eating, sheltering, mating, dying—those may be good enough for the rest of foxes, but not for me. I'm not content with mediocrity."

"You could really make a name for yourself," I added. Silver wanted the food. I wanted to study humans and gain skills that I could use with them. Perhaps Chestnut wanted fame. If so, I could appeal to that desire.

"That wouldn't be so bad," he agreed, scratching an ear with his hind paw. "Oh, I know what you're thinking. I've heard it all before. I'm vain, proud, too good to live the life that nature charts for us, the one that's been good enough for all our ancestors. Well, I don't know what to say other than that I'm not interested in settling."

"I didn't mean to imply anything," I said, lowering my ears slightly. "I'm sorry if that came out wrong."

"I won't settle," continued Chestnut, as if he hadn't heard me, "not because I think I'm better than anyone but because it's boring. That's it. Call me whatever you want."

"Well," I said, changing tactics, "one thing I can promise is that our team won't be boring. The training is repetitive, of course, like all training is, but the thrills!"

"It's high-risk?" he asked.

"High risk," I said. "Sneaking, hiding, running for your life. Dangers you'd never encounter in the wild or normal city life."

"I can't wait."

"All right, then," I said, trying not to smirk. "Sounds like you belong with us. If it's a challenge you're after, something never before attempted, that's what we're about."

"That's me to a T," he quipped.

"Plus," I added, "as I said before, the payoff is a lot better than this garbage you're eating. If you don't want to settle, start with your diet."

Chestnut ended up coming with me. As we traveled, we chatted about his own exploits and other legendary achievements he had heard of. With the exception of Aurora's father, he looked like the strongest fox I had ever seen. His whole stout frame radiated energy, yet his demeanor was beyond detached, like he could face a dozen wolves with the indifference of sniffing out mushrooms. Contrary to my earlier assumption, it was hard to imagine he had any opinion of himself at all. His whole focus was outward, on goals to be attained and obstacles to be overcome.

Just before dawn, we curled up to rest at a midway refuge, the underside of an old iron structure grafted to a building, which Silver explained was to give the humans a way out in case of fire. In this particular case, the rusty metal looked ready to collapse under its own weight, like a log consumed by termites from the inside out. Chestnut seemed to have no problem sleeping out in the open. Despite the frigid weather, he started snoring the moment his brush fell across his nose.

By mid-afternoon it was dark, which made for easy travel through the city. The roads were clear, and there was little traffic. We reached the basement den by evening. I sensed that Silver was out, so I showed Chestnut around and told him to make himself at home. In truth, I was uneasy about how Silver would handle another fox. The idea of a team had pleased him, but even though he was brilliant in his own way when it came to planning and training, the older fox was also mercurial. I wondered how Chestnut would handle his moods.

"Nice basement," Chestnut called to me from the far corner. "Really spacious."

"It is," I said. "Silver and I typically sleep over here beneath this desk."

"Seems like there's no need if this building is really un-used, as you say."

"No humans so far," I said. "But I prefer the desk any-way."

"Suit yourself. I don't suppose you two will care if I tend to lounge around different parts of the building, then, or is it imperative that we sleep together in the basement?"

"I never thought of it," I said. "Actually, I've never even seen the upper floors."

"I like to rest in different places," Chestnut explained. "I find it gives me new ideas."

I heard claws tapping down the back staircase. Silver stepped into the room. "Sleep wherever you like!" he called, "at least during the probationary period."

Chestnut trotted over to us, wrinkling his muzzle. "Pro-bationary period?"

"Of course," Silver said, casting me an accusatory glance. "What did Nimbus tell you?"

"Well," I tripped over my tongue. "I figured the three of us should sit down and figure this out. Chestnut here seems quite capable, and he's willing to give us a chance."

"Chestnut, is it? Well, you know that I'm Silver, the founder of our coalition. Nimbus is my first, er, *colleague*. And you, Chestnut, are a candidate to join us."

"If what Nimbus tells me is true, I'd like to, but I'm not too keen on preconceived rules. It's my view that we should all get to know each other, get to know the objective, and then determine how things are going to work. So, maybe you can tell me what you mean by this 'probationary pe-riod.'"

Silver looked irritated. I could hear him trying, unchar-acteristically, to keep his voice level. "It *means* that I have developed a certain repertoire of knowledge and skill. Some of this I've imparted to Nimbus. But, as you just said, we don't know you yet, and you don't know us. A probationary period is our way of saying that we don't owe you anything as such. If you can give us something we need, great. If not, then we'll cut you loose. This is a collective undertaking, not a family."

Chestnut continued, unfazed by Silver's directness. "I'm not sure there is such a thing as a 'collective undertaking.' That implies that we have our own lives, our own contributions to make, and then come together for mutual benefit."

"Yes," Silver muttered, gritting his teeth, "that's the idea. So what's your point?"

"So I don't work that way. I chose to do this because it's never been done and, more importantly, because *I've* never done anything this big. When I commit, I go all in. If you're telling me that my membership is temporary or partial, maybe I should find something else to invest myself in."

"That doesn't make any sense!" challenged Silver. "You can't be in and out at the same time. You're either committed or you're not. I don't have time to waste training you only to have you flake out at the last moment. Nor am I interested in offering charity if you can't deliver."

"And, I'm not interested in compartmentalizing," Chestnut explained. "So maybe we actually agree. Your project is interesting and challenging. I want to be part of it. If I am part of it, then my commitment is total. You get *me*, not just my work. And because we're working together, I get you—unconditionally. It doesn't make us a family exactly, but we'll be bonded, with obligations to one another. Being fickle only leads to failure."

"You're in no position to be making demands," growled

Silver. "You haven't done a trial run or proved yourself in any way. You're asking us to divide our spoils with you, which is a big request."

"Don't you get it?" Chestnut rejoined. "I don't care about the food. You and Nimbus can have it all."

For the first time since I had met Silver, he was speechless, as if Chestnut had spouted pure gibberish. His eyes pored over the younger fox's face. Chestnut's gaze remained steady, his posture and tail relaxed. It was clear that he was not exaggerating. Silver's stance softened, and his eyes widened. He saw it, too. He didn't comprehend it, but he saw. The older fox had been drawn by his appetite for rich food for so long that he couldn't really believe that a young, daring specimen like Chestnut was standing before him. Chestnut was driven by nothing but ambition. He didn't want the prize so much as the effort of getting it.

"All right, then," Silver said at last. "Let me confer with Nimbus. Would you excuse us for a moment?"

"Sure thing," Chestnut chimed nonchalantly. "I want to explore the rest of your building anyway."

Chestnut trotted off to the side exit and ascended the stairs. Silver turned to me. "Well, you were pretty silent there," he hissed.

The hair raised on my back. "There wasn't much opportunity to speak," I said. "I brought in an obviously capable young fox eager to join up with us, but you grilled him— quite rudely—the first chance you got."

"He's not 'obviously capable,'" Silver insisted. "Ability must be demonstrated before full acceptance. This isn't a game for cubs. We risk our lives. Are you ready to entrust your life to some starry-eyed hotshot you just met? I hope you've learned better than that."

"Silver," I said, slumping to the floor. "I just got back.

I don't have the energy to debate you right now. We both want more foxes on board, and Chestnut is the only one who's agreed. Honestly, from my perspective, we're lucky to get him. You keep insisting that he has to prove himself, so let him do it. There's no need for rigid formality."

Silver's eyes flashed in the dim basement light. For a moment, I thought he might snap at me, but I was too tired to care. His moods had frightened me before. Now they only exhausted me. The decision was made, and we both knew it. Silver slinked away grumbling. I curled up on the rug to sleep.

Chestnut joined our team. For several days, I treated him with extra kindness, taking every chance to compliment him and deferring to his ideas during our planning sessions. I did this not to be obsequious but to make up for Silver's surliness, hoping that he wouldn't get sick of it and leave. In truth, the older fox's demeanor confused me more than usual. Everything he wanted was coming together. For the first time in his life, his goal was actually within reach, and yet he acted as if Chestnut had robbed him of his last morsel in the dead of winter. My young compatriot carried himself as always, never reacting to Silver's hostility, but I had to believe he noticed it.

By the end of our first week, Chestnut had mastered the basic maneuvers. I was more than a little jealous, since it had taken me nearly three times as long to learn the same. He had also done a test run and proved himself by stealing a large slice of pizza from a child's hand. Even Silver couldn't hide his admiration at the young fox's talent and courage. In contrast, I found myself in a rut. With Silver's attention occupied in Chestnut's intense training and Chestnut able to withstand greater and greater abuse, my own training had plateaued. Each day I repeated my darting, leaping, and running exercises and went over tactics and strategy, but I no longer experienced steady growth. At least I enjoyed one advantage over Chestnut—my longer legs. This meant that at full speed I could outrun him, a fact I highlighted whenever possible.

I felt most engaged during our planning sessions, when the three of us would lie down on the basement rug to discuss when and how to make our first big strike. I favored waiting for the spring, and I even suggested that we continue looking for new recruits to build some redundancy into our system and improve our chances of success. Silver wanted to move as quickly as possible. Chestnut's abilities were winning him over, and I noticed that the older fox was treating him better every day. One afternoon, after some light scavenging in the nearest park, Silver even let Chestnut eat first—which he had never done for me—saying that Chestnut deserved it for all his hard work.

Our group continued to transform in the weeks that followed. Silver seemed to have reversed his earlier position, acting less and less businesslike. Chestnut not only surpassed me in innate ability but had caught up to me in knowledge as well. By late winter, we were more like a pack than I thought possible. Our tactics and teamwork were more like those of wolves than foxes. An implicit hierarchy was developing.

That was what worried me. Silver ranked first due to seniority and knowledge alone. Chestnut was rising fast, and some days I got the sense that he was considered my superior already. He seemed as aloof as ever to such matters, which only irked me more.

I had taken a few more trips lately in the hopes of finding more recruits, in case I had missed any adults still unattached from the previous season. With spring approaching, it was time to get our full complement ready not just for one strike but for repeated hits of the new carts that would pop up in the warmer weather.

All three of us agreed about the need to expand our group, but I had two reasons of my own for doing so. First of all, I had begun to question the value of maintaining a relationship with Silver. His almost exclusive focus on Chestnut proved that he had no special attachment to me. That in itself didn't bother me, as it kept me relatively safe from his temper. The problem was that Silver wasn't teaching me anything new, and although I liked the food we stole, I wasn't addicted to it like he was. I remained in the city because I wanted to understand humans not just live off them. So, I thought, if I could bring a few more foxes on board, Silver wouldn't need me and thus wouldn't give me any trouble if I left.

My second reason served as a hedge against the first. If I stayed, new foxes would put me relatively higher up in our new hierarchy, especially if I took care to bring in weaker specimens. I could even make myself more needed, if I so chose, in the management and training of the team. So far, I was undecided. The temptation to give up on Silver and leave once spring came grew stronger, but I also felt that Silver had more to teach me, if only I could win back his attention.

One night I found myself far from our home base, over a day's comfortable journey toward the city's northern edge.

I had never come this direction before, but the warming late-winter air made travel pleasant. The streets were different from those near the city's heart. They were not paved but made of hundreds of interlocking bricks. There were also many fewer vehicles out and about. Perhaps, I reasoned, they did not like the rougher surfaces. But, then again, why would the humans create roads unfriendly to their own cars? Another mystery.

I was again searching for foxes willing to join our group. I met no resistance when I announced my intention to go out looking. For one thing, all three of us desired more members. For another, Silver didn't seem to care where I was anymore. True, on the rare occasion that he wanted something from me, he would snarl and curse if I was absent, but otherwise I felt superfluous.

I hadn't had any luck in my mission so far. On several such trips, I had tracked down an unattached fox—I avoided those who smelled of family—but none had any interest in our endeavor. Their cocked heads and curious, pitying eyes no longer bothered me. I came to expect such reactions. It had always been clear that we were deviating from traditional fox customs, but it was getting harder and harder to make our group intelligible to other foxes. I felt like I had changed species.

I was well into the suburbs, and I expected soon to find myself beyond the city's bounds altogether. I realized all at once that I had not left the city in several moons. I even thought of the fields and forests beyond as "the wild" in a way I never would have as a cub. My former homeland, once so ordinary, had become exotic. A strong temptation to return there gripped my heart, and I changed my walk to a trot. In an instant, I no longer cared about Silver, no longer cared about the ease and comforts of the human world. A crisp, fresh breeze ruffled my fur, like a caress from freedom itself.

My mind was nearly made up to leave, to run beyond the suburbs and never return. I would have done it, I think, if a thousand curious odors had not surrounded me and choked out the scent of the land beyond. That confusing cloud of animal smells so distracted me that I almost ran muzzle-first into a stone wall. The aroma was so intense that it seeped right through the thick, cold rock and pulled me by the nose. Dozens of animals—more than dozens—were behind this wall. Some smelled ordinary enough, but many were species I had never encountered, with odors ranging from sulfury musk to nectar kissed by honey.

Overcome by curiosity, I sniffed along the stone wall until I came to an iron gate. The complex was large and secure. I peered through the gate, studying the scene with care. Despite the presence of so many animals, not yet visible from my current vantage, I detected minimal signs of violence. There were fear smells, mating smells, and the sinking stench of malaise, but little blood and no fresh kills. This puzzled me. Even though I had seen time and again how city animals tolerate one another much better than in the wild, toleration only goes so far. So many distinct species in a concentrated area should have caused a frenzy, yet it didn't.

Slowly, trying to remain undetected to anyone who might be observing, I wriggled under the large gate and hugged the inside of the stone wall. The cloud of smells and the darkness hid me well. The enclosed space was large. I couldn't see how far the walls ran in each direction. There were also well-defined paths spreading out like a spider's web. Several months ago, the rough pavement would have scraped my paw pads. Now, hardened by city life, I paced down the nearest side path without discomfort.

Broad, antler-like lamps illuminated the path every dozen yards or so. Thankfully, the humans had enough sense to keep them dim, unlike the city streetlights, whose intensity could easily daze incautious creatures. I passed several long single-story buildings, all dark. One radiated with the smell of food. I looked for a way inside but found none. Rows of large enclosures lined the path on each side ahead of me. There were even trees and grass within these tremendous structures. For a moment, I wondered why humans would take the trouble to cage such things. I had been through city parks but had never seen plants caged before.

As I approached the first enclosure, however, I realized where I was. This was what Silver had called an "animal park," a place where humans kept animals just to look at. Judging by the smells I recognized, they didn't apply much logic to the arrangement. Nocturnal and diurnal creatures both suffered under the dim lights. Predators and prey were neighbors.

Some of the imprisoned animals noticed me as I walked past, but few seemed interested. No one called out begging me for freedom. No one barked or growled. An eerie languor haunted the place. To my left, a family of raccoons lazed openly behind a thin wire mesh. To my right, some large spindly bird of unknown species shot me a glassy eye.

The path and the enclosures, sometimes close together, sometimes generously spaced, continued as far as I could see. Up ahead, another path shot off toward the park's center. I decided to turn around and leave, and I would have if not for one scent. Out of the dense fog of smells, one gripped my heart. I froze. It was a pure reflex action. My thoughts swirled like a gathering storm cloud, but then they crystallized into the single, clear idea that I might have died.

CHAPTER

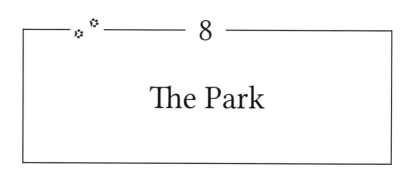

8

# The Park

I shook my legs back to life and ran deeper into the park. Dashing past cages of strange animals, I inhaled so sharply that I fell into a coughing fit. No matter how many times my brain processed the scents, I knew I wasn't mistaken: Three foxes, and one was Aurora. If I lived till the stars burned out and the seasons no longer turned, her scent would be as fresh to me as on the last night we sang together. Even slightly changed in a way I couldn't account for, that spiced musk was unmistakable. I tracked it at top speed.

Eventually I reached where the foxes were kept. A male, two or three years of age, lay on his side, lounging on the ground. Through the hexagonal wire mesh, I could see that the enclosure's earth floor was no more than a few inches deep. In a few places, it had worn through to reveal the hard pavement beneath. When I approached, the fox's ears perked up and he rolled onto his stomach. Haphazard brush and large rocks as well as a wooden structure filled the space behind him. Somehow the imitation of nature made the whole thing seem even more artificial. Despite the tight confines of the enclosure—maybe twenty-five feet in length and certainly no deeper—I could see neither Aurora nor the other vixen I smelled.

"Hello, brother!" the fox called to me cordially. I noticed that he was missing the tip of an ear.

I stood right in front him. I sniffed as best I could at the mesh dividing us, but I was still panting from my run. Everything felt unreal. Was this a dream, one of those nighttime fantasies that still sometimes seized me? The dreamworld held charms and terrors of its own, often intertwined. Perhaps in a moment I would jolt awake and Silver would nip and curse at me for oversleeping.

The fox's eyes glinted in the dim light. "Are you friendly?" he asked. His manner seemed curious and hearty. When I continued to stare, he cocked his head to the side and added, "Is something wrong?"

"Where's Aurora?" I asked once I had caught my breath enough to speak. "Is that her? Is she here?"

"You know Aurora?" asked the strange fox. He thought for a moment and then added, "I'd better wake her." My interlocutor rose and headed toward the wooden structure, which I realized served as a den. "She sleeps a lot these days," he called back to me, "but she won't want to miss a friend from the outside."

He stuck his head into the dark opening. I heard muffled speech, and a moment later he trotted over to me with a grin. "I'm Blaze, by the way," he said and sniffed at me through the mesh. "We don't get a lot of visitors here, as you can imagine. What's your name?"

Before I could answer, Aurora emerged from the wooden den and gasped. Her voice, the voice I expected never to hear again, caressed my ears and broke my heart. "Oh, Nimbus!" she cried, choking as she pronounced my name.

"Aurora," I said in disbelief. "Aurora, it's me!"

Her golden eyes peered into mine as she swaggered toward me. When she reached the mesh that divided us, Aurora lay gingerly against it. Absentmindedly, I dropped to the pavement.

"Nimbus," she said again, "It really is you. I can't believe it."

I pressed my muzzle into the wire hard, desperate to touch her. We managed only to rub noses through the cold metal. From the corner of my eye, I saw Blaze watching us in curious silence.

"You're alive," I said and repeated the fact several times as if trying to convince myself.

"Yes," Aurora affirmed. "And *you're* alive, and you're here. I never thought I'd see you. You're like a forest spirit from those old stories we used to tell."

"*I'm* the ghost?" I balked. "Aurora, you died. The gun. The fur. You sank wounded and bleeding beneath the ice, and you never came out."

"No." She shook her head. "I didn't fall in, not all the way."

"How?" I cried. "You mean you climbed out? But if you survived, where did you go? Why did you leave? You had to know I would come after you, that I would look for you. And I did. Your father and I tracked you to the pond, but—"

"I didn't leave," she interrupted. "At least, I didn't mean to." Aurora sobbed, burying her muzzle in her paws. "Oh, Nimbus, it's all so overwhelming."

For several minutes, neither of us spoke. Aurora's body shook with grieved moans. I could only watch, inches away, beyond the barrier. Every time I opened my muzzle to say something comforting or ask a question, her sobbing silenced me.

"Excuse me," Blaze interjected in a gentle tone as he sat beside Aurora. "Maybe the rest of us can get caught up on this?"

He glanced over his shoulder. Another vixen had poked her head from the den and was listening cautiously. At Blaze's invitation, she stepped out from the darkness. Even with a thick winter coat, she looked thin and delicate. The vixen kept her crisp, green eyes on her paws as she padded over and stood behind him.

"This is River," said Aurora, forcing out the words. "She's Blaze's sister."

In the interval that River's introduction provided, my dazed consciousness caught up with the situation. I studied the three foxes through the wire. I again sensed something different about Aurora's scent. I noticed how her belly swelled beneath her thick winter coat and the way Blaze sat so close.

"You're pregnant," I stated at last.

"Yes," affirmed Aurora.

She and Blaze exchanged a glance. "So," Blaze asked, "you're not just an acquaintance from the old days, I take it?"

"No," I said. "I'm certainly not."

Aurora stifled another sob.

"I lost her," I continued, "on the night meant for our wedding."

"I- I'm sorry," said Blaze gravely. "I didn't realize."

"You didn't do anything wrong," Aurora reassured him. "How could you know?"

"Indeed," I said and cleared my throat.

"If I had known," added Blaze, "I wouldn't have been so casual in introducing myself. Of course, this must be difficult for you."

"Oh dear," whispered River. I felt the pity in her gaze.

"Difficult doesn't begin to describe it," I stated, holding back a growl.

I breathed in slowly, attempting to hold myself in check. If I spoke further, the bitterness welling in my breast would pour out uncontrollably.

Aurora slumped against Blaze's side. We sat in silence for a long time. The dim light shone through the wire mesh, casting crisscross shadows on the dirt. Aurora avoided my gaze. River stood back, wide-eyed. After a while, Blaze murmured something to Aurora.

"What was that?" I barked.

I expected Blaze to snap back at me, but he just looked up, his expression sullen.

"He asked if I wanted to tell my story," Aurora replied. "I suppose I should." Blaze and River's reflective eyes peered at me. "Would you like to hear it? This is a big shock for all of us."

"That's an understatement," I muttered.

"I know," she said. "Yes, it's awkward, but it really is good to see you, Nimbus. It's a gift I never thought I would get. And it's an opportunity to explain what happened back then. I still can't believe it. It feels like years ago."

"Yes, but it's only been a few months," I said pointedly, "not much time at all."

"You're right," she said, "but it was another life."

I swallowed hard, hoping that the shade was hiding my trembling. Part of me wanted to growl and curse. Part of me wanted to run. A dark, guilty part of me even wished that Aurora really had died. I wanted an explanation, but I wasn't sure I could bear it. Hemming and hawing would do no good. "So, what happened, then?" I grunted at last.

"Do you remember the dream you had, the one with the daisies?"

"How could I forget?" I grumbled.

"Obviously, I couldn't fasten flowers to my fur, but I got it in my foolish head to bathe myself in their scent, which meant, of course, that I risked a trip to the farm to see whether the daisies behind the shed were still alive. It turned out that they were—the last of the season. I felt so lucky when I saw them. Now, I'd been to the farm before, but this time I was in a hurry, and I didn't take all the precautions." She paused. "It was supposed to be a surprise."

My stomach wrenched. Once again, I cursed myself for ever sharing that stupid dream. As practical-minded as Aurora was, I should have known she might do something like that for me. At the same time, my skin burned with an urge to scold her for gambling her life and our future on something so silly. She should have known better. If only she had come back those three or four months ago, we would be free and happy together!

As if replying to my thoughts, Aurora said, "It's not your fault, and it's not my fault. Or if it is, I forgave myself. Mostly, it was just an accident."

For the moment, my curiosity won out and I kept silent so that Aurora could continue. She explained how the farmer had caught her off guard, shot at her, and sent her scurrying in desperation toward the highway. The bullet had grazed her, drawing blood but doing no internal damage. In her haste, she had leaped onto the road right in front of an oncoming car. It had swerved to miss her—like the one that had avoided me but hit the coyotes. She had tumbled down the embankment and slid onto the pond's frozen surface, which cracked beneath her weight. With her hindquarters sinking into the icy water, Aurora had clawed and struggled enough to pull herself out. After this, she said, her memory failed her.

I listened in near disbelief as Aurora then described waking up, dazed and wounded, inside a human vehicle. I could taste her panic as she recounted her primal drive to escape, how she had scratched all around and thrown her body against the plastic walls surrounding her. She had tired herself out, which had been easy to do in her weak state. The vehicle must have been designed for the exact purpose of containing animals. In fact, it had been thick with the lingering scents of various species previously captured and transported.

She told me how she had drifted in and out of sleep, faint from blood loss and from struggling. Men had carried her—restrained somehow in a way she couldn't remember—from the vehicle, into a building, and down a long concrete hallway to a bright room. There she had fallen into a deep sleep.

"I awoke with a great thirst," Aurora continued. "I was in a small cage then, but there was water and some kind of syrupy liquid in front of me. The humans had stripped the fur from my hind leg and closed up the wound."

"They mended you?" I asked in surprise.

"Yes. Somehow they did. They kept me in that small cage, I think, for several days. There was no sun or moon, and I couldn't rely on my sleep-confused body to know the time. I waited for them to kill me with their strange, metal instruments, but they never did. They did not retaliate when I snapped at them, and they sometimes made soothing noises when I cowered."

"Remarkable," I whispered.

"Once I felt strong again, they brought me here, to this enclosure with Blaze and River. I didn't know where I was, but I could smell the other creatures all around. So many strange species. Actually, I had smelled some of them before from inside the building."

"I could tell she was a wild, country fox right away," interjected Blaze. "She carried herself like a vixen who's used to earth and grass beneath her paws with trees or open sky over her head. I myself have always been a city fox."

"In fact, I didn't understand at first that we were *in* the city," explained Aurora. "All I knew was the farm, the roadside, a disorienting trip, the small cage, and then this enclosure. Blaze and River had to explain the bigger picture to me several times. I'm afraid I wasn't too friendly when I first arrived."

"I tried to see it from your perspective," Blaze replied. "The wild foxes I met before I lived here always took a while to adjust to city life. River and I had trouble, too, when we were first brought to the animal park. So, I figured that those two factors together would make it pretty rough on a young vixen."

"I didn't think you were unfriendly," said River to Aurora. "Adjustments take time."

"Truthfully," said Blaze, "I found you rather endearing."

"That's kind of you to say," said Aurora, "but learning to live in confinement is not easy. I never thought I'd see this as my home. I still don't, not really. It's only good company that makes it tolerable." She nipped playfully at Blaze's ear, the one with the missing tip. He flinched, then smirked at her.

All the while, pressure was building within me. Aurora's survival. Her captivity. Her pregnancy. It was too much to process. Hot and cold warred in my breast. I wanted to bark or cry—maybe both—and throw my body against the wire mesh in frustration. I felt miles away, watching Blaze and Aurora, unable to divine their conversation. They played and chatted while I remained frozen.

Only River noticed. She eyed me curiously and finally spoke up, albeit bashfully. "Nimbus, are you all right?"

My throat was dry. Several times I opened my muzzle to speak and could not. "How could you do this to me?" I hissed at last.

Blaze, who had been speaking, fell silent. Aurora turned to me, looking hurt. "Excuse me?"

"How could you do this to me?" I repeated.

"How could I do what?" she asked coolly.

"Choose another mate," I spat.

"Nimbus, you can't be serious!" Aurora scoffed. "I understand you're upset. Of course you are. So am I. But surely you're not upset with *me.*"

"I am upset with you," I said, clenching my jaws. "I thought we were in love. I thought we had decided to be together. But you just *replaced* me."

"I didn't replace you," she insisted. "I lost you. Don't you see? They brought me here to spend the rest of my life in this cage. I might have been half the world away for all I knew. I had every reason to believe I would never see you again, just as you had every reason to believe the same."

"*I* didn't take another mate," I said flatly.

"That was your choice," she said. "You didn't, but you could have, and you can."

"How could I?" I exclaimed. "The very same season? Like you never existed? No." I shook my head. "I'm not like that."

Blaze opened his mouth, but Aurora shot him a look and he kept quiet. "Nimbus, I loved you... I love you," she said. "Seeing you tears my heart wide open. It really does. But you have to understand that Blaze was *here*. You weren't. I love him, too. If things had been different, I would have chosen you. I know you know that. But I couldn't, and I can't."

My ears burned, not only with anger but with the embarrassment of arguing about such an intimate matter in front of two strangers. I thought about leaving and never coming back. I thought about telling Aurora that I could move on as quickly as she had. But the pavement gripped my paws, locking me in place. Blaze stared—or glared—at me. I wondered what he thought, what he felt when he looked at me. Contempt? Pity?

"You know," I said, "since I've been in the city, I've learned so much. I've studied. Look how healthy I am! I have skills that almost no other foxes do. I know how to live in the human world, how to get around their dangers. I could have provided for us. We could have been city foxes, like you always wanted, if only you had waited for me."

"Honestly, Nimbus," Aurora replied, "we're not children anymore. Be realistic."

"Then I wish I had never seen you again!" I snapped. "Then at least I'd have remembered you as faithful. Now you've taken that from me, too."

The statement surprised me. It felt like spitting out a ball of venom from deep in my belly. I simultaneously felt relief and horror at what had come out of me.

Aurora's face fell, her eyes widened, and I thought she might start sobbing again.

"Now listen here," interjected Blaze with a firmness he had not yet shown, "Aurora hasn't done anything wrong. You have no right to accuse her."

"I didn't mean that," I said.

"But you said it," insisted Blaze. "You should be glad to see Aurora alive, not causing her grief."

"No," I said, "I mean, I don't know." My head was spinning. Aurora peered up at me, looking broken. My anger had given way to confusion and shame. The pavement released its grip on my paws. I backed up, muttering excuses and turned to leave.

"Nimbus, wait!" Aurora called out.

"Yes?" I asked, already several yards away. My mind screamed at me to apologize, not to waste the chance to leave on good terms, but I couldn't translate the impulse into words.

"I know you're hurting," she said. "I'm hurting, too. And, it hurts me even more to say this. It's the worst time, but it's the only time." She swallowed hard. "I need to ask you for a favor, not for myself, but for my cubs."

I cringed but held my peace. "What is it?"

"Will you try to release us from this cage? You just said that you've learned how to deal with human things."

I began to protest, but Aurora interrupted me. "River knows how the locking mechanism works. She's watched the humans carefully. The trouble is that it's on the outside, so we can't get to it. Please, Nimbus. I don't want my cubs to be born here, not if there's any hope at all."

"And yet, you conceived them in that cage," I growled. "You're not the victim here. You may have been forced to live here, but mating with Blaze was your decision."

"You're right," said Aurora. "And you may not accept that decision. Even if you don't, even if you think I'm at fault, please see that it's *my* fault, not my children's. I'm begging you. You might be able to free us, and we won't get another opportunity like this. Will you have mercy on them? Will you at least try?"

I stared at my paws in the dim light, not wanting to look at Aurora, much less to see Blaze and River judging me. If I left, I would never have to face them again. Despite my training, there was no guarantee that I even could help them to begin with. In any case, I needed time. My poor brain was overloaded. With dawn approaching, it made no sense to keep myself in danger of being captured and ending up their fellow prisoner. Aurora, Blaze, and River weren't going anywhere. They could wait. I didn't owe them an immediate answer. I didn't owe them anything.

Silently I walked away.

CHAPTER

9

# Freedom

It took a day and a half to return to home base. I arrived in mid-afternoon and found Silver and Chestnut discussing a timeline for executing what they were calling "Operation Apex." After some prodding, I learned that it was meant to be the culmination of a series of hits directly on the food carts.

"We'll hit a *truck*," said Silver lustily. "A full truck!"

"That's right," affirmed Chestnut, "but we're going to work up to it. There's quite a bit of strategy to account for." Chestnut's expression was intense as he explained the details. It was like he saw the whole spring and summer's worth of maneuvers unfolding fluidly before him and was only reporting the event, not planning it.

Once Chestnut had finished, Silver snapped back to his usual self. He scolded me for returning without a new team member. I barked back at him, in no mood to tolerate the usual abuse.

Chestnut must have sensed that something was different about me. "Nimbus, what's wrong?" he asked.

"Nothing. Well, I mean I can't really explain," I muttered, unsure whether I wanted to talk about it.

"Good," spat Silver, glaring at me. "We don't need any excuses. You've gone over half the city and still haven't found us any help."

"I found *Chestnut*," I scoffed, incredulous. "Did you forget that already? And, speaking of forgetting things, did you forget that we're equal partners? I'm not your slave."

Silver's expression revealed that he might actually have forgotten the terms of our deal. Perhaps he had never meant to honor them. But it was my fault for not being more assertive. Silver's respect was never given without cost. Proving myself once wasn't enough, especially with Chestnut around.

"Oh, well, I meant you haven't brought us anyone *new*," sputtered Silver, ignoring the rest of what I had said. "We need at least two more, I think. Surely there are foxes around."

"It's almost spring," I said. "You know that. Most foxes are busy with other things."

"I don't care about most foxes!" retorted Silver, "only those with talent who aren't tied down by family or other nonsense. That's who you need to look for. You were away nearly a week this time. Where are you even going?"

Chestnut leaned over and sniffed hard at my coat. "Where *have* you been?" he asked. "It's faint, but I can tell you've been around animals I never smelled before. Lots of them."

"I was—"

"The animal park!" Silver interrupted. He rushed over to me and pressed his nose against my neck. "Yes, that's it. But you visited some foxes as well."

"So what if I did?" I snarled, fur bristling.

"No need for anger," Silver cooed mockingly. "Did something upset you?"

"Nimbus," Chestnut added, casting Silver a harsh glance. "It's okay. Why not get some rest after your long trip?"

He was right. I was exhausted, and Silver would only goad me on. I excused myself and withdrew to a far corner of the basement where I curled up. I was quite worked up, but I did my best to ignore Silver and Chestnut's planning session and the occasional muttered remarks about me till I fell asleep.

A few days later, Silver was out on some errand, and Chestnut cornered me as I returned to the basement after a brief trip out for some water. "I didn't want to bring it up with Silver here, but you were whimpering in your sleep again."

"Again?" I asked.

"You've done it ever since you got back from that long trip."

I shouldn't have been surprised. We were back on a diurnal schedule, and I woke up repeatedly each night. Aurora plagued my dreams more than ever. I saw bright lights and metal bars, ugly human faces laughing and gawking at imprisoned animals. I saw Aurora cowering, pleading, scrambling in vain to scoop up a litter of cubs and keep them safely hidden. Sometimes the cubs were alive, themselves struggling to break free. At other times, they were dead or malformed. I found little relief in the waking world, for Aurora haunted me there as well. Her scent lingered on every breath; her golden eyes begged from every dark corner.

"Oh. I didn't realize," I said. "I'm sorry if I'm disturbing your sleep." I was also puzzled because of Chestnut's habit of sleeping in a different part of our basement each night, sometimes even the building's upper levels. He could simply move if I was bothering him.

"No, that's not it," Chestnut said. "I'm worried about you. Ever since you got back from your last trip, you've deteriorated. You're not as sharp. Even your physical appearance. Frankly, you look terrible."

I knew I had been aloof, speaking to the others even less than usual, but Chestnut's concern surprised me. I had grown to see him as a rival, a usurper of Silver's tenuous favor.

"Silver hasn't said anything, has he?" I asked. "I mean, I don't seem to have woken him up. I'm sure he would have given me an earful if I had."

"Silver's quite a heavy sleeper," said Chestnut. "And, no. He hasn't said anything out of the ordinary about you." Chestnut's voice held no tone of condescension, but that only made me feel even more inferior. I was falling apart while he excelled. If I hadn't been so desperate to vent my frustrations, I might have resented his solicitude even more.

"I guess I'm glad you brought it up," I admitted with a sigh. "Since I have no reason to think he'd respect my privacy, has Silver told you why I came to the city?"

"Yes."

"Well, something happened on this last excursion."

I told Chestnut all about the animal park, about finding Aurora alive and pregnant. I had intended to describe the bare events in as matter-of-fact a way as possible, but once I started speaking, I found myself inserting more and more details along with personal commentary. He listened patiently as I rambled about my nightmares, about the rage that I carried in my breast, about grief, envy, and everything else.

When at last I fell silent and crumpled to the cold basement floor, Chestnut lay down beside me. He radiated warmth. In contrast, I lay breathless, empty, like a pelt drying on some hunter's wall.

"Nimbus," he said, "you've told me a lot of things. Now, I know we're not exactly friends and you haven't asked my advice, but isn't it obvious what you have to do?"

"I have to go," I whispered, my throat raw.

"That's right. If you don't at least try to help, if you leave things the way they are, it's going to eat you from the inside out."

"How do you know that?" I asked.

Chestnut snorted. "You all but said it yourself. You came to the city because you wanted to get back at the humans who had taken Aurora from you. Well, you can see now that that never happened."

"No," I interrupted. "They *did* take her from me, not in the way I first thought, but they've stolen her nonetheless."

Chestnut shook his head. "They haven't stolen her. She's there, waiting for you. She won't be your mate. That's true. But you have a chance to make peace. If you don't, *you* will be the one who drove her away."

"This isn't fair," I groused.

"It's not fair or unfair. It just is," said Chestnut. "But think about this. Based on what you've described, what do you think will happen if Aurora has her cubs in that enclo-sure? They can't live in there forever. There isn't enough space. So, either the humans will release them into the wild without the proper training, or else... Well, we can guess."

I began to mutter something but couldn't summon a co-gent reply. Chestnut said nothing but rose and left me to myself.

I knew he was right. I was angry and confused by the humans and angry at Aurora, but I couldn't live the rest of my life thinking of her caged in like that and wondering whether I had sentenced her cubs to death.

Silver returned about an hour later. Chestnut still had not come back to the basement, so I was alone with the old fox. Summoning my courage, I told him where I was going and why.

"Go on then," he grunted. "I'm sick of your selfish mop-ing."

"Selfish?" I objected. "None of this is for me."

"It's all for you. You're just doing this to make yourself feel better." He glared at me and added, "It won't work."

"How dare you," I hissed. "Why are you always putting me down?"

"I'm just telling you the truth, kid. The conscience is as base an appetite as any other, nothing more than a lust for self-approval. If you can't live without thinking of yourself as a hero, then go on."

Silver had struck a nerve. I growled, keeping my eyes locked on his. The old fox squared his stance and lowered his head. I couldn't tell whether he was preparing to lunge at me or steeling himself against me. I relished either possibility, imagining my claws slashing him, splashing blood across his gray snout.

"I'm stronger than you," I said.

"Look at you," he scoffed. "You're pathetic. No sense of control. The best thing you've done here is bring in your replacement."

"I do all your silly exercises and most of the real work on our raids. All you do is give orders and complain. I contribute so much more than you."

"You would be lost without me."

I scoffed. "It's just the opposite. Without me, you'd be scavenging for trash, leering at rich food, but deprived and totally alone."

"Listen to yourself," Silver retorted. "You and I sound pretty similar, if you ask me."

"Hardly!" I barked. "You're crass, and self-absorbed, and... and hateful."

"And what do you think all your noble feelings are? I'll tell you. They're sentiments. Stuff in your own head that doesn't even rise to the level of an idea. But what have you *done*? What have all the nice, pretty thoughts in the world done for anyone but yourself? You lost your mate, so you formed some childish vendetta against humanity. Now you've found her—against all odds, I might add—and you act like you're making some big sacrifice to help her. You got more than you ever wanted, and you're still not happy."

I stood still, breathing slowly till my pulse returned to normal and my fur lay flat once again. Silver continued to brace himself, but he did not attack. I no longer felt the urge to strike him, even though he deserved it.

"I have very little I want," I said. "I'm going to help Aurora if I can because it's the right thing to do." I padded away and called over my shoulder, "I might not be back."

"Don't feel bad about it," said Silver. "That's what I've been telling you. Slake your thirst. Satisfy your hunger. Live your own life. And if you don't? Doesn't mean a damn thing to me."

Two days later, I arrived back at the animal park. It was night, and I trotted along the wide, paved walkway lined with cages. The ranks of imprisoned animals again ignored me. I found their myriad scents quite distracting. Or maybe I was looking for a distraction. In other circumstances, I might have visited just to indulge my curiosity and sniff around. Instead, whatever had forced me to come back also urged me onward. And yet, the closer I got to the fox enclosure, the stiffer my joints and the heavier my paws became.

When I got to the cage, Aurora was waiting. She sat upright by the wire mesh and trained her eyes on me. "I knew you'd come," she said. I could hear the relief in her voice, and it warmed my own heart, confirming me in my decision.

"I'm sorry," I said. "I never should have left." I forced myself to use a calm whisper. I believed the words I was saying, at least the better part of me did, but the old pressure, like steam when hot meets cold, pressed against my ribs. I had resolved that if I came back to Aurora, I would not let her see my anger. Chestnut had been right. This was my chance to leave things in a peaceful way. Even if my own internal struggle was not yet resolved—or never would be—Aurora didn't need to know that. I had the power to leave her with the memory of a gallant Nimbus, a noble Nimbus who accepted her choices and life's twists of fate without resentment.

"That doesn't matter now," she said. "By the way, I never got a chance to ask you more about what you've been up to these last few months. You mentioned learning some special skills."

"Oh," I said, sitting down across from her, "let me fill you in."

I explained my run-in with the coyotes and moving to the city—though I didn't mention wanting to avenge her. I told her about my time living in the suburbs and how I had met Silver. As I spoke, River and Blaze emerged from the wooden den and sat a few yards off. When they saw that I didn't fall silent or express any discomfort at their presence, they drew closer and listened. Aurora and Blaze both gasped when I told her about the training I had gone through and Operation Apex. River kept quiet, seemingly lost in thought.

"Who would have thought?" exclaimed Aurora. "*You* of all foxes involved in something like that. Blaze has told me about those food carts. Apparently they wheel them out around here in the warmer seasons. I can't imagine the risk of attacking one, much less climbing inside. What if you got stuck? What if it fell and crushed you? No matter how predictable humans can be, they are dangerous. They keep us here in the park to look at us and feed us, but they'd just as soon shoot us or run us over."

"I wouldn't have guessed it, either," I said. "Actually, to be honest with you, Silver doubts my ability. If he finds a replacement for me, he may cut me from the group. If he does, it's hard to say whose side Chestnut will take. I think he likes me. Sort of. But his first commitment is to the project."

"Only in the city," interjected Blaze. "You'd only see something like this in the city. Foxes aren't meant to be gregarious. It's not in our nature. But when you take us *out* of nature and put us in this man-made environment, we adapt."

"That we do," I said. "In unexpected ways."

"So," said Blaze. "I hate to be businesslike about this, but do you think you can free us? With all your training, I mean."

"I'll try," I said. "You mentioned that River has worked out the locking mechanics?"

"*Maybe*," said River shyly. "I don't want to get everyone's hopes up. I've done my best to watch how our handlers do it, but, well, you know how humans are clever about that sort of thing."

"Not more clever than you," said Blaze, giving her a lick on the cheek. Turning to me, he added, "My sister may just be the smartest fox alive."

I thought of Amber and almost objected, but there was no point. It was time to get to work. "All right, River," I said. "Show me what to do."

The lithe vixen led me along the perimeter of the cage. After about ten feet, the cage turned at a right angle away from the walkway. I followed River to where the wire mesh met a wooden fence at the back of the enclosure.

"The fence prevents visitors from going where they shouldn't," River explained.

The fence was high and sturdy. All I could see beyond it were a few treetops, which had been trimmed back so that they did not overhang the enclosure.

"We don't know exactly what lies beyond the fence in that direction. It's not all trees. There must be some human buildings back there, since our handlers go in and out this way," she said. "There are two doors. Entering from where you are, they first have to unlock the wooden gate. They carry a special tool for that. It has many loose metal pieces and jingles when they walk. A few feet past the wooden gate is the second door, which is metal—steel I think. If you look through the mesh, you can see it. The steel door opens just by squeezing the latch in a certain way. Once you get past the wooden gate, you'll see what I mean."

"Obviously, we don't have the tool to unlock the first gate and probably couldn't operate it if we did," I remarked. "So, I presume you want me to dig under the fence?"

"Yes," River affirmed. "There's pavement beneath us in the enclosure, so we can't dig out. But there's only dirt between the wooden gate and the steel door. I figure that the fence is to keep the wrong humans out, but the metal is to keep us in. The humans haven't considered that animals might want to break *in*."

"Does it happen often?" I joked.

River didn't react to my attempt at humor, so I put my paws to the dirt and began to dig. Pavement covered much of the ground, sometimes running right up to the fence. This meant I had little space to work with. More than once my forepaw slipped and struck the pavement hard, causing me to wince. I shuddered to think how much worse the pain would have been if the city streets had not toughened my pads.

It took me the better part of two hours, maybe more, to dig under the fence. As they looked on, the others called out occasional words of encouragement. If I had been digging for myself alone, I could have done it a little faster, but I had to create extra space for Aurora's swollen belly. Thankfully, the early-spring weather had thawed the ground.

Once I had dug through and popped up on the opposite side of the wooden fence, I studied the steel door built into the side of the enclosure. It was flush with the wire mesh and had a strange sort of handle about four or five feet from the ground. Twin metal rods, thin and long, split from it and ran in opposing directions under several metal braces. River explained that they locked the door in place so that it could only be opened if each rod was twisted and pulled out from beneath the braces. I had trouble following her explanation of the mechanism, but she promised to walk me through it step by step.

"The first thing you need to do," she said softly, "and I'm sorry about this, is to climb up on the enclosure if you can. I'm afraid it will hurt, but there's no other way to reach the lock."

I stood up on my haunches and leaned against the enclosure. It gave way slightly, which threw me off balance for a moment. Then, I wedged a front paw in between the wires that formed the mesh. In the end, there wasn't enough space, so I had to splay my toes outward so that metal pressed in between them. I did the same with my other forepaw and then pulled myself up. My hind legs flailed behind me, and reflexively I kicked against the cage, knocking myself to the ground. I cursed under my breath and then got up to try again.

"Nimbus, are you okay?" asked Aurora. She and Blaze had taken a step back.

"Yes, yes," I muttered and began the procedure anew. Suppressing my instinct to kick or claw, I forced my hind paws in between the wires so that I could push myself up. The handle stood less than a foot from my muzzle. The cold metal sliced into all four paws, pressing fur and flesh hard against the bone. I grunted and snorted with the effort to push and pull myself higher. Several times, I thought I would fall.

When the lower locking rod was just inches above my

muzzle so that I could nearly taste it, my ears perked up. Footsteps. Aurora and Blaze glanced suddenly toward the main thoroughfare. River didn't move. A man was fast approaching from behind me. If he looked through the enclosure at a sharp angle, he would see me. Giving up my grip on the mesh would mean losing all my progress as well as making a noise that might attract his attention. Even if I withdrew to a hiding spot behind the fence, there was no way to conceal the hole I had just dug. It took all my energy to keep still.

From the corner of my eye, I could see the sweeping beam of a flashlight drawing closer step by step. The wires cut into my aching flesh. The heavy footsteps paused. If he saw me, the guard would have no trouble catching me trapped between the cage and the fence. I would never make it back through the hole in time. I imagined large human hands grabbing me, wrapping around my body, choking me, and carrying me off. Would I awake in the cage with the others to live out the rest of my days in captivity? Or would I never wake again? Stifling a whine, I pressed my hind paws down into the wire even harder, struggling to hold on.

Just then, Blaze ran to the far edge of the cage and yipped. The flashlight's beam swept over to him, causing Blaze to shut his eyes and turn away from the blinding light. For a moment, I thought his gamble had made things worse, but Blaze remained calm, and the man continued down the path, glancing back only once.

Aurora sighed in relief, and after several agonizing minutes River whispered that it was safe to continue. It was just in time, too. My hind legs were trembling from exhaustion.

"I can't hold on," I grunted and then lunged upward, chomping onto the lower rod and jerking my head down.

The metal scraped my teeth, the fresh pain distracting from my bleeding paws. Somehow, I managed to dislodge the lower rod before falling backward onto the pavement. The impact knocked the wind out of me, and I gasped for a few breathless moments before I was able to twist myself back onto my belly.

I licked my paws while Blaze and Aurora praised my efforts. When I was able, I rose and repeated the same procedure with the upper locking rod. It took me several lunges and some grappling to nose the rod upward, free from its braces, but eventually I fell to the ground again, landing on my sore feet, and saw the gate fall slightly inward.

"You did it!" cried River with more enthusiasm than I had thought possible for her. The others likewise cheered before Blaze wedged his muzzle into the opening and swung the gate fully open.

One by one, they filed out, into the area between the cage and the wooden fence. Blaze was the first to pull himself under the fence. He insisted on surveying the area before the rest of us followed. Once he announced that the coast was clear, River, Aurora, and I exited through the hole. We wasted no time in heading for the park's side entrance. Though they had ignored me before, the other caged animals took notice as the four of us trotted toward freedom. It was a heady, whirlwind escape, and before I knew it we were standing outside the park's high stone wall.

We congratulated one another once more. Then, one by one, we all fell silent. Awkward, downward glances and somber expressions replaced cheering. The reality of our situation sank in. I had been so focused on the task at hand that I had not truly considered what would happen next. Obviously, Blaze and Aurora couldn't stay with Silver and me, nor would they wish to.

"So," began Blaze. "We should be going."

"Yes," I said flatly. "Yes, of course." I glanced to River. "And you'll want to go off on your own, I suppose?"

"Actually," she said. "I'd like to go with you, that is, if it's all right."

"Come with me?" I asked. "You mean back to Silver and Chestnut?"

"Yes," said River. "I'm interested in studying with your group. I'm not very strong, but I'll do my share of the work, and I can fit into places that others can't. Besides, my brother and Aurora are starting their family. They don't need me around."

"River," interjected Aurora. "It's okay. Really. You can live with us. I don't know where we'll go. I'm too far along in the pregnancy to return to the wild, so we'll have to stay in the city. You've been with us all this time. We'll be glad to have you."

"No," said River. "You have your own life. I want to do this. I really do. If Nimbus will take me, I mean."

"If you're serious," I said, "I'll take you there."

"I guess that's it, then," said Blaze. "We should leave before it gets light out."

He was right. The moon was sinking, and soon there would be no need for streetlights. The escape had taken all night. I was exhausted. Blaze and Aurora had not worked as I had, but they had the task of finding a new home ahead of them.

It was time for us to part. None of us wanted to be sitting out in the open when the sun came up. Blaze and Aurora said their goodbyes to River. By unspoken understanding, the two siblings continued down the street, giving me a moment alone with Aurora.

"Nimbus," she said, fixing her wide, golden eyes on me. "Can you forgive me?"

I should have wished her well. I should have told her that I was sorry and that I wasn't angry with her, but I couldn't find the strength. The last ember had died within my breast, leaving me cold and spent.

Aurora again asked my pardon. With supreme effort, I mustered a single word, "Goodbye," before giving in once more to my tired, silent gaze.

The vixen's ears drooped and her tail sagged. A lifetime's seasons turned at once all around me. I saw the daisies bloom and wither in a single heartbeat, and by the time I realized it, Aurora had caught up with Blaze. Then she turned, rosy fur glinting as the first rays of dawn broke over the horizon. I saw her final, pained expression before she walked away.

CHAPTER

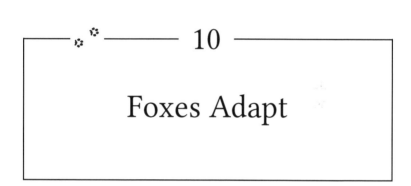

10

Foxes Adapt

River sat beside me just outside the park. Blaze and Aurora had left, and the new day was beginning. My muscles were spent from digging, and my teeth still hurt from clamping onto steel. River seemed to be in fine condition, lithe and unscarred. I assumed she was tired from our escape, but she gave no indication of it. I felt a certain responsibility toward her, as if I had found an abandoned cub. I reminded myself that such paternalism was purely instinctual and silly. After all, River was older and probably smarter than I was.

"Are you certain you want to come with me?" I asked, still exhausted but in less of a stupor with Aurora and Blaze gone.

"Yes."

"To be honest with you, I wasn't even sure I would go back myself."

"Why is that?" asked River.

"For one thing, Silver may not want me. The other fox I mentioned, Chestnut, he's become the favorite. And I'm not sure Silver has much left to teach me."

River trained her green eyes on me. In the growing daylight, they seemed sharper than ever. "Will you stay, though, once you take me there?"

"Yes, I think I will," I said, "at least for a while. Maybe bringing another fox will improve Silver's mood. Besides, it's something to do, which is what I need right now."

"You don't have to," River said. "I'll be okay on my own."

I sighed. "No," I said, "I want to give it another chance. I feel that you'll bring some interesting knowledge to the group. I could lie down here and give up, but I've done that before and it leads nowhere. I came to the city to learn, so that's what I'll do."

River didn't push it further, and so we began the trip to home base. There wasn't enough time before full daylight to get to Silver's nearest refuge, but we had to put as much distance between ourselves and the animal park as possible.

River was quiet as we trotted through the streets and neighborhoods, but her perked-up ears and scanning nostrils told me that her senses were fully engaged. I tried to imagine what the outside world felt like to her after a long captivity. When I asked, she told me that everything smelled cleaner and larger than she remembered. The wonder in River's voice made me glad I had freed her.

When I could travel no more, we curled up at the base of a tree in a suburban backyard. It wasn't the most secure resting place, but I trusted that if we drew human attention, they would either study us quietly from a distance or else approach so noisily that we'd have plenty of warning. For the moment we were safe.

We reached home base two days later. I had kept our pace to about three-quarters of my usual speed out of consideration for River's inexperience. Despite her quiet demeanor, she proved tough and didn't panic, even at a few difficult passages through the city. I could tell that she had refrained from indulging her curiosity at the world outside the animal park, avoiding unnecessary sniffing and exploring in order to keep up with me on the trip.

When we arrived, there was an another fox sitting with Silver and Chestnut. He appeared to be my age. He was large with a full winter coat. Dark marks peppered his otherwise rusty pelt, including a prominent black streak that ran from his forehead to the back of his neck. All three turned toward River and me as we entered the basement.

"Who's this?" asked Silver.

He sounded calm, which took me aback. I had spent the last leg of our journey rehearsing to myself how I would handle Silver's reaction. Even though he had wanted me to bring back a new fox, I feared that River, a thin and meek-looking female, would upset him.

As it turned out, Silver seemed quite interested in River, walking up to her and sniffing around just a bit longer than customary for a first meeting.

The vixen stood there uneasily. "Th-thank you for taking me in," she said.

"With pleasure!" Silver bellowed, uncharacteristically cheery. "At five members, our team is finally complete, and I think introductions are in order."

With that, we all greeted those in the group whom we didn't yet know. The newcomer—whose name was Ash—was bubbling over with enthusiasm. Even when introducing himself to me, he repeated no fewer than three times how excited he was to be with us. His dancing eyes and great, grinning face made me think he might pounce on me and lick my face at any moment.

Once everything settled down, Silver explained that after an accelerated training program for the new members, we would execute our plan. He seemed to have forgotten that I had ever threatened to leave the group. Before I knew it, we were all discussing our roles in the next phase of the operation.

In the end, the consensus was that Silver would typically direct and divert the crowd's attention. Chestnut and I would run up and into the cart or truck from either side. Ideally, both Chestnut and I would make it in and toss food out to Ash, who would relay it to River for caching. On jobs where River's small size could provide an advantage, she might go in instead.

An energy emanated from us. I caught a sense of Silver's old leadership—never totally benign but certainly less spiteful than it had become in recent weeks—and the eagerness I had once felt. I tasted that first hamburger again and salivated dreamily. I thought of unraveling further human mysteries and gaining the upper hand against them. It was thrilling. All that training and talk had not been wasted.

For two more weeks we trained, learning each other's movements till they were second nature. I came to expect Ash's barreling approach a consistent two seconds earlier than I would have liked. I relied on River's silent, snaking movements to keep her invisible till we met up after the strike where she would present us with the carefully stowed spoils. Naturally, our training was on a much smaller scale—park benches, trash cans, and the like—only practice for the real thing, but we took it seriously.

From time to time, Aurora would invade my thoughts, pouncing into my consciousness from nowhere and ravaging my attention till I shook my head and lashed back at my vain curiosity. I told myself that it was natural to wonder where she and Blaze had ended up, whether she had given birth yet, and to how many cubs. It was natural to wonder about such things as one might wonder whether it would rain tomorrow, but a cruel fire lingered in my breast whenever I entertained those thoughts. I was getting better at channeling that fire into my training. The others rebuked my lapses in attention whenever the thoughts gripped me at an inopportune time, but they also noticed how I ran faster, bit harder, and risked more in our skirmishes and sorties.

Ash and River also did individual exercises with Silver till he was satisfied with their physical and mental abilities. I marveled that they did not collapse, given that they were doing in two weeks what I had done in three times that. Still, Silver held his head and tail high, projecting a confidence I had never seen, even in him. Soon we had set a date for the first strike leading up to Operation Apex.

When the day came, our team of five huddled together beneath a stone footbridge in the city's largest park. A light breeze tickled the lush spring grass, and the trees oozed with healthy sap. Everything was about to burst with life, and we felt like one fox, a many-eared, many-footed titan about to emerge from long hibernation, roaring into an unready world.

Today, we would strike a cart, not just to steal from it, but to despoil it of everything we could carry. We had chosen the target carefully: a small one-man vendor of hot dogs and sausages. His cart was open in the back, a roll-up operation, with coolers large enough to hold a day's supply of the meats and a grill right behind the counter. We had two special advantages. First, River's careful observation told us that the lids of the coolers had no latch and could probably be nosed open. Second, because the back of the cart was fully exposed, we would not have to climb into anything and risk getting stuck inside.

At Silver's command, we broke from our huddle and darted like bolts of lightning to our assigned positions. River disappeared. Ash ran to a nearby tree and held steady. Silver, incapable of maintaining a sprint, trotted into the thick of human activity, while Chestnut shot to the left and I to the right. Speeding through the park in a long-ranged pincer move, I heard a few gasps and children's cries but did not slow for a moment. The timing was crucial. Silver had learned long ago how to gauge human reactions with precision, and so Chestnut and I had to arrive together at the right moment following his diversion. Besides, after months in the city, ignoring the surprised stares of humans was easy. Their eyes no longer burned into me or ignited instinctual fear. I was in control. They reacted, but I acted.

Once out of the park, the pavement became a blur beneath my paws. I began to close the arc. A hundred yards away Chestnut was doing the same. He was out of view, but I felt his energy, complementing me, as we raced toward one another. I was the faster runner, owing to Chestnut's shorter legs, but we had practiced enough together that I could maintain a pace equal to his even without seeing him.

I saw the commotion up ahead. Silver was lying on his

back in the street, rolling around, kicking his paws in the air, and making a spectacle of himself like never before. The humans ate it up. They had formed a growing ring, laughing and pointing at his antics. As desired, the hot dog vendor had stepped away from his cart to get a better look.

My eyes met Chestnut's, only a few dozen yards out, as we zoomed toward the exposed back of the cart. His tongue lolled from the side of his muzzle, and he grinned more broadly with each lusty bound. I felt truly kindred to him in that moment. All rivalry had vanished from my heart. He was magnificent, but so was I. His strength was mine, and mine was his.

As we closed in the last five yards, we slowed, silent paws dancing across the pavement. The scent of our prize grabbed my nostrils and pulled me in, but I steeled myself against desire. Rushing in could ruin us, could waste the opportunity Silver had bought us. The vendor was laughing and gawking with the others, but long practice, like an unseen tether, kept him no more than an arm's length from his cart.

Chestnut and I reached the cart within a half second of each other. Without pause, we each started on a cooler. It took me a few seconds to find the small notch used as a handle for opening the lid, but once I got my nose into it, the cooler opened with ease. It was filled with hot dogs, but to my surprise they were packed in ice.

"Chestnut!" I whispered. "It's all cold!"

"I know," he grunted back. "The grill's too hot. We can't grab the meat there without getting burned. What do we do?"

"Let's take what we can," I hissed. "We don't have much ti—"

I was interrupted by a shout and a sharp blow to the

back. The vendor had discovered us. I fell forward, the cooler's lid slamming down and crushing my head into the ice. I gagged and dropped the cold meat. Sputtering, I snapped out of my confusion and flipped my head up, knocking the lid open. Thankfully, either shock or indecision had prevented the vendor from striking again. I grabbed one of the sausages I had dropped and turned to run.

In my peripheral vision, I spotted Chestnut beside me, muzzle packed with hot dogs. He shot me a look like a rabid beast and headed straight for the vendor. In shock, the man screamed and lurched backward, stumbling and flailing his arms. The crowd of perhaps a dozen was in a frenzy. I couldn't find Silver, but I saw Ash, ready to receive the first relay of spoils. I tossed the sausage to him and doubled back, confident that Chestnut had bought me time to grab more.

I raided my appointed cooler twice more with ease, each time passing the prize to Ash, who scooped it up with ready jaws and bolted off for River. Just as I turned for a fourth pass, however, a piercing yip from Silver rang out in the distance—the cry to fall back. Immediately I broke away and headed for the park.

After some precautionary zigzagging, I exited the park on its far side and sprinted till I reached our rendezvous point, the rear loading dock of a department store several blocks away. Panting, I crawled into the shade underneath.

The others were waiting—all except for River. Chestnut, too, was out of breath when he showed up a few moments later. No one spoke in that musty darkness, till claws scraping through the dirt and a familiar scent alerted us that River had arrived. She pulled herself under the dock with ease, and before she could utter a word, we all cheered.

After we had calmed down and rested a bit, River led us back to the park's far side. It was exciting to watch her trot with confidence along the city streets knowing that just a few weeks before she had been the humans' prisoner. I marveled at how the shy, slender vixen had already memorized the city's layout. Not once, to my recollection, had she gotten lost during training or even taken a sub-optimal route.

An image of Aurora flashed in my mind. I flinched at the intrusion and forced myself to concentrate on the pitter-pattering paws before me. Once we had reached the park's edge, River halted amid a tangle of saplings, freshly planted, and proceeded to uncover the cache.

"I chose this place," she explained, "because the soil has been disturbed recently, so extra digging goes unnoticed."

She was right. The dark soil even somewhat masked the scent of the assorted meats. It wouldn't remain safe from other animals for long, of course, but humans wouldn't notice. It was an excellent hiding place given the constraints of time and distance.

"Good work!" barked Silver, barging forward. He shoved his snout forward and attempted to gulp down a whole sausage. This caused a coughing fit, and Silver was forced to spit it out and bite off a single chunk. I could hear his muffled grumbling about its coldness. He turned and glared at the four of us, who were still sitting by silently. "What the hell happened?"

"They store the meat cold," said Chestnut. "We didn't know that before."

"So, they're not just warming the flesh and adding ingredients?" asked River. "In that case, we need to reflect on this and analyze the cooking process more closely."

"You don't say?" said Silver mockingly. Whether the remark was directed to Chestnut or River, I couldn't tell.

"Now wait a minute," interjected Ash. "This was a valuable learning experience. Besides, we all got away safe, and we got enough food to last for days!"

"Always the optimist," Silver groused. "Yes, we can live for a few days off this meat, but that was never the point. Where's the savor? How can we *feast* with these dirt-covered scraps?"

Ash's muzzle was agape in disbelief. River had turned away, looking hurt. Pride and a sense of camaraderie welled within me. We had done well. There was no reason to let a bitter old fox spoil our victory. We had proved our ability and would do so again.

"We'll feast," I said, squaring my shoulders and pushing out my chest. "Maybe not this time, but we will. This is only the beginning."

"Nimbus is right," added Chestnut. "There's no reason to complain. Let's take this back home and start working on the next phase."

Ash echoed his agreement, and River nodded. We began to gather the spoils, stacking as much as we could carry in our muzzles. From the corner of my eye, I caught Silver struggling to suppress a grin, and it struck me that the coy old fox might have been feigning disappointment all along. Maybe it was his way of inciting us to try even harder, or maybe it was to unite the rest of us in our resentment toward him. Perhaps they amounted to the same thing, since unity had become our strength, and only trial and error would tell us how far that could be pushed. Silver had already done what no other fox had by making us into a team. We were no longer beggars. We saw what we wanted and took it.

That night, we ate well. I realized as I ripped off mouthfuls of the now-lukewarm meat that I had not experienced lasting hunger in weeks. Hunger had changed for me. It no longer threatened starvation but had become the prelude to indulgence. In fact, since I was shedding my winter coat, I saw clearly that I had gained weight. I was a year old, so I attributed some of my increased mass to a final growth spurt as I entered full adulthood. At the same time, I couldn't deny the role that rich fare had played. My speed and stamina hadn't suffered, so I pushed the thought aside and continued eating. After all, I needed energy, and I deserved the reward of my labors.

My belly growled again, begging for more. I devoured another hot dog. Judging by the loud smacking and slobbering muzzles, the others were enjoying themselves as well—all except for River. She was batting lazily at a sausage with a single, narrow paw. No one else seemed to notice. If I hadn't paused to count the number of remaining morsels—to make sure I wasn't being cheated—I wouldn't have given it a second thought.

"Something wrong?" I asked.

"I was just thinking about my brother and Aurora," she said softly.

"Oh, well, I'm sure they're doing fine. They've probably found a nice home, and I'll bet Aurora's had the cubs by now."

River's quivering muzzle and sorrowful eyes caught me off guard. She looked astonished, even betrayed. Was she upset with me? I struggled to understand what was happening.

"Don't you think it's strange," she asked, "that we haven't talked about them at all?  Not once since we left the park."

Our teammates were still devouring their supper, although I glimpsed Chestnut's ears pricking up.

"Uh, River," I fumbled. "Do you want to talk about this now?"

She nodded.

"Well, can we go somewhere more private?"

River agreed and followed me up the stairs and outside into the alleyway adjacent to our building. Silver and Chestnut glanced up as we left but soon went back to eating. Ash ignored us completely. He seemed to be savoring each bite as long as possible, chewing the cool meat into a pulp before letting it slide down his throat.

The night air was warm, but not hot.  A slight breeze twisted through the alley, stirring up scraps of paper and other debris. Before I could ask River what was on her mind, she glared at me and said, "Don't you care about them?"

"I don't understand," I said, startled by her accusatory tone.

"Don't you wonder where they are and whether they're all right?"

My heart beat faster.  I pressed my forepaws into the cracked pavement and tried to remain calm.

"Of course," I said. "It's natural to be curious. But, River, we have to focus on the task at hand. We are really building something here, something that will make for an exciting, successful life that most poor foxes would never dream of.  I used to stalk through fields hoping to catch a stray grasshopper, but now..." I trailed off and thought a moment before continuing.  "It's not like we don't earn those delights, you know. We're perfecting our skills well beyond normal. A month ago, you lived in a cage. Look how far you've come!"

"Yes," she said. "This is better than the park. I couldn't bear another year in that space. Actually, I might have tolerated it, if I had known that freedom was coming. The real imprisonment is the routine, the never-ending, never-changing routine—pacing, sleeping, always waking to the same wire frame around you. They fed us predictably. There was no danger there."

"See," I said. "Now you have all this excitement! And the food is better, isn't it?"

"Yes," she agreed. "The food is better, and I do enjoy the challenge."

"You're better off. So, don't you think that Blaze and Aurora are, too?"

"I'm sure they are," she replied. "That's not the point."

"Well, what is it, then?"

"It's that we just let it all go. How could we do that? Like they never existed—"

"We have a memory," I interrupted, "and so do they. Their memory of you, at least, I know is a good one. Besides, you're the one who wanted to join me. I was about to leave Silver for good. I came back because of you."

River was silent, eyes cast down at her paws. I sensed anger mixed with fear, but I couldn't tell whether these emotions were directed at me or at something else.

"Why did your parents name you River, anyway," I asked, "seeing as you're from the city?"

"Don't change the subject," she retorted but then answered anyway. "My father insisted on naming one of his cubs that. He grew up in the wild near a beautiful river. I've never seen one myself."

"They're overrated. Trust me, you're not missing anything," I replied, even though I had never seen a river either. "We've got it made right where we are."

"And *this* is enough for you?"

"Enough? It's more than enough! All those starving, desperate beasts out there, living in fear of humans or at their mercy—like in the park. We left all that behind."

"Maybe." She shook her head. "Only, I don't want to forget. I love my brother and Aurora. I'm glad for my freedom. I want to be glad for them as well."

"Then be glad," I said. "What's the problem?"

River's eyes met mine. She looked disappointed. I thought she would scold me again. Instead, she studied my face for a long time then turned in silence, her brush flagging as she descended the basement stairs.

I had a dream that night—a nightmare. I was running, but not from anything I could define. Dread coursed through me. At the same time, I struggled to carry sausages, hamburgers, pizza, and many more scraps of food than I could possibly hold. Each new morsel forced me to drop everything else I was holding and scoop it up with my mouth. When I slowed to do this, never stopping, I found that I couldn't get back up to my former speed. Eventually, I was scrambling around in a circle, shot through with terror, my muzzle empty but snapping frantically at every turn. Wide-eyed, I looked up to see tightly spaced metal bars surrounding me. They closed in till I was trapped in a space barely the length of my own body, so that my brush inevitably smacked against the bars when I moved. Points of light shone all around me in the dark. At first, I thought they might be stars, but they were eyes—ugly, mocking human eyes.

I awoke gasping, confused and ready to bolt till I recognized my surroundings. A thin bar of light filtered into the dark basement from the alley streetlight. By it I saw the undisturbed, slowly heaving bodies of my teammates. Even Chestnut was there, sleeping. In a break from his former practice, he had begun sleeping in the basement most nights. I was grateful that my nightmare had not awakened them.

For the next few hours, I lay on the concrete floor by the corner desk, shifting positions often. Despite being tired, I could not sleep. My breathing and heart rate had returned to normal. My body was calm enough, but my mind busied itself with a hundred needless thoughts. I curled my brush across my muzzle once again and, under my breath so that no one else could hear, began to sing, "*I saw my love. I saw the rising sun!*"

CHAPTER

## 11

# The Alpha Fox

Our next attack went well. And the next. And the next. We stole food from carts and stands throughout the spring and summer. We were so successful that it only took a full raid twice per moon to restock. There were setbacks, of course—the time Ash got lost or the week we were all laid up with some illness—but we always came back stronger.

Our reputation must have spread among the humans because Silver's diversion technique ceased to be effective after our fourth or fifth strike. This forced us to vary our approach, since as soon as a food vendor spotted a fox, he would guard his cart jealously, often arming himself with a broom or a heavy stick. The first time it happened, Chestnut was lucky to escape with just a sprained paw.

We all agreed that any viable plan had to include a diversion. Even Silver—who had also suggested attacking the humans themselves—acknowledged that we should distract them first. River pointed out that the diversion did not necessarily have to be a *fox*, and her insight provided the foundation for a new strategy. In the end, we came up with two variations on it. First, we could use the vendors' suspicion against them by feigning an attack on one cart in the hopes that the owner of another might abandon his own cart to aid the false target. Second, we could take advantage of seasonal food sales. Since late spring, the number of vendors had increased greatly, especially around the parks. The large crowds, the presence of pets and other animals, and the scores of children were all potential sources of distraction.

The first method proved unsuccessful. The vendors did not assist one another as predicted. Instead, if one was threatened, each guarded his own supply even more carefully. This surprised most of us, but Silver dismissed the behavior as typically human and reiterated that we should have been using physical threats all along. Despite its failure, he heaped praise on River for the idea. It struck me that the old fox rarely criticized her—only in his worst fits of rage.

We had better luck with variations of the second method, especially once we observed how interested most children were in us and how they, in turn, drew the adults' attention. This sort of behavior was not unique to humans, of course. Foxes and many other creatures are highly solicitous for their offspring and will abandon other duties to look after them. So, we learned to draw crowds of children, either by Silver's usual antics or—when the opportunity arose—by stirring up other animals, such as squirrels or flocks of indignantly honking geese.

My own role in our sorties became second nature. The sprints and dodges took less of a toll on me. Adrenaline no longer pumped wildly through my veins. The whole endeavor had become routine. There were advantages to this newfound comfort, such as less stress and freedom from slavish focus on the task at hand. There were also disadvantages. For example, I accumulated more flab than ever, fully perceptible beneath my thin summer coat. Even Ash, already stocky, was putting on weight.

By mid-autumn, when the carts were becoming scarcer as the days shortened and the weather cooled, our team found itself in a rut. Success had made us lazy, altering the same approach time and again. It wasn't long before we were complaining of boredom to each other. Silver took the occasion to remind us how we had once aspired to strike a food truck, not merely a cart but a complete, self-contained vehicle. "Remember Operation Apex?" he chided one evening. "We've let it drag out in this middling phase for too long."

It was too late for the present year, but the idea rallied our spirits and raised our hopes for the spring. It also led us back into a discussion we'd had before, namely, whether to expand our enterprise further and bring in some new recruits. Silver was open to the idea, as was Chestnut. River was wary, and Ash said he would follow what the majority wanted. I was against it. The reason I gave the others was that additional foxes would over-complicate our strategies, rendering them less effective in the long run.

What I didn't tell them was that my mind still wandered to Aurora. If we went out searching for foxes to join our group, I might run into them or their cubs. I felt sick imagining myself living and working with one of their adolescent offspring. It would be too *real*, too much a reminder of my stolen life. Thankfully, I succeeded in convincing the others that we needed to remain agile and that any additions to our group would only prove cumbersome. And so, we passed the winter—and I completed my second year—still scheming and training for our biggest raid yet.

One early-spring night, just days before we planned to strike the truck, I awoke to a rough whisper. Several weeks had passed since my last nightmare. I had been hoping that they were finally past, so when I realized it wasn't a dream, I was relieved.

The whispering continued. It was River. She and Silver stood together on the far side of the dark basement. I could just barely see them from behind the corner desk where Ash and I slept. He snored as loudly as ever, chest rising and falling with each breath, undisturbed. Chestnut wasn't there.

Raising my ears, I could make out River's words. "Silver, I'm not interested," she said, her voice wavering. "Besides, it's not even the right season."

"Even better," he replied. His voice trilled, as if in a growl or a purr.

"Maybe for you," she said. "Please leave me alone now. I'm going to sleep."

"River, wait," he whispered. "I'm sorry. It's just that you're so *pretty* and smart."

"Stop right there!" River hissed. "I don't know what gimmicks have worked for you in the past—if they ever *have* worked—but you're not going to win me over with cheap flattery. You're not going to win me over at all. Look, I've enjoyed our work. It's challenging. But you don't own me, and if you continue like this, I'm just going to leave."

"And go where?" Silver began to ask but fell silent. Footfalls, soft but audible, echoed down the exterior stairs. I couldn't see from my vantage point, but my nose and ears told me that Chestnut had returned from whatever errand had engaged him outside. "So, you're back," said Silver flatly.

"I'm free to take a nighttime walk if I like," replied Chestnut, "although based on what I suspect is going on, I wish I hadn't."

Chestnut looked toward the desk as he entered. I dropped my head to the floor and shut my eyes, pretending to be asleep. With my ears down, I could no longer understand the conversation, but I heard all three arguing in muted but stern tones. Eventually Silver grumbled something and left the basement for the upstairs. Afterward, River and Chestnut continued speaking as they headed for the exit.

When they passed the desk, I heard River say, "I don't believe his moods for a second. This wasn't passion. He's not like that, no matter how much he pretends. He's deliberate and cold. I wonder if he feels anything at all."

I thought for a long time about what that meant and whether River's assessment was correct. Over the last year, I had gone from fearing Silver to respecting him to being disgusted by him and back again. I had wanted to impress him, but I was coming to realize that I had outgrown him. He had taught me nothing of substance since the winter. His physical ability had declined even further—shorter sprints, longer naps. If River was right, even his temper and impulsiveness were a facade. He was just an old fox desperate for control. Silver's contribution had been made. He was only holding us back.

The day we were to strike the food truck was overcast, not gloomy like a cloudy day in the fall or winter but full of promise. I could smell and sense from the moisture in the air that a heavy spring rain was coming. Chestnut suggested putting off the strike till the weather cleared, but Silver insisted that the impending storm was all the more reason to act quickly. Foot traffic was lighter than usual, and rain would drive nearly all the humans indoors. River thought that we could use inclement weather to our advantage, but I pointed out that we had not trained for it. In the end, we followed Silver's lead and stuck to our plan.

This particular job required something special. Chestnut and I normally raided the carts together, but a truck would be different. One of us had to get inside. That was how I found myself panting nervously as I scratched at the metal door of a kebab truck. Already my mouth watered at the scent of roasting meat and vegetables. Besides the delicious spices, an advantage of kebabs is that they are easy to carry.

One man ran the truck alone—unusual but good for our purposes—so when he came to the side door to investigate the rough grating of my claws, my attention was all on him. He was large with a dark complexion. The instant he cracked the door wide enough, muttering angrily at the disturbance, I nipped at his legs, not his flesh but only the heavy outer garments that humans wear. My teeth caught the frayed edge, close to his ankles. I pulled.

Shouting, he flailed his arms and tripped forward. Deftly, I shot between his legs into the truck. Every compartment in the small space was packed with food or human gadgetry. The walls were lined densely with more supplies than I had anticipated. It distracted and confused me long enough that the vendor, still yelling, stumbled back inside.

Ideally, the man would have been shut out. Ash was standing by to rush in and slam against the door to do just that. I feared that he had missed the chance. I shook my head and focused on the vendor. He grabbed something metal from the shelf and swung at me. I retreated till my backside bumped against the opposite wall. Only then did I realize I had trapped myself.

At the window, two more men were pointing and calling to the vendor. A woman shouted, and they pressed in to see what was happening. I ignored the commotion and ducked another blow. The metal implement struck a shelf beside me, knocking pots and paper plates to the floor. I scrambled through the debris, heading for the door. The large man stepped aside and let me pass. I bolted into the daylight and then halted.

A quick glance to the side confirmed that Ash's big, shaggy head was poking out from beneath a bush. I met his gaze and knew he was at the ready. Sure enough, our gamble paid off and the kebab vendor lunged outside, thinking he was driving me off. Instead, I doubled back instantly and leaped up once more into the truck.

Before the man knew what had happened, Ash had body-slammed the door shut, and I was alone in the truck. The loud snarls and the ruckus outside told me that Ash was keeping the vendor at bay and—I hoped—distracting the small crowd of onlookers.

With renewed zeal, I rifled through every niche and container I could. Where a compartment or lid proved difficult for my paws or muzzle to open, I moved on. Haste was the highest priority. Any moment the door would swing open, and I would have to bolt. We couldn't risk using the same deception twice.

By accident I knocked a large pot from the stove and sent boiling water cascading across the floor. Some splashed against my right paw, and I jerked away. Snaking my way past, I grabbed a piece of raw meat and threw my neck to the side, hurtling the food through the open window to the outside. I repeated this again and again till there was nothing left. I also emptied a smaller pot of warm meat and a cooler of chilled meat. It was hard work, grabbing the meats in my muzzle one by one and tossing them through the window. I worked as quickly as I could.

The door handle clicked, and the vendor, clamoring furiously, leaped at me. The attack caught me off guard—humans rarely strike unarmed—and before I knew it, we were wrestling on the truck's wet floor. Thankfully, the water had cooled enough that it didn't burn. I wriggled and kicked my way to freedom. As soon as I was loose I headed for the door, still wide open, and turned sharply to my left upon exiting. Ash was nowhere to be seen, but I glimpsed Silver approaching from the opposite side.

The crowd's eyes were partly on me, partly on the pile of food I had thrown from the truck. A quick assessment told me that Ash and Chestnut had successfully ferried a large portion of the spoils away to River, whose task was to cache it. They were long gone. Silver was running as fast as he could, heaving and fixated on the remaining meat. I was sure we had more than enough already, so I nearly called out to him to fall back and start the rendezvous. Just then, a woman, stout and with a severe look, swung a black umbrella. She struck Silver in the neck, and he lost his footing, skidding to the side a few yards from the truck.

By this time, the vendor was back, glancing wildly in

every direction. He held a heavy iron bar. I was at least thirty feet away, so I curled up behind a large blue mailbox and peered beneath it, ready to flee if necessary. The man looked right at me. He might have seen me, but he did not pursue. Instead, he turned back to Silver and wound up for a swing.

Silver had picked himself up and, after a few staggers, was coming at the food from another angle. His eyes were focused straight ahead like a viper's, and I could tell he was not aware of the vendor's presence. The man was still a few seconds away. I opened my muzzle to bark a warning, but something about Silver's face—his drooling lips or ghoulish stare—kept me mute. He had the look of one consumed. Silver had often vexed me, had angered or even frightened me, but now he disgusted me. In that moment, I didn't even pity him. I wanted the blow to land, and a wave of hot pleasure swept through me when it did.

The metal cracked into Silver's rib cage, eliciting a banshee-like shriek and knocking the old fox to the wet pavement. The onlookers gasped. Some cheered. Silver bleated, and the man struck again. Any illusion I might have entertained about Silver's survival or recovery was shattered along with his legs, back, and head as the beating continued. All the cheering and hooting stopped, and the vendor alone continued to yell and curse, landing blow after blow.

I saw a baby bird once, when I was small—a blue jay fallen from its nest. It twitched, broken inside, squeaking for help from above till it died. I thought of that as Silver writhed and pleaded in his last moments. The hot scent of blood filled the air. I watched a long time after the noise had ceased.

Eventually, after the crowd had dispersed, I headed for our meeting place, the space behind a large receptacle for plastic bottles on the park's far side. When I entered, Chestnut was prone, muzzle flat on the ground, ears drooping. River lay beside him, her tail draped across his haunches.

"We took a lot of risks," the vixen was saying. "It was bound to happen eventually. Silver knew that better than all of us."

"I suppose," murmured Chestnut, "but that's just it. We were at our peak, and now... Well, now what's going to happen? I mean, I'm just in shock, I guess."

"So you know about Silver?" I asked.

"Yes," said River. "Chestnut is taking it hard."

"It's strange," said Chestnut with a sigh. "I had serious issues with Silver. We all did. But it's still a loss. For all his faults, he brought us together and pushed us toward success."

"Not to be callous," I said, "but today *was* a success in terms of the payoff. Silver would be glad for that fact." Chestnut looked at me puzzled. "What I'm trying to say," I went on, "is that Silver got what he wanted. I'm sorry, I'm not putting it very well because I'm upset."

"He got what he *wanted*?" gasped Ash. "Silver wanted to be alive. That's what he wanted."

"You're right, Ash," I interrupted. "I hate to lose Silver. I really do. Yes, he was strict, but he's the one who took me in and taught me so much. I think he would have been the first to tell us that we need to think bigger, that now's the time to set our sights even higher."

"It's too soon to think about anything like that," murmured River.

"You're right," I said. "I guess I'm just trying to live up to what I think Silver would do. He would say that we should use this as a learning opportunity."

"That's right," agreed Chestnut. "That's what he would say."

"Did anyone see how he died?" asked River.

"I didn't see it," I lied, nipping at my paw, "but I heard it, even though I was too far off to get to him. The owner of the food truck was yelling." I swallowed hard, pretending to find the memory overwhelming. "And he was hitting him with something hard, again and again."

River buried her narrow muzzle in Chestnut's fur. "That sounds horrible, just horrible."

"Yes," I said, "it was monstrous."

CHAPTER

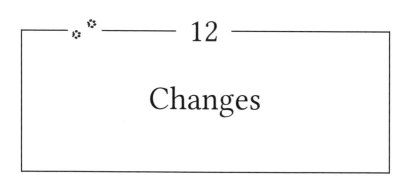

12

# Changes

For the next week we did no training or foraging, surviving on what we had stockpiled. At times one or another of us would be absent without informing the others. The days of a rigid routine were gone. After the prolonged intensity of our campaigns, the rest and freedom felt unreal. Life was so different without Silver.

Chestnut and River were often in each other's company, leaving me alone with Ash, who seemed to be taking Silver's death rather hard. He would go the whole day without eating and then binge. I think he even had trouble sleeping.

Foxes sometimes hold simple obsequies for the deceased—a few songs and ritual movements—but we did nothing for Silver. The body was irrecoverable. Even if someone had been willing to risk going back to the scene, it would have been too late. Humans may leave our corpses on their roadsides, but they will not tolerate dead animals in their public squares. I had more than once witnessed the removal of deceased fowl or rodents from the city streets. Silver had told me once that they were incinerated in a large building at the city's eastern limit. I had to admit that observing his death had exhilarated me. Even so, I took no particular joy or sorrow in imagining his remains being pulverized and consumed in flames. A pathetic creature had come to a pathetic end. It was an event, a brute fact, nothing more.

Foxes have hardy stomachs, not like humans, who, I had observed, preferred rich fare not only out of decadence but because they couldn't tolerate much else. Nevertheless, once our stockpile turned rancid, not even Chestnut could choke down the last portions, and so hunger eventually drove us out to gather food. The problem was that Silver's death had also made us skittish. Chestnut, River, and I stole from a few bins here and there, but we avoided the large parks. The city's eyes were on us, wary of the fox menace. We were used to humans' gawking and cooing when they spotted us in the daylight, but recently there had been shouts and even a glass bottle thrown, which had shattered into many fragments and cut River's paw. I could taste the humans' fear in the humid late-spring air, and fearful humans are dangerous.

I set my mind to thinking up a plan to move our group out of the city. With Aurora and Blaze free, there was always the chance that I or one of our team would run into them—or their children—if we stayed in the city. Besides, there wasn't much left for us to do in the city. A move elsewhere, ideally with me cemented as leader, made the most sense.

Several weeks after Silver's death, when the four of us happened to be together, I spoke up. "I think we need to talk about our future," I said. "It's been long enough. We have to decide what our next steps will be."

River's twitching muzzle and stiff, down-turned lips betrayed concern, but Chestnut, who had polished off his food and was lounging beside her, looked relieved. "I wondered when one of us would broach the subject," he said. "Obviously, we're all thinking about it. Normally, Silver would have put it in the open and sorted it all out, but, of course, he can't. I almost said something the other day when River remarked how she never finished her last bit of training, but I figured that you all assumed I would be the one to push us on and, well to be honest, I'm not sure I really want to."

Ash's ears perked up. "Oh?"

Chestnut nodded. "I enjoy what we do—or, what we used to do—but I feel like we've reached the limit. Frankly, I'm just not interested in stealing food from carts anymore. It was fun while it lasted, but, in my opinion, continuing with it would be juvenile."

"Well," I said, "I would agree that we're ready for something more. Silver saw that as well, which is why we went after a full truck. But, let's accept that we need an even bigger shift. No more business as usual. What sort of project would you be interested in?"

Chestnut glanced to River. "Well, I don't want to speak out of turn, but it might be time for a change of scenery. Maybe we could think about moving to the suburbs, for example."

"Interesting idea," I agreed. "And I'm not looking to impose myself, but I *have* been at this the longest. In fact, as you know, Silver and I were technically partners. I often deferred to him because of his experience, but now that experience is mine as well." I looked to each of them in turn. "You all have talents, too. I recognize that. We've lost something in Silver, but this is also an opportunity. The four of us can really go in a fresh direction. I promise I won't be autocratic or capricious like Silver often was. We all have skills, and those skills will be rewarded when used for the good of the team."

"You sound like you've thought this through," said Ash.

"I want to be totally honest," I said. "I have thought it through, and I think I would make a good leader."

"You want to be in charge?" asked Chestnut.

"No need to worry," I said. "I'm not looking to be a dictator or anything like that, more of a first among equals."

"Who says we need a leader at all?" challenged Ash.

"That's what I thought at first," I said, casually arching forward and scratching behind my ear with a hind leg. "But, for the sake of group cohesion, there has to be someone who takes on the burden of finalizing our plans. All with full consultation, of course."

"And you're that fox?" asked Ash.

I felt my ears and forehead warming, but it was essential to appear calm. "I could be. I'm willing to accept the burden, anyway."

"Well," said Chestnut, "I wasn't expecting this exactly, and I have to say that the wheels in my own head have been turning in a different direction, but you've piqued my interest."

"That's the spirit," I said. "Let's give it a try. A change of venue and a change of leadership. It will be a new beginning for us. I wouldn't want to impose myself, but I would be a natural choice to take responsibility for our next step. Certainly, I'd be no worse than Silver was, and we all accepted him."

Chestnut piped up. "We accepted Silver for a time," he said. "That's true, but it's because we were getting results. Operation Apex is over. Robbing food carts is over. Frankly, it went on longer than I ever thought it would."

"Right," Ash agreed. "Silver's dead. This group died with him. Or, at least, it's dying. Silver might have kept us together. Now that he's gone, I do question why I ever tolerated so much abuse from him. No matter. You're right, Nimbus, that this is an opportunity to move on, and it's one that I'm taking."

"Let's take it together, then," I said in a friendly tone. "Each one of us is free. We've always been so. If you want to leave the group, you can. No pressure. Nothing to lose. Just give it a chance."

"And where would you like to go?" asked River.

"There's a place on the north side. I once saw it while out recruiting. There were no foxes that I noticed and many fewer humans than within the city."

"You mean somewhere on the outskirts?" asked Chestnut.

"Yes. You may know that there are hard metal tracks in parallel stretching as far as can be seen toward and away from the city on that side. There is a place near those tracks that I believe would be quite comfortable."

"What are the tracks for?" asked River.

"They're rails," I explained, "for the largest vehicles you've ever seen, like tremendous iron snakes that charge along faster than cars." The vixen's eyes widened, and she pressed against Chestnut. "But," I continued, "like the cars, they never deviate from the path the humans have set for them. As long as you're not caught on the tracks at the wrong time, they can't harm you."

"I've been there," said Ash. "I know where you're talking about. Say we do go there together, what's the point?"

"Well," I said, "it would be a change of pace. Like Chestnut, I'm tired of stealing from carts. That was Silver's obsession, and it's better laid to rest with him. Besides, here in the middle of the city, we're too exposed. The humans are still on the lookout for us. Why not go somewhere we can observe them instead?"

"Observe the humans?" asked River. "I've spent my whole life observing humans."

"So you know how strange they can be," I said. "There may be opportunities we don't know about yet. A little more breathing room there on the outskirts and we could really come into our own." I didn't mention that I wanted to lower my chances of running into Aurora or her family.

"It's okay with me," said Chestnut. "We do need to get out of the city, and we have put a lot of effort into training together. It would be a shame to split up just because we've lost Silver. I'll give you a chance, Nimbus. I think that's fair."

River nodded her agreement. I turned to Ash, who sighed and said, "All right. It won't hurt to stay together a bit longer, I suppose."

The next day we left the basement behind. I felt strange leaving the place I had spent the majority of my life, but I relished the opportunity. Silver's time had ended; it was up to me to lead us into the next stage. Our journey took a few days because we had to be cautious, stealing our way out of the city. Summer was upon us. The streets and buildings radiated heat throughout the day, so we traveled at night. The others were less enthusiastic than I, and I made an effort to check in with them regularly. They had agreed to follow me, and I had to show that I was ready to direct them.

As we drew near to the outskirts, shrill whistles occasionally sounded in the distance, until at last we reached the tracks. It was night, and the long, straight rails flashed in the moonlight. They were surrounded by white gravel and ran from left to right into the darkness. River sniffed inquisitively at the steel tracks, the spikes that held them fast to the ground, and the wooden beams that braced them every yard or so. I warned her not to tarry between the rails. Once River was satisfied, I led us parallel to the tracks.

After about half an hour, a powerful rushing sound like a windstorm suddenly bore down behind us. Metal raced along metal with the force of lightning. "Don't worry!" I shouted, "we're safe as long as we're not on the tracks!"

Although I knew I was right, even fifteen feet away from the rails it felt as if the train was right behind us. Within a matter of seconds it roared past, sending a strong gust of wind at us. We all leaped away into the bushes, myself included, until a good two minutes after it had passed.

"Instincts are hard to resist, aren't they?" I asked to break the silence that followed in the train's wake. Despite my best efforts my voice trembled.

"Wow," said Ash. "It stayed on the tracks, though."

"I believed it would," agreed River, "but I couldn't help diving for safety."

"That's why humans are worth studying," I said, shaking myself off. "They built this. You know how weak they are—they would be just as scared as us—and yet they keep control. Imagine if we could learn that power? The power to overcome instinct by force of will?"

"Humans are special," said Chestnut. "No animals like us have ever made something like this. It's so far beyond us."

"Isn't that what's exciting?" I asked. "You're a risk-taker, aren't you? A lover of challenges? The best is yet to come." I took a few steps and saw the reflective eyes of my team follow me. "Let's keep going. There has to be a juncture somewhere. I'm hoping we'll reach one before daybreak."

Sure enough, the track eventually led into a large gravel yard populated with rough-looking buildings, both large and small. Bright lights shone down from atop tall posts. We crept carefully through the shadows. In the midst of it all several other tracks met the one we had been following. Unlike roads, which often intersect at sharp angles, the metal tracks curved toward each other and gradually melded together.

"It's like an enormous spider's web," whispered River, "except with fewer lines. I wonder how large the network is. How high up would you have to be to see it all?"

"As high as the stars," remarked Chestnut.

"Let's get higher up," I said, indicating a hill with my nose.

From the hilltop, we studied the scene below us. It was nearly dawn, and the first rays of light showed how the surrounding landscape was littered with brush and debris. Only a few plants dotted the landscape here and there. Several roads led from the rail juncture toward the city.

"I thought there would be more humans around," said River. "Aren't the trains meant for transport?"

"Yes," I said, "sometimes for themselves, but these seem to be trains meant for carrying other things. I noticed piles of wood and metal on the train that raced by us earlier."

"You're right," agreed Ash. "See those large metal buildings along the road over there? Those aren't residential.
They're probably for storage."

"How do they get the piles from the trains to storage?"
asked River. "They must be terribly heavy. They couldn't
possibly lift them, even with those hands of theirs."

I didn't want to appear ignorant, so I redirected her
question. "That's why we're here. Not just to steal from
the humans, but to learn from them. They enjoy a power
that other animals don't understand. Fear has kept us from
getting close enough to study, but we are a team that has
conquered that fear. Now we will truly begin to grasp what
the humans have to teach us."

"To what end?" asked Chestnut.

I wondered whether his question was more than it
seemed, since he knew I wanted to avenge Aurora. As far
as I could tell, neither Silver nor Chestnut had told the others. In any case, I felt that my desires had evolved. I still
wanted the satisfaction of getting back at the humans on
that farm, but the city had revealed something more. "Think
of this," I said. "It's obvious that the humans are not physically stronger than other animals. We've seen that. They're
not faster. They have pitiful teeth and no claws. Not even
fur! Haven't you wondered how they survive the winter?"

"Actually," said Ash, "I used to ask myself that, but I realized that it's the buildings. They live inside those large
buildings, which keep them safe."

"Right," I said, "but where did those buildings come
from? They didn't grow like the grass and the trees. The
humans made them—from materials like those carried by
the trains, from wood and steel and glass. How do they do
it? That's what we're here to find out. If those weak crea-

tures can tap into such deep ability, who's to say that we can't?"

"You think that some day foxes will be building warehouses and driving cars?" asked River skeptically.

"No," I replied, "I'm not going *that* far. Foxes may never do what humans do. Would we even want to? I just mean that we have more potential than we realize. Who knows what we're capable of unless we try? The humans ought to be our model. One day we might learn to organize even more, to absorb the territory of a dozen foxes around us, rid ourselves of wolves and coyotes and all other enemies, and be free."

"Aren't we free already?" asked River. "No cages hold us. We can go where we please and do what we choose."

"No," I countered. "I mean the liberty of really free animals, those who are not slaves to hunger or fear, who rule the land around them with all its creatures, who will bequeath that same hard-won privilege to generations yet to be born."

"You're talking about an *empire*," scoffed Chestnut. "No fox has done something like that. Our lives are wedded to the seasons. We come in with the seasons and go out with them. Each litter renews that cycle."

"We may yet become something more," I said. "That's what the humans do. No single one of them built that city. It took generation after generation, passing down the fruits of hard work and knowledge. We could do that, too! Our team has already done more than most foxes by coming together for study and training. Why shouldn't we expand? Imagine the power of a dozen of us, or a hundred! One generation teaching and forming the next, not just for a few months of cubhood, but for a lifetime."

"A fox empire," said River incredulously.

"A fox empire," I repeated. "Humans have built one, why not foxes?"

"I have to admit, it does sound exciting," said Chestnut. "It would be something new. But, how do we do it?"

"First things first," I said with a yawn. "We have to find a place to rest."

"I didn't smell any other foxes," said River. "But I did notice a trace of something that might concern us out here."

"Coyotes," said Ash.

"Exactly," said River. "I don't think they live here, but they have definitely come this way."

"I thought so, too," I said. "We should move on a little to be safe. I can see a bridge over that small creek past the scattered buildings. That might be a good place."

"The sun is getting higher all the time," observed Chestnut. "I, for one, am ready for a rest."

After exploring the nearby options, we settled on a thicket of bushes uphill from the creek. The land was grassier there, more like what I remembered from the country. I would have preferred an underground den, but the foliage provided a little cover, and the others agreed it was secure enough. The bridge was about a hundred yards downstream. It looked old to my eyes. Its dull red paint had nearly flaked off completely, revealing the worn steel underneath. I had an odd feeling about the area, but I was too tired to investigate further. I dismissed the thought, and we laid down for the day.

CHAPTER

13

# Enemies and Friends

I awoke to distant laughter and raised my head, brushing against the foliage above me. Small points of light filtered through the thick bushes. It was late afternoon. My companions were still slumbering away, Ash snoring loudly, so I crept out and stretched. I felt like I had slept for a week. The sound was coming from the beyond the bridge.

I walked quietly downhill toward the creek. A mourning dove stared at me nervously then flew to safety. Only a thin, winding stream of water snaked its way over the rocks. It was barely deep enough to cover a paw, but it quenched my thirst. When I was satisfied, I followed the water downstream toward the bridge.

Climbing the hill toward the gravel road that ran along

the bridge, I kept my ears erect and my nostrils open. I saw the railroad tracks in the distance, parallel to the gravel road upon which I stood. The bridge before me was narrow, just wide enough for a single vehicle. Once I was sure that no cars were coming, I trotted to the center and peered over the side.

A group of men, wilder and dirtier than usual, were encamped under the bridge. I counted six in all, conversing in sharp human tones punctuated by laughter and exaggerated gestures. I had never seen humans lounging in such a place before. Was this a different sort of park? I studied the men, trying to understand.

Eventually I heard a rustle at my backside and turned. It was Ash. "There you are," he whispered, dropping prone to the ground beside me. "Did you find anything good?"

"Have I been gone that long?" I asked.

"Long enough. We woke up and you weren't there, so I tracked you. What's going on?"

"These humans," I said. "They fascinate me."

"Well, that's obvious!" Ash chided. "I'm surprised you haven't been hit by a car, lying here in the road like this."

"It's not a big road," I replied. "I don't think there's much traffic."

"Fair enough," said Ash. "So, what are those men doing anyway?"

"I'm not sure yet. That's why I'm watching them. They seem to be relaxing on the banks of the creek. But, do you notice the bags and other things they have with them?"

Ash craned his head lower to get a better look. "Yes," he said, "it's more than humans usually carry for sure."

"I think they might live here," I said, "or at least spend a lot of time here."

"Well, then they'll still be here later. Come on, let's get some food and meet up with the team!"

My stomach growled at the mention of food, and I realized how long it had been since I'd eaten. "You're right," I said. "Let's go."

In the days that followed, the other foxes and I explored the surrounding territory. Scent trails and markings chronicled the land's population. Deer and small game frequented the area. Coyotes and even a bear or two had crossed through recently. We traded the cluster of bushes for a pile of debris farther from the creek, in the direction of the city. Weeds growing up amid the wooden beams and sheet metal indicated that no humans had disturbed the area recently. I hoped it would prove an adequate den for four foxes.

The transition back to wild food was harder than I expected. The first few days, the cravings nearly drove me mad. It wasn't just my belly, but my whole body that cried out for the tastes and smells of the city. Roots and berries made me sick, and I could feel myself losing weight. I noticed it in the others, too, especially Ash. But eventually we adapted, and I felt better than ever in my thin, summer coat without the excess fat.

After our first week, I called a meeting outside our den. The other foxes gathered, curious to hear my plans.

"I thank you again for joining me and for your confidence," I began. "I promise I will not abuse that trust. You may wonder what we'll be doing out here. I've already explained a little, but I'd now like to formally articulate two areas of focus, two major tasks for us. First, I am instituting a sparring regimen. We have to remain fit, and beyond that, we must become better fighters. Silver taught us many things, but not combat. I'm sure we all did our share of play-fighting as cubs, but I'm talking about serious, methodical training. I want us to be ready to defend and expand our territory."

"Expand?" asked River.

"Yes," I said. "As I mentioned before, I feel we foxes have set our sights too low. The four of us have proved that foxes can work as a team, so why shouldn't we start working toward what Chestnut referred to as an empire? I have to admit, I like the word."

"You're serious about taking over territory from other foxes?" asked Ash.

"I won't rule it out," I said, "but if that makes you uncomfortable, keep in mind the coyotes. We'll have plenty of work eradicating them. That would actually *help* our neighbor foxes. Who knows? They may want to ally with us for protection after a favor like that."

"And how will this sparring work?" asked Chestnut. "Surely we won't turn our fangs and claws against one another."

"No," I said, "not in earnest. We'll have to be careful, but the experience in footwork, maneuvers, and acrobatics will be valuable. There's plenty we can practice without seriously hurting each other."

"I see," said River, "and we'll rotate sparring partners?"

"Yes," I said, "as I envision it. I think we'll learn a lot that way."

"Well," she said, "it's not what I was expecting, but seeing as I've never lived in the wild before, it would be good for me to work on such skills. I'm willing to try it."

"If River agrees, then I'll try it, too," said Chestnut.

"Okay with me," said Ash, "but don't expect me to go easy on you!"

I laughed. "Thank you all. I appreciate that. Now, as you already know, I'm sure, our other focus will be observation. I want us to take turns scouting out the juncture as well as spying on the men by the bridge and any other areas of human activity that we come across. We'll report back to each other, and I'll ask River especially to think carefully about the information we recover and search for patterns or anything of interest."

"I'd be glad to," said River shyly.

"It's no secret that you're the smartest of us," I said. Then, turning to Ash and Chestnut, I added, "Remember, in this group talent is acknowledged."

Things continued amicably for the next week or so. Our group's spirits were high, lifted by the excitement of our new home and new endeavors. It felt good to hear the others joking and encouraging one another, free from the negativity Silver had engendered. Anything seemed achievable.

One day, after his regular patrol, Chestnut reported something of interest. "I was near the juncture," he said, "and a train stopped. After a while large trucks came and men began to unload its cargo. It was quite a sight. They opened up the large cars pulled by the train and carried out piece after piece of metal."

"How did they lift them?" I asked.

"With their hands," he said, "two men at a time. They were also wearing gloves."

"The gloves protect their hands," explained River, "like the clothes they wear."

"Right," I agreed. "So, the metal must not have been that heavy. What did they do with it?"

"They loaded it onto their trucks and eventually drove away one by one."

"Good reconnaissance work!" said Ash.

"Yes, good job, Chestnut," I said. "What you saw doesn't solve the mystery of how they move heavier loads, but it does give us a lead. This was at the juncture, you say?"

"Yes."

"Then I'd better go there. In fact, I should stay a few days. Perhaps a train with heavier materials will stop there."

"That's a good idea," said River, "but why not commute back and forth? It's not that far."

"I want to be ready," I said. "In the hour or so it takes to get from here to there I might miss something crucial. I'll find a secure vantage point where I can respond at a moment's notice. The trains will wake me as they come in."

"Be mindful of predators," cautioned River. "We're not alone out here." Chestnut nodded his agreement.

"Do you want one of us to go with you?" asked Ash.

"No," I replied. "You all are doing good work. Carry on with your regular schedule here. We have to keep our eyes and ears open. There's always more to learn. Don't worry about me. I can handle myself."

My first day away was uneventful. I had arrived in late morning, found where I would sleep, and caught some mice before slinking down toward the tracks for closer observation. Two trains stopped that day, but neither unloaded anything. They only rested for about half an hour while men buzzed around them conversing and examining equipment.

By the third night I was ready to give up. None of the trains had held cargo heavier than what could be carried by hand. My patience was at its end, so I had left my post for a bit of nighttime hunting. Here and there fireflies lit up, and the stars were just coming out. The cooling air was a pleasant break from the summer heat, and I was sniffing along leisurely when a pair of red glowing eyes caught my gaze.

I froze, heart pounding. Whatever it was remained still, as if waiting for me. The animal had an oaky, non-threatening scent. Curiosity won me over and I approached. Once I was about twelve feet away from the silent creature, I saw that it was a raccoon.

"Be careful out here, fox!" hissed the plump stranger. "There are coyotes, you know. They were just here this very day. Meaner than normal, I think."

"Yes, I know," I said, annoyed. "I have a nose, of course."

"You didn't smell me!"

"Well, you're upwind, and I wasn't looking for raccoons in any case." I was ready to dismiss the little beast and get back to hunting when I realized what was so odd about our conversation. "Wait," I asked, "how can you speak my language?"

"A long story. I traveled once a long way with a rail fox. You see? We have been to many towns along these rails. Some foxes travel. So do some raccoons. It is not the way of us all, but it was my way once and that of my friend. From him it is I learned some of your language."

"I'm impressed," I said. "What's your name?"

"You would translate it to 'Sturdy.'"

"Sturdy?"

"Yes, yes. In raccoon-speak, it is more elegant— *Chitchigitch.* It was my father's name. But it means 'sturdy.'

That is what Comet—my old friend the fox—called me."

"Where is Comet now?" I asked, wondering whether he could be an ally.

"He still travels. Or is dead now. I do not see him for one year at least."

"But you stayed here?"

"I am older. I saw too many towns. Too many country-sides. All the same. When I was young, I did not know that. I thought the world was big. Now I know. Why go farther?"

"I see," I said. "And did Comet learn raccoon-speak as well?"

Sturdy laughed. I had never heard a raccoon laugh be-fore. It made me shiver, like fangs biting sheet metal. "Poor fox. Only some broken words. I think our language is very hard for you. Very complicated. Many rules. Many excep-tions. Not simple like fox-speak."

I felt a little offended and almost said something but decided against it. Sturdy was the first animal I had met who could converse with others beyond their kin. As a fox, I could understand the dialects of coyotes, wolves, and other canids—except domestic dogs, whose speech had bro-ken down through human conditioning. I assumed that the case was similar for birds and other beasts, that mountain lions could understand bobcats, and so forth. But Sturdy had really gotten me thinking. "Do you speak any other languages?" I asked.

"Bah!" said Sturdy, waving a paw dismissively. "A little of a lot. I spent most time with Comet, so fox-speak is my best foreign language."

Sturdy's gesture drew my attention to his paws. They were like tiny human hands, delicate but flexible. Some-how seeing another animal with such an endowment made me consider the importance of hands to human beings. It had become clear that the humans' ability to make things, whether vehicles or large buildings, stemmed ultimately from their ability to work on fine details. Even the tallest structure in the city depended on the ability of many workers to manipulate small tools. I wondered why raccoons had not accomplished so much, nor squirrels or any of the few animals who had paws like this. Just how like humans could we become?

"I'll bet you could help me," I said.

"Help?"

"Yes," I continued. "You have a certain dexterity that I don't, and maybe some knowledge as well. But first I want to ask you something."

"What do you ask?" replied Sturdy.

"Why were you waiting here for me? I think I'm glad to make your acquaintance, but it's obvious that you were seeking me, not vice versa."

"Yes," said Sturdy. "It's no secret. I have seen your group around. I like to know what is going on here. Four foxes can be a little—how do you say it?—*intimidating*. So when I saw that you are out on your own these few days, I wanted to meet you. What is your name? Where are you from? I want to know these things."

"Oh," I said, "I'm Nimbus. Most recently, I've come from the city. Now, as I was saying, you may be able to help—"

"Help, help," said Sturdy with a sigh. "I see. That is all you are thinking of right now. Fine. What do you need?"

"Can you understand the language of humans?" I asked. "Or use their tools? What do you know about them?"

"I see," replied Sturdy. "You want to learn about humans? All about them, I suppose?"

I nodded.

"Of course," said Sturdy. "It happens that I know about many things. I will be honest with you, since I am an honest raccoon. I do not speak their language."

"Well, that's no worry," I said, interrupting. "You or I wouldn't be physically capable of speaking their language to begin with. What I'm really interested in is whether you can *understand* what they're saying. Like their dogs do, for example."

"The dogs understand, yes. But at what cost? They are almost human themselves," said Sturdy, shaking his head in disgust. "No, I never tried to learn that. I knew I would never speak with a human, so for me there's no point to bother with their language."

"It could help me out a lot," I said. "I'm studying humans. It would be revolutionary for my research to know even a little of what they're saying."

"And what do you offer me?" asked the raccoon.

"Strength and speed. You mentioned coyotes. My team can protect you."

"Bah! Are you sure? They are very powerful. Many underestimate. But I don't need you to help with the coyotes. They are more a threat to you than me."

"What would you like, then?"

"I am interested in culture," said Sturdy. "Where were you from before the city? You said you came recently from there, but that means you were somewhere else before. Where was that?"

"I came from the east," I said. "The countryside near woods and farmland."

"Comet was a rail fox, a traveler, as I said. I have never known a country fox. So, I would like to learn from you. You tell me about your home, your myths, your poems, whatever you have. That is what I want."

"You'd be interested in that?" I asked.

"It is all I am interested in anymore," explained Sturdy. "The world is small, but it is old. What has been passed down can be of great value."

"I know some of the old stories," I said, "and some songs, though I don't much feel like singing."

"I want to hear them," insisted the raccoon. "I will help you if you give them to me."

"Fine," I said. "Do we have a deal, then? You help me with the humans, and I will teach you our stories and songs."

The raccoon raised both paws to his mouth in thought. "Yes, it's a deal."

"Only," I added, "don't talk to the other foxes. I don't want them to know about you just yet."

"Oh?" asked Sturdy. "Why is that?"

"I have my reasons," I said. "Do you agree?"

"Yes, yes. That's a deal, too."

When I returned to camp the following night, the others were eager to hear my news. Ash had just come back from his assigned shift, and they were lounging outside our den.

"So," asked Chestnut, "did you learn how they unload the trains?"

"No," I replied. "It was a disappointing stakeout. I didn't figure out any more than you and River already had."

"Nothing of interest?" asked Ash.

"No," I said. "It was completely uneventful."

"That's too bad," said Chestnut, "but speaking of River, she has some news that might lift your spirits."

"Oh?" I asked.

"Well," said River, "I noticed something about the men who live by the bridge. They camp there every day without fail, but it's not always the same people. Most of them go out during the day, but each evening four to eight return. Sometimes one shows up for a few days before disappearing again."

I thought for a moment, trying to grasp the significance of the report. "What does it mean?" I asked.

"I'm not sure," said River sheepishly. "It's just a pattern I've identified. I suppose at a minimum it indicates that they don't consider that a permanent living space. That would fit with what we know about humans in general. They don't live outside. This group seems to be anomalous, but maybe they're not so different from the others."

"Could they be traveling?" I suggested. "Maybe they're just passing through."

"I considered that," replied River, "but what's strange is that the group remains stable, even though not all of its individual members do. Anyway, I don't know what to make of it just yet."

"Good work," I affirmed. "Anything we learn is helpful. Let's keep going. I'll be back on my regular rotation as well, and I'll make it a point to pay careful attention to those men."

I thoroughly enjoyed the weeks that followed. My sparring sessions with the others bore fruit. I could feel myself reacting more quickly, striking harder, and dodging better. Each of my teammates called for a different approach. Chestnut's short legs gave him a low center of gravity, making him hard to topple. River was lithe and quick, like a fast-moving liquid. I took special pleasure in my matches with her. For his part, Ash had the advantage of bulk. His big, shaggy body absorbed blows with ease. No matter who I fought on a given day, each bout left me panting and exhilarated.

I also met Sturdy when I could, away from the others. I shared stories and songs with him and told him all about myself as well, from the time I left home through my life in the city. Though he loved to talk, Sturdy was also an attentive listener. In return, he taught me what he had learned about humans in his years of travel. At times, he would go off on a tangent about other animals and their languages and cultures. I pretended to listen patiently, even though I was only interested in humans. The silly creature had spent his life gaining this knowledge and seemed desperate to share it.

Sturdy agreed to observe the men who lived by the bridge and try to understand their speech. I warned him again not to let the other foxes find out he was working with me. For the time being, they were still my team, but my position as leader was vulnerable. I had disappointed them with my failed report from the juncture. Silver had maintained control not because of his gruff personality but because of his knowledge. I had to show the others that I knew more than they did. That was how Sturdy could help.

Unfortunately, Sturdy wasn't able to learn the human language. "It's no use with the words," he said one day. "It will take me a long time to understand anything. Probably never. But I have made some observations with my eyes instead of my ears. That is the best I can do."

"And what have you seen with your eyes?" I asked, annoyed that the raccoon was giving up, especially after I had humored him with so many songs, stories, and long conversations.

"They are rail people," said Sturdy, "like I was once a rail raccoon. They come and go sometimes, but they like to stay near the trains."

"I thought humans lived in buildings," I countered. "They build towers higher even than trees! Why would they choose to live in a ditch?"

"You spent time in the city!" Sturdy balked. "You never did see a human living in an alley or a park? I saw it in many towns."

I thought hard. "Now that you mention it, I suppose I must have. I saw people who would stand at intersections and beg."

"Cast-outs," said Sturdy. "Some by choice, others not by choice."

"But those I saw like that were usually alone," I added.

"Here they are a group. It is safer. They come and go. They take their turns."

"And share their resources?" I asked.

"They share," affirmed Sturdy. "What one has, he gives to the others. Like your little fox-band."

"If they're outcasts, I assume they have fewer resources than other humans. They seem to be in worse condition. Have you noticed them sharing anything significant?"

"Yes," said Sturdy, "something I saw before with other humans. They share food and drink, as one expects, but they have a kind of drink that is special. They enjoy it a great deal."

"And what's special about it?" I asked eagerly. "Could it be part of the secret to their power? I've sampled many human foods, but never any special drinks."

"These men are not powerful," said Sturdy, shaking his head. "I have tried this drink before in another town. One must be careful. It is strong. And there's the glass, too. Very sharp."

Sturdy went on to describe the drink's effects in detail. His words reminded me of a story Silver had told about consuming some overripe apples before he had moved to the city. According to him, it had produced a strange sensation, so pleasant and comfortable that he had fallen asleep right out in the open beneath the tree! Telling that story was one of the few times Silver laughed at himself, and I always got the impression that he would have liked to experience the same effect again.

"I get that it's pleasant," I said. "But what good is it? What does it actually *do*?"

"In my experience," replied Sturdy, "this drink can give one—what's the word?—*insight*."

"Well," I said, "I could use some insight, and I'm here to learn about humans anyway."

"You want to try?" Sturdy said with a chitter.

"Yes," I replied, "I think I would. For my research."

"Research!" Sturdy cackled at me. I just glared.

It was a late-summer afternoon, and all four of us were relaxing near the den. The others still had not found out about Sturdy. Chestnut had sighted him once, but there was nothing unusual about seeing a raccoon out and about. They still had no idea that he could speak our language or that he was helping me. In fact, despite his failure to understand the humans, Sturdy had proved invaluable. I had enlisted him to scout out the broader region for neighboring foxes. Within me stirred a sense that the time was nearly right for expansion. Sturdy's report indicated, however, that the nearest fox territory was back in the direction of the city. He reasoned that this was because of the coyotes, who controlled the woods beyond the tracks.

A comment from River interrupted my thoughts. "In my opinion we've made some important advances over the few months we've been here," she said as we lounged, "discoveries about the humans and improved fighting and survival skills. I feel like a much more well-rounded fox, now proficient in city and wild living."

"Thank you, River," I said. "I agree. We're beginning to understand the humans more—their physical traits, their social structure, their habits. We should also concentrate on motive."

"Motive?" asked Ash.

"Yes," I said. "What moves the humans? Why do they do what they do?"

"I suppose," said Chestnut, scratching his ear casually, "that they wish to eat, to mate, to rear strong children, and so forth."

"Like all animals," I said. "But, Chestnut, you of all foxes should appreciate why those things aren't enough. The humans clearly want more. Why the buildings, the vehicles, the cities?"

Before Chestnut could respond, River spoke up. "Ants build, too," she said, "and beavers, I've heard, though I've never seen one myself. Birds certainly do, as do we foxes."

"Not on the same scale," I said.

"No," continued River, "but ants are much smaller. To them, their mounds must be like great cities."

"Not the same," I insisted. "I see your point, but other animals work with nature. Ants pile up dirt. We dig it out to make holes and tunnels. But humans go far beyond. They make their own materials. Either they have tamed nature, or risen beyond it. There's something special about them. The normal drives of hunger and blood do not limit them. They want more than food and healthy children. They do more because they *want* more. That's what makes them great."

"Are they great?" asked Ash. "At first I thought I understood your interest in humans, but you've taken it to such an extreme. Why idolize them? They're not gods. We could be living a normal life with plenty to eat instead of spending all our time watching them."

"What are you implying?" I asked, annoyed.

"Nothing!" said Ash defensively. "I enjoy our group. It's fun enough living out here. I just wonder sometimes, that's all."

"I've explained it," I said. "The humans have a power that other creatures don't. They certainly *are* like gods compared to us. All animals fear them. I want to understand that."

"And use it," observed Chestnut. "What would we do with this knowledge? Or this power, if you're right that we can take hold of it in some way?"

"Patience," I said. "For now, you need to trust me. Silver's problem was one of vision. He taught us many novel methods, but they were just means aimed at the same basic ends set by nature—in his case food, which was all he cared about. I say that we need to go beyond nature."

"Do you think," asked River softly, "that that's really possible, or should we just be content with what we have? I was just saying how much I feel that I've grown—we all have—but we're at a plateau. We've peaked. It's hard to see what the next step is. If *you* see it, Nimbus, then I think you should let us in on your vision a little more."

I almost barked at her for doubting me, but I held my tongue. *This is an opportunity*, I told myself. *Don't be irritated. This just means that it's time!* "River, I'm glad you asked," I said calmly. "You're right. We should be planning the next step, and I'll tell you all just what that is." The others listened with rapt attention as I explained what I knew about the coyotes beyond the tracks. "There are about a dozen of them. It's the same group whose members sometimes cross through our own territory one or two at a time. Remember that coyotes have wide hunting grounds. They live in those woods, but they roam far and wide. That's also why there are no other foxes around here. I'm sure they only leave us alone because there are four of us, and our markings indicate how strong and healthy we are."

"I see," said Chestnut. "And how do you know all this?"

"Repeated spying," I said with a smirk.

"And why didn't you bring this up before?" asked River.

"Our observational focus has been on the humans," I said, "but if you all are ready for some *action*, I think we should launch a sneak attack against the coyotes. Goodness knows they'd get rid of us if they had the chance."

"A sneak attack!" repeated Ash. "That could put us in real danger."

"What do you think we've been training for?" I said coldly. "Those claws aren't for show. Besides, we can definitely win, even against twelve of them. For one thing, they're not expecting it. Plus, we can disable one or two while they're out hunting. That will be easy. A few from the group may even flee in fear. And they won't all be in their prime, either, like we are."

It wasn't easy to convince the others, but eventually I did. My tongue had never been so slick. Words swam out like upstream salmon, overcoming all resistance. Killing a few coyotes and driving out the rest—pure benevolence. We would free the area for foxes. In a few months, newly mated pairs would move in to rear their cubs in peace the following spring, all thanks to us. Some of those cubs might even join up, there being no need to maintain the barbaric old custom of exiling them from the territory at adolescence. In a few years we could grow an army, with the four of us at command!

"It sounds grandiose," said River as I finished my speech, "and I don't know what to think about the long-term vision, but in the short term, I *would* feel safer with those coyotes gone. You haven't led us astray yet, so I'm willing to fight with you."

Chestnut and Ash likewise agreed, and before I knew it we had planned an attack on the coyotes for two weeks hence. I could see the confidence in my companions' eyes. All our work was bearing fruit. We were strong. We were ready.

Finally, the time came for us to hunt for the night. As we departed, I made a final announcement to the others. "And one more thing," I said. "Next week I'll have a surprise to celebrate our progress."

A week later, the time for our surprise had arrived. Having canceled all assigned duties, I led the other foxes down to the creek. It was a balmy evening, and the earth's moist breath wrapped all around us. On the dark grass amid the fireflies and mosquitoes sat a white plastic bowl, which Sturdy had stolen for me.

"Where did this dish come from?" asked River. "The men by the bridge?"

"Yes," I said, "I borrowed it to help with a little surprise."

Ash perked up his ears.

"Yes," I continued, "I've been too business-like. I want to thank you for trusting in me. I'm really glad we're sticking together, and you all deserve a treat for your commitment."

"What sort of treat?" asked Chestnut.

"Something pleasant," I said, "a taste of what the humans have to offer. Just hold on a minute."

I crossed the shallow creek and headed for a nearby bush. Hidden there was a large glass bottle. I gripped its neck in my muzzle and, tilting my head to balance its weight, carried it back to the others. Sturdy had loosened the cap—an advantage of his raccoon hands—so I had to be careful not to spill the drink. Once I had fully removed the cap, I picked up the bottle again and filled the dish with a sweet red liquid.

"It looks like blood," remarked Ash.

"This is wine," I said. "As you can tell, it's a human drink. This is why we're out here, to learn and experience things like this. Who knows what else there might be? I think we're doing quite well, so let's celebrate!"

The others stared at me.

"Well, who's first?" I asked.

"Why don't you go ahead, Nimbus," said Chestnut with a skeptical look on his face.

"Sure," I said and lapped up a mouthful from the dish. The wine was sweet but strong-tasting and heavy in a way I wasn't used to, like sap. I liked it and wanted more but decided to give the others a turn.

Soon we had all tried it and discussed our first impressions. Everyone seemed to enjoy the taste, and most of us took a second and third drink right away. It wasn't long before I started to feel a pleasant haze. It was relaxing yet made my face feel hot. Humans, coyotes, keeping the respect of the others—all these anxieties drifted far from my mind.

I looked at River. She took another drink then grinned, the white of her muzzle stained red. She was usually so quiet and dignified. I had never seen her looking silly before, but I liked it. Chestnut had his glacial eyes fixed on her, too. Ash was in his own world, but soon he and I were reminiscing about the city. Somehow even the old abuse we had suffered under Silver felt like a cause for joy. I even missed him and wished that he could have shared our revelry.

I can't remember the details, but I think Ash and I conversed late into the night. At some point the bowl was emptied amid the stories and jokes. I had never felt so close to Ash, like we were good friends. But something else happened that night—something forever lost to my memory—which ruined everything.

CHAPTER

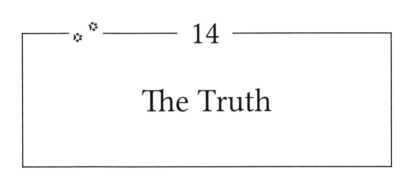

14

# The Truth

The day after our drinking party, we all felt terrible. I awoke in the afternoon desperately thirsty and exhausted. I could barely crawl down to the creek for water. I was hungry but didn't want to eat. Only after a long time were the four of us able to get up and do a bit of foraging. There was no question of going out on rotation that day or of doing anything else worthwhile.

I noticed that throughout our waking moments Ash seemed to be watching me. All of us were out of sorts, so I didn't think much of it, until he followed me down to the creek while River and Chestnut were napping. In place of his usual friendly demeanor, he wore a grave expression.

"Well?" he asked sharply as I gulped down a mouthful of cool water.

"Well what?" I replied, lifting my aching head.

"What you said last night."

"What do you mean?" I asked. "I don't remember much of our conversation."

"We were talking about old times with Silver. It was all a lot of fun reminiscing, but then you started going into detail about his death. And well, it became clear that you were *there*, that you saw it happen."

"I don't recall," I said, rubbing my eye with a paw.

"I do," said Ash. "You said it quite clearly. You watched Silver die. You *let* him die. You could have warned him, but you didn't. You wanted it to happen!"

"Are you sure?" I retorted. "Maybe your memory is mistaken. If I did say such a thing, why haven't River or Chestnut confronted me?"

"I don't think they heard," said Ash. "They were both pretty drowsy by then. But I know what you did. To be honest, I sensed that something wasn't right." He shook his head. "This whole thing—moving to this place, obsessing over humans, all of it—has just been about you and your weird fantasies, hasn't it? It's so obvious. Well, I'm done with it. I'm going to tell the others, and then you'll be all alone again. I'm not going to waste any more of my life with you."

I looked into his eyes and saw an intensity uncharacteristic of Ash. He looked afraid, like he had had to work up the courage to confront me, but resolved. How sure was he of my guilt? Could he persuade the others?

"Look," I explained, "it sounds like we don't have much clarity about what happened last night. In any case, when Silver died there was nothing I could do. I got there too late."

"No," said Ash. "That's not what you said. You admitted everything. You *bragged* about it." He fell silent, as if his mind struggled with the concept of betrayal. "I have to tell them. I *have to.*"

"You sound like you're trying to convince yourself, not me," I said. "It's clear you're not sure about this."

"No," said Ash. "I'm sure. It's just that my head hurts. But I've thought about it. I'm going to tell them."

"Think carefully," I said, stepping toward him. "None of us really liked Silver to begin with. They may not be so upset."

"Silver was tough, but that doesn't make it okay to kill him. We're supposed to be a team. We've trusted each other with our *lives.* I think Chestnut and River agree with me on that."

Ash studied me for a moment. I considered tackling him, but attacking him would only make me look guilty. My head throbbed. It was hard to think straight. Finally, I got an idea. "Look," I said and sighed, "the things I said last night weren't true. You're absolutely right: I *was* bragging. I was trying to impress all of you."

"Impress us?" asked Ash skeptically.

"Yes," I continued. "It's embarrassing to talk about, but, well, I feel that I'm not a very strong leader, not as good as Silver. I mean, I've got such high aspirations, but I just can't shake the sense that I've let you all down. I thought that at least if I could show some strength—that Silver got killed and I didn't—maybe you'd have more confidence in me."

"Confidence."

"Confidence," I repeated. I had begun walking casually down stream, toward the bridge. Ash was following me, apparently without thinking. I aimed to keep it that way. I had to keep the conversation going. "I even thought that because we all didn't like Silver, I might look like a hero for getting rid of him. That's why I lied yesterday."

"So you *weren't* there when he died?"

"I got there after it happened, like you did. So, no, I didn't survive a situation that took his life, and I didn't contribute to his death. I realize now that it was silly to try to take credit for that. It sounds ridiculous to my own ears even having this conversation. I must have come across like a cub last night. No doubt the wine was behind it."

We started up the embankment leading to the gravel road and the narrow bridge. I kept Ash focused on me as we crept higher and higher toward the bridge. Almost there.

"I'm not sure I understand why you thought we would be impressed that you watched Silver die without even warning him," Ash had been saying. "That certainly wouldn't make me think of you as a good leader."

All of a sudden, a man coughed from beneath the bridge. Ash's his eyes widened and he shook his big fuzzy head. "Hey! What are you doing? Where are we going?"

"Going?" I asked innocently. "We're just talking."

"No," he insisted. "You're trying to manipulate me. You got me up this hill. Why? To knock me over the edge into the creek? It won't work."

"Ash!" I gasped, as if indignant. "I would never do such a thing! Here I'm confiding in you about my insecurities, and you keep making me out to be a killer."

"Why are we on the bridge, then?"

"We're not on the bridge," I corrected him. "Okay, look, I do want to show you something. If you're willing to at least keep talking with me for a moment, I'll take you to what I discovered the other day. You'll really be surprised. It makes all our time out here worthwhile." My aching brain kept my tongue going almost automatically. *As long as I keep Ash away from the other foxes, I have a chance!*

"What is it?" he asked.

"To be honest with you, I don't know. That's why I couldn't just tell you about it before. It's something human, something I've never seen. But I know it's very important."

"And *where* is it?" asked Ash, sitting down by the gravel. "I'm not taking another step until you tell me where you're trying to get me to go. You know you can't move me."

"It's just across the train tracks," I said. "We're almost there."

Ash again studied me and sighed. "So that's it, then? If you can't push me off the bridge, you'd break my leg and strand me on the tracks. Nope. I'm not having it, Nimbus. Not another second."

With that, Ash bounded down the hill and back toward our den. I cursed and followed.

I arrived moments behind Ash. He had awakened River and Chestnut. They looked groggy, fur matted, as they emerged from beneath the sheet metal roof of our den. The evening sun cast their shadows far across the grassy hillside. My mind raced. What to do?

"We can't trust Nimbus," Ash had been saying.

River stared at him, seemingly unable to absorb the message. "Wait a minute. Ash, what are you telling us?"

"I'm telling you," said Ash, "that Nimbus lied to us."

Chestnut shook his head. "Huh? I don't understand," he said.

I kept silent. Ash was practically prancing as he spoke. His tail swung excitedly. "I'm saying that Nimbus killed Silver! He admitted it last night."

"I didn't hear that," objected River.

"Neither did I," added Chestnut.

"You two had already dozed off," insisted Ash, "but he said it. He told the whole story and bragged about it!"

"What?" I interjected with a dismissive laugh, as if hearing this for the first time. "Ash, don't joke about something like that."

"He *killed* Silver?" repeated River, shaking her head. "I thought that kebab vendor killed Silver."

"Nimbus was there when Silver died," explained Ash. "He could have saved him. He could have warned him or tried to help him. But he didn't."

"Why didn't you say something before?" asked Chestnut.

"I wanted to confront Nimbus first," said Ash. "Like all of us today, I'm not feeling quite myself. So I wanted to be absolutely sure that I was remembering correctly."

"And you're sure?" asked River.

"I'm sure," said Ash. "Nimbus has showed his true colors. He's got all of us serving his childish fantasies, out here watching these trains and this pitiful camp of humans for some unknown reason, but in reality he doesn't care about us at all. He'd get rid of any of us who might be inconvenient."

"Wait, wait," interjected Chestnut. "What's your basis for that?"

"I can't prove it," said Ash, "but just now he would have killed me if he could have. No doubt he would have pushed me off the bridge or onto the tracks and told you two that it was an accident. He probably would even have feigned a guilt complex over giving us that wine and gone on and on about how it might have impaired my reflexes and so forth. I'm telling you, he's more selfish and manipulative than Silver."

"Let's back up," said River, watching Ash and me carefully. "Nimbus, were you there when Silver died?"

"I certainly was not," I growled. "I was on my way back to the rendezvous point. Yes, it's true that when I heard Silver cry out I ran back toward the sound, but by that point it was too late. Don't you think I feel badly enough about what happened without being accused all of a sudden? I *thought* we had found closure. There's no need to open all this back up."

River kept quiet, studying Ash's face intently. Chestnut scooted closer to her. "So *you* were there, Ash?" he asked.

"No," said Ash, surprised at the turnaround, "I wasn't there. I arrived after Silver was already dead." His ears flicked nervously. I seized the chance.

"How could you accuse me of murder, Ash?" I asked, trying to sound hurt. "Are you really so jealous? Is that what this is about?"

"*Jealous?*" Ash barked. "You're a liar, Nimbus. And a murderer. Silver was a scoundrel, but that doesn't justify what you did."

"It sounds like you had a lot of problems with him," I said, softening my voice and folding back my ears.

"We all did," Ash retorted, fur beginning to bristle. "That's the truth, and everybody knows it."

"Yes," I said. "That's fair. But we all followed him."

"We followed him because of his skills," said Ash.

"Precisely," I affirmed, "and those skills surely would have saved him if he could have been saved. Now, I didn't see what happened, but it must have been unavoidable. I don't want you to blame yourself, Ash. If you've been living with guilt all this time, I'm sure it's eaten you up inside."

I paused, trying to sound benevolent. "It's not your fault. None of us could have saved him."

"*You* could have," he seethed.

I slumped to the ground. "You know," I said, "I can deal with the personal hurt, but you're letting down our team. We're just days away from driving out the coyotes and making this area safe for foxes, but now you're sabotaging us. If you're afraid to fight, just say so."

"How dare you," growled Ash, stepping toward me. "I'm stronger than you, and I can make you feel it!"

"That's enough!" interrupted Chestnut. "It won't do us any good to be at each other's throats for real."

"I don't have to listen to this," spat Ash. "I'm done. The rest of you are okay, but I won't work with *him* anymore. You shouldn't, either. He's going to lead us against a dozen coyotes? It'll be another death sentence."

Chestnut studied me a long time then suggested that he and River needed to eat and that we all take some time to think. He rose and headed for the creek. Ash followed. River stood but lingered till she could have a private word with me.

"Nimbus," she whispered, "please forgive what I'm about to ask. It's not fair. I know that. But you really didn't do it?"

"River," I said, trying to sound hurt, "you of all foxes shouldn't grieve Silver's death. Think of how he treated you—that filthy cad. It was only going to get worse with time. But, to answer your question, no, I didn't kill him."

River nodded. "I see," she said. "You know more than I realized." Turning, she followed the others to the creek.

"Oh please," called Ash, who had heard my response. "You're a poor liar, Nimbus, despite the practice."

Once the others had left, I trotted off to find some supper. Night had fallen, and I ventured toward the tracks. Hunger tore at my belly, but I knew that food would only bring limited comfort. I could see on Ash's face that he wasn't bluffing. His membership in the group had ended.

Just as I was pondering whether I might convince River and Chestnut to stay with me, a set of red eyes flashed before me. A few more steps, and a familiar oaky scent filled my nostrils.

"Sturdy!" I called, "it's good to see you! You won't believe what happened." I paused and sniffed hard at the raccoon's dark fur. "Wait, what's this? Why do you smell like coyote?"

"Bah," said Sturdy, spitting, "I ran into one today, you see."

"And you got away?" I asked. "I'm impressed."

"Yes, yes. I got away. I'm not so fast, but I talked myself out of it. It wasn't hard. That coyote was looking for something tastier than me anyway."

"I'm still impressed," I said, "*especially* if you talked yourself out of a pinch like that. It smells like you were in close proximity, so no doubt he could have torn your throat pretty easily. I wish I had your persuasion skills! They would have helped me earlier."

"Then you were in a pinch also?"

I sighed. "Yes, something happened last night."

"Last night," repeated Sturdy as if he were trying to recall. "Ah! The wine. Yes, I want to ask you how you enjoyed the wine I helped you with."

"I enjoyed it at the time," I said. "We all did. But it did cause a certain... misunderstanding. The long and short of it is that I think my group is splitting up."

"And why is that?" asked Sturdy.

"They blame me for the death of our former leader. They're terribly confused, but I can't get through to them."

"Yes, yes," murmured Sturdy thoughtfully. "The wine can make confusion. But remember what I said, it also gives insight."

"In a way that may be true," I said. "The truth is that I think the other foxes wanted to leave anyway. They don't share my interest in the humans—not really. But they would come to see things my way if only they gave me a chance."

"You are very focused on humans," agreed Sturdy, nodding his head. "Why is that, Nimbus? It's a strange hobby for a fox, no?"

"Look at you!" I countered. "You've spent your life studying the cultures of a dozen species. So what if I want to know about humans."

"I never said I wasn't strange, too," said Sturdy with a chuckle. "No need for anger. But, I think for you there's something more, is there not? You want to revenge yourself against them."

"You know all about me," I said. "You're partly right. At first I just wanted to get back at the humans because of losing my mate. But once I realized just how great their power is, my interest grew for other reasons. It's extraordinary to me how little we other animals settle for, how narrow our vision, when these creatures with less strength and speed than we have can accomplish so much."

"You want to become like them," observed Sturdy.

"I think," I said, "that as I speak to you, I realize I already am. I would have led our team to victory over the coyotes, our four against their dozen. I feel deep in my belly that we would win, like the humans do, through smarts and determination, through thinking and wanting bigger. Every other species, no matter how powerful, falls to their empire. All I wanted was a chance for us foxes."

I returned to the den just before dawn. River and Chestnut were curled up together, drowsing amid the lumber and metal. They sat up at my arrival, eyes opening and reflecting in the dark.

"Ash is gone," I observed, breaking the silence.

"Yes," replied Chestnut.

"I hope you don't believe him," I said. "I'm telling you, it's not true."

"I do believe him," said River flatly. "I wish I could say I'm sorry, but I won't apologize for telling the truth. I don't want to think it, but I do."

"I see," I said. "And you, Chestnut?"

"I agree with River."

"Of course, you do," I said, rolling my eyes. "So, what does this mean for us?"

"We're leaving tomorrow," Chestnut continued. "We talked about it, and we'll let you have this territory. We're not interested in fighting. We're going to start a family, and it's not the ideal place for us to settle anyway."

"It's hardly the season for that!" I protested. "Besides, once you help me remove the coyotes, we'll have plenty of room here. There'll be territory enough for a dozen foxes! Your family could be one of the first to live here in peace and freedom."

"No," said River, "I don't want my children to be part of this. And, I don't want to be part of this any longer."

"She's right," agreed Chestnut. "It's over. We'll move far away, and we won't cause you any trouble. I think that's reasonable on our part. I don't wish you any harm, but our time together has ended."

"No use arguing, then," I said, suppressing a growl. "You're obviously not going to listen to me, no matter what I say. Well, if some cold winter day you're starving out there in the wilderness, longing for the old days, whine as loud as you want, I won't be there to help you. You'll have to face it all alone. In fact, why don't we start now? If you're too good for my team, then you're too good for my den. So, get out."

"Nimbus," said River, "it's not your den. Don't be petty."

"No," I snapped, "it's the *team's* den. And you're not on the team anymore, remember?"

Chestnut licked her cheek. "Come on, love," he said. "The sooner we go, the happier we'll be. Let's leave Nimbus be." They rose and crept out from beneath the metal. The sun had not yet risen. As they left, Chestnut turned to me one last time. "The kingdom's yours, Nimbus. You can have it all. Everything you've worked for."

# CHAPTER

## 15

# The Consequences

I was too angry to sleep. For most of the day I roamed around snacking on a berry here or there. By afternoon, with nothing else to do, I headed for the bridge hoping that the men were back for the evening. Perhaps they would be up to something interesting. Perhaps Sturdy would be there, too. As my paws hit the dusty gravel, a gruff-looking fellow jumped up and pointed at me. His companion—the only other who had returned from his daytime excursion—shouted at me and threw a rock. It struck the ground beside me, and I easily side-stepped it. I had the high ground, and at that distance rocks weren't a real threat. Grabbing an empty bottle, the first man threw it at the edge of the bridge. It struck the old steel and exploded, spraying glass all over.

I dashed to safety and shook myself vigorously, trying to rid my coat of any small shards that might have hit me. I seemed to be unhurt, but the attack had unnerved me. Never before had the men been on such high alert. They had seen me or Sturdy in the past, just as they might spot any number of animals, without hostility. Could the humans somehow have realized that we had been spying on them? Or, more likely, had they become paranoid after the theft of their bowl and wine?

Puzzled and still upset, I returned to the den. That pile of debris, now empty, felt like a tomb, and I was like a ghost. I needed to rest and reevaluate my next moves. As I finally drifted off to sleep, I thought of the men I had so often observed. I was more like them than I had expected. They were not god-like or great. They were just misfits, driven by rejection and mediocrity out of sight and mind, left to scrounge in the long shadow of the city.

I awoke around midnight and decided to go for a walk, hoping to find Sturdy and ask his advice. I looked and looked but could not find him. After a bit of wandering I found myself beyond the railroad tracks. Suddenly a coyote descended the hill by the woods. He was a male, several years old, and in good shape. He glared at me as he approached, but I maintained eye contact. I sniffed the air hard to see whether I could pick up the scent of any others.

"Alone?" he called.

"Yes," I said, deciding not to bluff and hoping that this would make me appear confident. "Though I'm not far from home, and there are several of us."

"I've noticed your little pack," replied the coyote. "Strange behavior for foxes."

"Not for coyotes."

"Not always."

"So, do you have a pack around now?" I asked. "I have nosed them out before, of course."

"Naturally. Our network is more extensive than you realize. We make it our business to know those who take up residence in our territory, especially the *irregular* cases."

"Are we going to have any trouble, then?"

"No trouble today, fox. We just had a nice encounter with your raccoon friend. I happened to see you trotting along so conspicuously and thought you might like to know. You won't be seeing him again."

So they *had* been watching. "He wasn't my friend," I said, bristling. "And, I won't miss him. I had everything I needed from him."

"Are you sure? You seem to have quite the enterprise underway." He stared me in the eye. "Watching those men for hours on end, stealing from them, drinking—whatever you're after, it's not normal."

"It's above your intelligence," I barked. "In any case, I can handle myself!"

"We'll see," the coyote replied. "By the way, I wouldn't risk attacking us, if I were you. I think you'll find you're quite outnumbered without your pack. You are all alone now, aren't you? Interesting development."

As he asked, another coyote stepped up onto the hilltop, becoming visible to me in the moonlight. Then another and another, till at last at least ten pairs of reflective eyes stared down at me. Their menacing silhouettes towered over me, and my blood turned cold.

"As promised," continued the coyote, "no trouble for you today." I made no reply and turned to leave, struggling to keep my brush from curling beneath my hind legs. As I crossed the rails and headed toward my den, the coyote called out, "But tomorrow is another day!"

I never saw Sturdy again after that, so I took the coyotes' threat quite seriously. Besides, there was nothing left to be done with the humans in that location. I had learned a few things, but, practically speaking, my research had been a failure. At the rate I was going, I would never possess a power like the humans had, would never build a dynasty like theirs. Without the other foxes, I could never drive out the coyotes. I wouldn't even be able to defend myself against them.

And so, after a little thought, I decided to return to the country. In particular, I would return to the farm where Aurora had been shot. Although I had grown out of my childish idea of revenge, part of me still savored the chance to cause some trouble for those humans. Who knew how I could apply what I had learned in my time away?

Of course, going back meant passing by my parents' territory. Just as I feared encountering Aurora and Blaze or their children in the city, I would rather have gnawed my paw off than see my parents again. I decided to cut around the woods to the north in order to give their borders a wide berth. I also couldn't violate the territory of Aurora's parents. I could pass through or possibly spend up to a few days there, but I couldn't set up a den.

As I began my journey, my brain continued to hunt and puzzle over how to negotiate with Aurora's parents. I had broken my earlier promise to return. Going back years later would not, of course, count as keeping the promise in any meaningful sense. Would Aurora's father be angry or offended? Would he care at all?

Another approach soon came to mind. Aurora's father thought that his daughter was dead, and her mother at least might know that she had gone missing those few years ago. If I were to inform them that their daughter was alive and had been found, they might be happy enough to let me stay—not in their den, of course, but within their boundaries. They ought to be especially grateful if I kept up the pretense of having returned all the way from the city just to share the good news with them.

Of course, they might assume I was lying. I had no proof. I thought hard. Was there some piece of information, some secret fact that I could provide as evidence? I shook my head in frustration. Everything I knew about Aurora beyond our childhood would be unknown to her parents and, therefore, unverifiable.

And then I remembered something Silver had taught me. One of the tricks to lying, he had said, was to embarrass oneself. Others assume that we lie to make ourselves look better because that's what they would do. So, a self-effacing story has the ring of truth. What if I could use Silver's advice about lying to tell the truth, or mostly the truth, with greater credibility? All I had to do was portray myself as incompetent, a failure returning home out of desperation. I had lost weight since leaving the city, but I was in excellent condition. If anything, I had gained muscle through my sparring practices with the others. But I could starve myself for the rest of the journey and leave my coat ungroomed. With any luck, I would look absolutely pitiable when I arrived.

I would say that I had found Aurora alive and that she

had rejected me. That part was true, and I cursed under my breath as I imagined admitting that to her parents. But I wouldn't have to give them any details about just what I had been up to. I would play the poor, vagabond cub who had nothing to lose in bringing good news to them and nowhere else to go. It was a good plan.

As I traveled, I ate nothing but insects and plants, just enough to maintain some strength. The fasting was harder than I expected. At times, I licked my chops, my body compelled to search out any old particle of nourishment stuck to my teeth. My pelt felt looser by the day. I could find no water clear enough to check my reflection, but I hoped to look sickly, maybe even on the verge of mange, by the time I reached my destination. I resisted the urge to nip brambles out of my thin summer coat, leaving them to tatter my fur and scratch my skin.

A week into my journey, I spotted a fawn, no more than a few months old, exploring a small grove of beech trees. It was so young that I had no doubt its mother would be nearby, but she seemed to have left it unsupervised for the moment. My blood ran hot, and I wanted nothing more than to kill the deer and gorge myself on its flesh. In the end, I succeeded in killing it, toppling it and tearing its throat before the mother's trampling hooves could catch me. But once I had slain the tender creature and chased its heartbroken mother off in triumph, I resisted the urge to eat so as not to spoil my plan of making myself look weak.

I continued farther north than I had ever been, far enough that before I arced back to the southeast, I could not even see the old woods. Part of me wished I could have visited our clearing with all its memories, but I couldn't risk passing that close to my parents' home. Already, I was keeping my nostrils trained for familiar scents in case any of my siblings had moved to the territory I was traversing. Running into one of them would not be as humiliating as encountering my parents, but I preferred to avoid it, especially in my disheveled state.

When I came within a half-day's trek of Aurora's old territory, I slowed and began to take extra care in my investigations. Old tracks here, fresh scat or urine-markings there—all these required examination and mental cataloging. Signs of a permanent vulpine presence, especially one sharing blood with Aurora, would have to be taken seriously. I thought about how to make contact with her parents. Should I arrange things so that one of them would happen upon me as if by chance, or should I trot up to her old den and announce myself?

The question became moot, since, to my surprise, I detected no foxes whatsoever, not even when I crossed what used to be the territorial boundary. In fact, there was no such frontier, no border-markings and no other signs of occupation. I had chosen to sweep the area in the daylight, when Aurora's parents would be resting. Curious, I scouted and sniffed around for the better part of the morning. No sign of them.

Finding nothing, I headed to the old den. My arrival there confirmed the total absence of any foxes. In fact, the lack of scent-markings and prey remains proved that none had lived there for several months at least. It was a no-fox's land waiting to be claimed. Even better, there were no coyotes to deal with!

At once, I scratched around the abandoned den, clearing out the fresh growth and getting it into shape. Tomorrow,

I would patrol the region and mark out the proper bound-aries. My stomach growled, and I realized that I could feed and groom myself as I liked. No need for deception. No one to answer to. For the first time, the land was mine and mine alone.

CHAPTER

## 16

# Life's a Game

I awoke late one evening in my new home, hungrier than usual and craving eggs. Yawning, I crawled from the earthen den, once home to Aurora's family, and stuck my head through its narrow hillside entrance into the twilight. The cicadas were already beginning their nightly chorus. To find eggs earlier in the season, I might have searched for a killdeer nest or thrown my weight against a few saplings. It was too late in the summer for that, nearly autumn. Instead, I trotted to the farm.

Upon arrival, I paused for just a moment to sniff the air. Over the past several days, I had stolen vegetables—cabbage and so forth—along with helping myself to scraps from the compost pile. I felt ready to escalate my thefts and make a real nuisance of myself for the humans. It would be safe enough. The farm dog was old and sometimes chained up. As for the humans themselves, I had detected only five: a man and woman with their three children. Two of the children were adolescents, essentially young men. The third was a younger girl. Like all humans, they were impossible to miss and easy to avoid.

At that moment, I detected no danger on my side of the farmhouse. Nearby, the humans kept about two dozen hens. The inelegant birds spent their days clucking around in the dirt. At night, they slept in elevated wooden hutches screened in with wire. Each day, one of the humans, usually the young girl, would gather eggs from the straw that lined the hutches. I had observed that the door latches could be flipped open with ease and were flimsy besides. I held my ears and tail high with confidence as I crept up to the nearest hutch and began to nose the latch upward.

As the gate swung open, a din of excited squawking erupted on all sides. At once I leaped inside. Beaks and talons flew in my face while a hurricane of wings beat all around me. Some of the hens fled. Others attacked. Those in the adjacent hutches continued their crazed screeching.

Unperturbed, I lay my head against the straw and crunched an egg open with my muzzle, quickly lapping up the goo inside. The pecks and scratches against my hide were not so bad. I had learned the importance of remaining calm in such situations. The hens' defense consisted mostly of alarm and commotion. They could inflict little actual injury. Taking two more eggs in my mouth and trying not to break them, I jumped down from the hutch and pranced away to safety.

One lone chicken ran behind me for a few yards in a final act of bravado, as if to take credit for chasing me off.

Just before I had cleared the premises, my ears picked up the sounds of the farmhouse coming to life. Distressed human voices called to each other. I left it all behind and, lounging safely atop my hill, cracked open my prizes. The creamy yolks and whites coated my throat, and I took my time licking the crunchy shells. Here and there fireflies punctuated the darkness.

The silence of the country enfolded me. The cloudless sky, pointed through with stars, drew me upward and pressed upon me all at once. The city's noise had been inescapable. Even the outskirts bore the regular rumble of passing trains. Here I was truly alone. This was my world, my territory, a place of pure freedom. Of course, it would have been better to have my former teammates around, but even alone I could enjoy myself. Here I could live in nature while also taking my share of the humans' abundance. And why not have some fun with them in the process? Opening a simple latch was just the beginning.

The next night, I repeated the escapade. The night after that, I had grown sick of eggs and decided to bring home a chicken. Such was my intention when I arrived at the hutches around midnight. Warm saliva poured from my lips as I thought of the soft, fatty flesh of poultry. I reared up, leaning my front paws against the hutch so that I could reach the latch. This time, however, a long, thin wire was wrapped tightly around it. Chewing and pawing did no good. Meanwhile, the chickens were rioting more loudly than ever.

The house lit up. A door flung open, and the dog ran out barking. I dropped to my feet and bolted, grateful that even

with adrenaline coursing through my system I had the mental clarity to flee in the opposite direction from my den. I
hoped I could wear out the dog with a long, parabolic course
around the field.

I was right. The chase that followed was uneventful,
at most an inconvenience. The old hound was soon whin-
ing and panting with exhaustion. I easily lost him and then
turned my attention back to my hunger.

I caught a stray rodent, and as I munched on it wishing
it were chicken, I thought hard about how to undo the wires
on the cages. They would have to be twisted and unraveled,
the kind of thing humans could do easily but other animals
lacked the dexterity for. I wouldn't have much time, either.
If I went back, the chickens would be just as noisy and I
would have to flee again. True, the dog wasn't a real threat,
but the humans might have a gun handy. In any case, I
would never be able to chew the wire off.

Could I get inside some other way? I concentrated, trying to hold an image of the hutches in my mind. The wooden
roof and sides were too tough to get through. So were the
latticed bottoms. I chewed the last bit of tough skin and
gulped it down. River probably would have been able to figure it out. As I thought of her, my mind wandered. Where
had she and Chestnut settled? And Ash, that big happy-go-
lucky fellow, would he spend this winter alone, or was he
out courting some vixen? I even thought of Sturdy. Coyotes are liars. He might still be alive, maybe even traveling
again.

I shook my head. Daydreams wouldn't fill my belly with
what I craved. Sighing, I rose to my feet and headed for
home. The cool woodland grass would soon be coated with
the fallen leaves of autumn. The earth would grow cold
and firm up. The farm would no longer produce vegetables.

I would have to resign myself to raiding what little trash there was around the farmhouse or to hunting through the scarcity of winter.

I avoided the farm for a few days, only munching on some vegetables at the peripheries. The unsatisfied craving for poultry gnawed away at me. Finally, I could stand it no more. I ran in during the day, when the chickens were out and roaming freely. I managed to grab a hen and carry her off with the dog at my tail. Even with my muzzle stuffed with feathery flesh, I outran him once again. I feasted more lustily on that hen than on any meal I had stolen in the city.

The next day, I had it in mind to snatch another hen, relishing the annoyance this would cause the humans as much as the meal. When I arrived, however, I found the chickens locked up and the dog nowhere to be found. Presumably, he was chained up in the backyard or else in the house. Near the hutches, a small wire cage lay open. Inside lay a portion of raw, stripped meat. My mouth watered, and I sniffed all around. A less experienced fox might have fallen for it, but to me the trap was obvious.

No doubt the humans hoped to lure me in and catch me. This would also allow them to salvage my pelt intact. Studying the device carefully, I determined that if I stepped inside to reach the food, a door would fall shut behind me. Instead, I pressed my nose up to the opposite side and pushed at an angle. With a little effort, I elevated one end of the cage, and the meat slid down toward the opening. Lowering the trap to the ground, I retrieved the bait with a single swift bite. I gulped down the morsel and skipped proudly home with my tail held high.

The small piece of meat had not sated my hunger completely, but the fact that I had earned it by my wits made up for that. All animals steal. To eat, after all, is to rob another of life. But I was a rarity among my race because I had forced the humans' hand. I didn't just take from them. They had come to *give* me what I wanted. I had learned that humans tend first to ignore the broader world, then to dominate it. That is why their mighty roads scrape across the landscape, obliterating the ancient animal pathways. That is why fresh corpses appear each day along those same roads, unnoticed by the vehicles that race along them. I had proved that humans could not ignore me, that they could not push me aside without notice. They had failed to dominate me. What they had set as a baited trap, I had made into a tribute, an offering on my terms, not theirs. But I was not yet appeased.

I reveled in the traps that followed. Each night, I patrolled my territory hoping for something new. I especially enjoyed the baited mechanical devices—cages with trick doors, snares, and so forth. The challenge of puzzling out how they worked gave me more pleasure than the food I stole from them. Once it was a trip-wire snare, evidently intended to coil around my leg. Another time it was a sharp steel jaw hidden amid the vegetables and meant to crush whatever limb pressed upon it. When I discovered it—in the nick of time—I defecated by the awful device as a taunt. The best nights were those when I could spring a trap deliberately without being caught. A few times, the young men of the family even kept watch for me with the dog and their guns. On those occasions, I kept my distance, resisting the temptation to let my fun deteriorate into foolhardiness, satisfied in wasting their time even if it was too risky to confront them.

A few weeks passed, and I had taken to randomizing my attacks even more. Just lately I had noticed multiple traps farther and farther from the farm. One steel jaw had snapped the neck of a middle-aged hare. When I stumbled across its corpse flies were already crawling over its faded, plaintive eyes. A voice that had not sounded in my mind for a long time—my father's—rang in my head, *A cautious fox beats a clever fox.* I vowed to be more careful.

I even explored the western boundary of my territory, which I had neglected till then for fear of coming too close to my parents. This kept me busy and away from the farm, and it gave me the chance to see what further food sources would be available in the bleaker months to come. Already cold winds had begun to ruffle my thickening coat.

Late one afternoon, on just such an exploratory trip, a growling stomach pushed me toward the old woods. The farm's fields lay barren, waiting to slumber under the coming snow, and I dared not approach the farmhouse, since I had stirred up a ruckus there the night before, spilling trash and marking all around so that even the old dog could smell. I wanted meat, and the woods were my best chance to get it. Squirrels busied themselves in rounding off their winter quotas. Subterranean vermin bored out fresh tunnels as the earth prepared to freeze. Any of them would warm a hungry fox's belly.

And so I skulked and skirted around the near-naked trees and crumbling leaves, sniffing and aligning my inner sense of direction, ready to pounce. The coarse late-autumn scent made me shiver. I exhaled hard and could just see my breath. It calmed me, like the ghost of winters past, evidence that I was alive.

A faint yip startled me. Sweeping my head side to side, I picked up a moan stifled by continuous rustling. It came from deeper in the woods. For a moment, I wavered, starting to head away from the sound then turning, ears and eyes straining, as if tethered to the distant commotion. Sighing, I gave in to curiosity and crept toward the noise.

At least I had the presence of mind to scan for familiar scents—my parents' in particular—as I approached the border of their territory. The risk of running into them would be minimal if I didn't go past the clearing where Aurora and I had spent so many hours all those seasons ago.

As I waded through fallen leaves, the moaning and rustling subsided, giving way to labored breathing. It struck me as familiar, even in its intensity, though I didn't know why. Hastening, I pushed my mud-stained paws over logs and around trees, nearer and nearer to the source. When at last I arrived, my fur stood on end.

Before me lay a fox—a vixen. Her small size made me think at first that she was an adolescent, but the late season made that impossible. Was she malnourished? A wire snare coiled around her right foreleg, cutting into the shaggy winter coat that enveloped her lean body. Blood seeped out from beneath it, matting her crimson fur.

Suddenly the vixen's scent registered in my mind. "Amber!" I gasped and raced toward her.

"Stop!" she groaned, eyes snapping open. "Be careful! There may be more of them."

At once I halted. "You're right," I said. "I lost my head for a moment."

"Nimbus, is that you?" she asked, sniffing the air.

"Yes," I said. "What a shock it is to see you, dear sister."

"A shock to me, as well," she muttered through clenched teeth. Amber heaved upward on her front paws but then collapsed. "Ah. I think my leg is broken."

"Just a moment," I called, tiptoeing toward my sister, checking the ground before each footfall in case there were more traps. Her hazel eyes held steady, fixed on me, even amid her groans.

When I reached Amber, I went straight to work, muttering little observations as I studied the situation.

"Your leg isn't broken," I said. "At least, I don't think it is. It looks like this wire is cutting off the circulation. If we don't get you free soon, you may end up losing it."

My sister grunted her acknowledgment, and I began to trace the wire back to its source. I expected to find a peg lodged in the ground, a trick I had seen before. Instead, the line ran to a nearby tree, up its trunk and over a limb.

"It looks like this trap was meant to hoist its victim in the air," I said.

"Then why am I still on the ground?" asked Amber between moans.

"It's not set up properly," I said. "It would work with a rabbit or a squirrel, perhaps, but a fox—even a smaller one—is too heavy. It can't lift you, but that's why it's cutting into your leg so badly."

"Can you do anything?"

"Normally, I would go to the source. A peg, for example, can be dug up. The problem is I can't climb this tree."

"Please, Nimbus," said Amber. "Despite the pain, I'm glad to see you. I'd hate for this to be the end."

"Me too," I echoed as I studied the wire loop, nosing my sister's fur aside. I lapped up some blood for a closer look.

"That feels soothing," she said, rolling onto her other side.

"Careful," I said. "Please hold still for a moment."

"I've lived here all my life," Amber said, "and I've never encountered anything like this. This is obviously human work, but why? In the woods no less. It doesn't make any sense. They hunt here from time to time, but with guns or bows, not like this."

"Don't worry about that for now," I said. "Let me see what I can do here. If we can't uproot the cord at the source, perhaps I can work the loop loose. The trick will be to give it more slack, which can only be done by pushing toward the snare. You see, most animals will panic and pull away, but that only tightens it."

"How do you know so much?"

"I'll explain once you're free."

Releasing Amber was a painful process. More than once she yelped for me to stop, and we had to take a break while she nursed the wound. My own gums bled as I gnawed at the thin wire again and again, slowly increasing the slack till Amber, scrambling with her front paws, just managed to pull her bloodied hind leg free.

She rose, took a few steps, and then collapsed into a pile of leaves. "I can't do it," she panted. "It's broken."

"It's not broken," I said, nosing at the wounded limb. "You're just tired and hurting. Besides, as I said, it will take a while for the circulation to return. Even then, there might be lasting damage."

"Can you get me home?" pleaded Amber.

"Where do you live?" I asked. "Is it far?"

"Our old den."

I swallowed hard, glancing away. "With our parents?"

"No," she said. "They're both gone now. Deceased, I mean. I live alone."

"Oh," I said, a strange wave of relief and regret washing through my breast. "Well, let's get you home, then."

I stood on Amber's wounded side, instructing her to press hard against me. Then, counting rhythmically out loud, we coordinated our steps so that she could keep weight off her injured limb. It was awkward and slow, but with a little practice, we made consistent progress. I had only assisted another fox in this way once before, when Ash had sprained a leg during one of our exercises. It was much easier with Amber's dainty frame in comparison to Ash's bulk. In fact, if Amber had been any smaller, I felt I could have draped her across my shoulders and trotted her home that way.

As we marched step by step out of the woods and toward the old field where we had played together as cubs years before, I almost led us the wrong way. Amber had to interrupt our counting and grunt out a correction. I felt foolish for forgetting, but Amber said nothing. The shrubs dotting the field's northern side seemed closer and smaller than I remembered. An early-winter wind rustled through the grass, and I shivered more than once as we crossed the field.

From time to time, Amber would burrow her head into my shoulder, moaning with pain. Once she even nipped me before murmuring an exhausted apology. Still, we persevered, bodies pressed together for balance, till at last we reached a familiar hole hidden amid the roots of an old oak tree. We were home.

CHAPTER

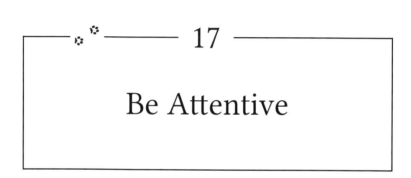

17

# Be Attentive

I tended to Amber for two days, cleaning her wound and bringing what scraps I could find. I spared her from conversation as she had little energy and preferred to sleep. At first, I feared for her life, both because of the blood loss and the risk of infection.

The third day, she felt a little better. We were curled up in the den, warm and dry. Daylight streamed in at the entrance. I had nearly fallen asleep studying the old root patterns of the earthen corridors, trying to determine how they had developed from when I was a cub, when she nosed my shoulder.

"Do you wonder," she asked, "how our parents died?"

"Yes," I said. "Do you feel well enough to tell me."

Amber nodded. "I don't know how our father died," she said, lazily pawing at a loose root. "One day last year, when their most recent litter was nearly grown, he went out to hunt as usual, but he never came back. Mom and I both looked, but we never found his body."

"You stayed here with them this whole time, then?"

"Yes," said Amber. "I helped with the cubs. I really had no desire to leave, and they seemed glad enough to have me. Once in a while we got on each other's nerves, but that's just part of family."

"No urge to start your own life?"

"Whose life am I living if it's not mine?" Amber quipped with a laugh. "Maybe it's because I was always physically weaker, but I was happy here, so I stayed. What is it our father used to say, 'A mouse in the muzzle is worth a rabbit in the field'?"

"Meaning," I said, "that ambition can lead to loss. Our father said a lot of things. He was right about some of them, this one included, but I take it in the opposite sense."

"Oh?"

"Yes," I explained. "The world is like a field, wide and full of prey. Risk is what grants us access. There is no true success without the possibility of losing everything."

"Is that how you understand life?"

"I don't claim to understand life," I said. "In fact, I don't think there's any such thing as 'life' in an abstract sense. There are just living beings, chasing and fleeing, exploiting and being exploited, striving for more."

"And what about you?" asked Amber. "You haven't said anything, but it doesn't take much detective work to figure out that you're not with Aurora. If she were waiting for you somewhere across the field, you would have left or at least mentioned her by now."

"Very observant," I said. "I suppose you want to know what happened?"

"If you feel comfortable sharing," said Amber. "You two were very close, so I'm sure there's pain involved."

"There's pain," I agreed.

I explained all about losing Aurora, moving to the city, finding her alive but wedded to Blaze, and everything else that had happened since cubhood. Amber listened patiently as I went on at length. The only detail I held back was my responsibility for Silver's death.

"It sounds like you've done it all," said Amber when I was finished. "Did you find what you were looking for out there?"

I snorted. "Well, I've contended with humans at their best and toyed with them like I would a field mouse before devouring it. I've done more than most foxes would ever dream of. I figure that's pretty good."

"Are you happy?"

My ears burned at the directness of her question, and I paused for a moment. I would have snapped at another fox to mind his own business, but Amber's eyes belied a keen honesty that made me want to answer. "No," I said at last. "I'm not happy. Now, don't get me wrong, I'm not particularly *unhappy*, either. Pointless to hem and haw about it. It makes no difference. Happiness is another abstraction. It isn't something you can bite into just because you want it. You think you're closing your jaws on it, about to sink your teeth in, and then it's gone, and you're left chomping at the air. I do what I can do, but even I can't change my luck."

"You know," said Amber, "we understand each other more than you think. Happiness *is* outside our grasp. You're right about that, but I would call it a gift, not luck."

"It sure seems like luck to me," I insisted, annoyed at her disagreement. "Just look at you. You didn't do anything wrong, but here you are living alone—and now crippled."

Amber seemed taken aback by my tone, but she recovered quickly. "I'm not alone," she said and licked my forehead. "I'm not happy about the leg, of course. But I'm happy overall, not completely but enough."

"Incomplete happiness," I murmured. "Is that the most anyone can hope for?"

Amber yawned and shuffled beside me. "A good question, but it's one I'm too tired to think about right now. We're frail creatures, you know."

"Yes, yes," I agreed before succumbing to a yawn.

The next day Amber had regained a little more strength. She still limped, but she needed less rest and could move a bit more. The den's main chamber was large enough for her to stand up in and turn around. Unlike me, she didn't have to keep her head low to avoid bumping it on the earthy ceiling.

"It must feel awful to be so cooped up," I remarked, "like being in a cage."

"It's not a nice feeling," said Amber, "but it's better than death."

"Maybe," I said. "I detest cages. Even staying here has me itching to race across the countryside again." I stretched my front paws, splaying my toes wide as if to illustrate.

"Not just racing, I gather, but fooling around with those traps, like the one I was caught in?"

"Well, yes," I admitted. "And, I'm sorry again about what happened. That snare was meant for me. I never dreamed they'd go as far as the forest. I must have really gotten to them."

"Which is what you wanted."

"Yep," I said. "No shame in that. They deserve it, and I enjoy tormenting them."

"They deserve it?" Amber flicked her ears in surprise.

"You don't think the humans have a little retribution coming to them? It's not much in the scheme of things, not compared with what they've taken from me—and countless other animals. I have no illusions about actually getting even. I told you what I learned in the city, that humans are on a different level. But, I can at least have some fun with them."

"And this will make you happy?" asked Amber skeptically.

"To some degree, yes."

"Which brings us back to incomplete happiness," she said. I detected from her voice that my sister was eager to reprise our philosophical discussion. "I thought your question yesterday was a good one. Can there be such a thing? It does seem like a contradiction in terms. But, if it isn't, then I'd say that we'll never know when we're happy, only when we aren't. If we were completely happy, we wouldn't be focusing on ourselves at all. We would be too joyous to worry about our own joy."

"No." I shook my head. "I've felt joy—strong joy, joy I would have died for." I paused, letting a sudden rush of emotion pass. "I wasn't *worried* about it, but I certainly noticed it."

"You mean with Aurora?" asked Amber.

"Yes," I said plainly. "You know, I forgot how wise you are."

Amber ignored the compliment. "Then think, Nimbus," she said with greater intensity. "Think hard. Which had greater value: Aurora herself or the fact that she was with you?"

"I suppose you're suggesting that if I really loved her, I'd accept that it's better for her to be alive than for me to have her."

"Correct. But I would go even further: it's better for Aurora to be in this world than for you ever to have met her. Wouldn't you agree?"

"The question backs me into a corner, which I don't like. Things could have been different. They *should* have been different. She should be alive *and* with me."

"I'm sorry," said Amber softly. "You're right. I've pushed too far on a sensitive matter."

"Thanks," I said. "I'd like to think I'm past grief. I've accepted that I'll never be completely happy. I don't resent it. I'll be okay."

"Your revenge—the tricks you play, I mean—won't make up for the loss?"

"No," I said. "I no longer pretend that it will."

"I'm glad to hear you say it, then. You know, I can relate to some of what you went through."

"You lost someone?" I asked. "Besides our parents, I mean."

"Not exactly. I feel more like I lost what might have been. I've never been in love like you have. But, it's more than that. It's this weak body of mine."

"The injury? You're getting better each day."

"No," said Amber. "I've never been strong. You know that. Ever since we were cubs, my spirit has been tethered by this frail constitution of mine. All the adventures you told me about—leaping and dodging through danger—I can't do that, and I never could. So, I'm acquainted with regret as well. I've spent my life learning to accept weakness."

"I would never settle," I said. "That's why I stayed with Silver, and that's why I tried to hold the team together after his death. And why I wanted to expel those coyotes by the tracks and bring in even more foxes. I wanted to *build* something, something that would become greater than myself. I'd still do that if I ever had the chance."

"But you must settle," said Amber.

"I won't."

"Then you'll never be happy."

"We've been over this," I said. "I know that. It can't be helped. But I'll take what I can. For now, I'll enjoy visiting with you and harassing the humans from time to time."

"Yes," said Amber, laying her head down on the cool earthen floor. "I understand that as well. It's just that you can't *receive* what you insist on taking."

"The pleasure's in the taking."

"I used to think so."

"If we have to receive happiness, then where does it come from? Does it well up like a spring or fall from the sky like the rain?"

"It's a gift."

"So, who gives it?"

"If I knew the answer to that," said Amber, "I really would be wise." She yawned. "Pardon me, I'm getting tired. The truth is, I couldn't say, though I've wondered a lot. Have you ever sniffed and sniffed and caught the scent of a mouse or some rodent deep beneath the surface and you were close to pouncing, only you didn't know exactly what it was, just that it was there? And whenever you would focus on it, you lost it? I can only think that there must be something, something good, a love greater than our hearts. What but love can give happiness? But, if it were in our hearts, it would be within our control, which it isn't. And yet, it can be put there. We are meant to look for it, and we can find it, but we can't take it. It has to be given. In fact, I can say nothing more precisely than that it gives itself if it wishes, and I think that it does wish that."

"You know," I said, "I used to have a friend who talked like you sometimes. You remember Sturdy, whom I told you about?"

"The raccoon?"

"Yes," I said sadly, "he wanted to know things and to share what he had learned. I didn't appreciate it so much at the time, but he really taught me a lot."

In the days that followed, Amber's leg continued to heal, though she couldn't hunt yet. I still raided the farm at times, which usually took most of the night because of its distance. Although prey and vegetation were growing scarcer in the late autumn cold, the truth is that I could have hunted more if I had wanted to. I preferred the pleasure of stealing from the farm.

My sister and I debated often. I rarely agreed with her—usually because I couldn't follow her arguments completely. She seemed to speak from a far-off place, and I joked that she'd lived alone for too long. Sometimes, even when I didn't disagree, I pretended to just for fun. I enjoyed watching the corners of her muzzle pull back in a stern expression when she realized I was toying with her.

One evening, as we lay quietly together, waiting for the late-afternoon darkness to become full night, I took a break from nipping at my paw.

"By the way," I said, "I just realized that you never told me how our mother died."

"Old age," said Amber. "Maybe loneliness. She passed on a few weeks after our father. She was ready, I think. It was a good death."

Amber seemed genuinely happy speaking about our mother's death, which struck me as a strange reaction. *A good death? Isn't that a contradiction in terms?* "I have no romantic illusions about death," I said. "Or life. I'm acquainted with their less peaceful side."

"I think our mother was at peace."

"At peace and lonely?" I scoffed.

"Yes," said Amber. "I think so. It was a longing peace."

"Well, I've seen death, but I've never seen anyone die at peace. I've seen a fox's bowels splayed out and trampled like any dead thing." I sniffed. "That's death, but it's also life. That's what's inside us, after all."

"Yes," said Amber, "those entrails are in you, but *you're* not entrails. And, you're not ears or paws or any other part."

"No, but I'm all of them put together."

"Rather," persisted Amber, "you're what puts all of them together. You're not a sum of things. You're what sums them. You're something more."

"How?" I asked. "I had no choice about the first breath I took, the first image I saw, or my first thought. I could hardly have put myself together."

"Right. You didn't bind yourself together, Nimbus. Just as I did not and no one does. Doesn't that make you wonder?"

"You're puzzling me again," I said, nipping an itch on my shoulder.

"Parasites?" asked Amber.

"Maybe." I continued nibbling till I had satisfied the itch. "Anyway, no matter how you or I or anyone started, we all know how we end, so it makes no difference."

And then my sister raised a question I hadn't expected. "*Do* we know?" she asked.

I was taken off guard. "I'm not in the mood for games," I said. "We both know what death is."

"I'm not being coy. Or naive," Amber said flatly. "I don't mean that just because you and I haven't died yet that we don't know it will happen. Nothing like that. Of course, we will die. But is that the end of us? Is it really?"

"Are you saying you believe in those silly ghost stories we used to tell? Honestly, you're a grown vixen."

"I'm not talking about ghosts," insisted Amber. "Here's another way of getting at what I'm pondering: can the greater come from the less?"

"Sure," I said.

"For example?" she prompted.

"Well, for example..." I fumbled for a moment. "For example, a tree grows from dirt, right? Surely, the tree is greater than the dirt."

"The tree is greater than dirt, and the oak is greater than the acorn. But is it greater than the tree the acorn came from? Or the water? Or the sun? Or all of them together? It only has what it has received."

For some reason, when Amber said, "the sun," that old melody came to mind, like a swallow squeezing into its nest after a long, lonely flight. *I saw my love! I saw the rising sun!*

"Nimbus?" Amber nosed my shoulder. "Are you okay?"

"Sorry." I shook my head, realizing I had fallen silent. "I got distracted. What were you saying?"

"I was talking about the seed. The seed *is* the tree, at least, it has the power to be. The tree is greater than the seed in one sense, but that's only because it's been given more."

"All well and good," I said, "but the tree dies, too. The seed has the power to be a tree. It's very moving—poetic even. But the tree has the power to be dead wood. So what's your point?"

"No," Amber yipped excitedly, catching me by surprise. "That's just it. The tree *doesn't* have the power to die. It *can* die, of course, but that only means something has gone wrong. As long as the tree's inner forces have their own way, the tree grows and grows. Something has to interfere for it to die. Or it has to fail in its receiving—water or sunlight or whatever else. The tree's death is the result of other powers, not its own."

"Once the tree is dead, do you think it cares how it happened?"

"The tree doesn't care about anything so far as we know," she said. "But I'll bet you care. Or if you don't, you should. You're sitting here right now, your heart beating, your blood flowing."

"And one day, I won't be. One day, the tree and I will be the same."

"There's a power within you, a power that holds you together and makes you alive. Yes, that power will no longer be able to do that someday, but that only brings us back to where we started: if that power *comes* from somewhere, might it *go* somewhere?"

Night had fallen, and the conversation was trying my patience. Besides, my belly was urging me to fill it. "Well," I said, rising, "it's all very interesting, but we'll find out what dying is like sooner than I'd prefer if I don't bring us some food."

"The farm again?"

"Of course."

"I wish you wouldn't go there," Amber protested.

"It's fun!" I quipped. "Besides, it's easy, and, as I've explained at length, they've earned the annoyance."

"That's what worries me. It *is* an annoyance. Humans can tolerate many things, but not annoyance. One of these days, you'll be caught in their traps—or worse."

"I know them too well for that. The day they catch me is the day I deserve to be caught."

"That's worse," said Amber. "The humans might never catch you. That's true. You are clever, after all. What I don't like is your debasing yourself into a creature that takes such pleasure in mischief."

"But you eat the food," I grunted. "You eat the food I bring you."

"Yes. I'm not perfect," Amber said with a sigh, "but that doesn't make me wrong. In any case, eating is one thing, but sadism is another."

"I'll be back later," I stated flatly.

"When you return," said Amber, "will you promise me that this is the last time you steal from that farm?"

"I'll consider it," I growled and squeezed through the knotted root entrance of our den into the cold night.

CHAPTER

18

# What Makes a Fox

Several weeks later, winter's fury had come. Prey were driven into hiding and edible foliage had vanished. As my hunting trips grew longer, I found that I enjoyed the solitude. Amber's company was stimulating, but our conversations were like seeds planted in my mind. Fragile, they could not bear too much digging. And so, I relished the silent growth that could only occur when I was alone.

I thought about happiness and what my sister had said about accepting limits. I had to admit that she seemed more at peace than I had felt in a long time. Despite what I had asserted, I began to suspect that Amber would find peace even in dying. We didn't talk about death much anymore—I got the sense that she was trying to spare me bad memories—

but I could tell that her whole way of living pointed to an end. Whatever this end was, Amber saw it not as life's cessation but its culmination. That was why she didn't clutch at health or security like most animals. I had seen that greed in Silver and in myself. In truth, I liked it. Without that lust for conquest, I felt life would be boring. I had told Amber as much, but she didn't understand. We had grown into such opposites, and yet I admired her.

My sister had expressed her desire to resume hunting. She had been able to forage on a few occasions, though there wasn't much food available to scavenge. Her recovery was steady, but the recent heavy snow had led me to insist she stay home.

I had been out for over a day, as my aching muscles and frozen paws bore witness. We had depleted our last autumn cache, and my belly complained loudly as I searched vainly in the northern woods. I had rested only a few hours the previous evening and then pushed myself through an early morning. I cursed as another circuit through the woods yielded nothing.

I thought of all the rich meals I had devoured with Silver. What I would have given for a hot dog or a taco! I thought, too, of Aurora's old farm with its livestock and stores of feed, but I was not yet desperate enough to return there. I had ended up promising Amber that I would no longer steal food from that farm. For once in my life, I wanted to keep my word if at all possible.

And so, I wove through the brush and fallen limbs farther and farther north. As I left the woods behind, a great barren field stretched out before me like a frozen desert. The afternoon sun glinted across the snow. Because of my journey back from the city's outskirts that summer, I knew that a small farm lay beyond this tract of land.

My breath clouded before me as I gazed toward that distant point. At a minimum, I could probably snag a few mouthfuls of feed for myself. Those loose pellets humans feed to dogs and livestock would be impossible to carry back to Amber, but there would also be garbage and maybe more. My stomach churned painfully, and I pressed on.

By the time I reached the worn wooden fence that marked the farm's boundaries, my head was light from hunger. My bones pressed firm against my skin. I tried not to think of how far from the den I had come. I consoled myself by remembering that Amber had eaten better than I and had not spent the last day and a half burning energy. She would not starve before nightfall.

The farmhouse stood on the horizon. It was hazy gray, almost invisible against the broad sky and snowy field that stretched out before it. Each heavy step seemed to bring me no closer to my goal. As I approached, the crest of the hill receded, sloping down imperceptibly. Painstakingly, I circled around to the back. No feed bins. No matter how I sniffed and sniffed, I found neither pellets nor garbage by the house.

I cursed but continued on toward the other buildings. With enough luck, there would be something farther along. I was past the point of no return. I could no longer make it back to the den without eating. A single thought, a single hope impelled my every footfall: *where humans are, there is food.*

Farther past the house and still nothing. My tail began to flag, but I shook my body and reminded myself that my frozen nostrils could not be trusted. Step by step, my view of the rear field became clearer. At last, a broad, metal-sided building flashed in the sunlight. It had no windows, only thin vents along the top edge. I recognized at once that its wide doors were meant for horses or other large animals.

Such animals would never serve as a fox's meal. I yipped in frustration. My vision was beginning to blur. Then I remembered that horses needed food, too. Perhaps their feed was stored near the stable? It was getting hard to think clearly. I had to rest. Even the stable was too far.

Not wanting to bury myself in snow, I looked around for cover. My best prospect was a medium-sized shrub about thirty yards from the house. I dragged myself to it and collapsed, my heaving breaths visible in the frigid air. In the spring or summer, the shrub—perhaps a rowan—would have formed a grand canopy, enough for birds to nest in. Winter had stripped its spindly branches of leaf and berry. I told myself it was better than nothing and curled up at its base.

How long I rested, I couldn't say. The experience was hardly restorative, filled with fits and starts. I feared falling into a full sleep—would I ever wake up?—and struggled to retain partial consciousness. Eventually I failed.

A cold nose against my shoulder roused me from a deep sleep. It was night. I opened my eyes with a start and gasped, an electric shiver running through my skin.

"What's that?" I cried, confused by my surroundings but better off than before my rest.

"Shh!" whispered the ruddy young vixen standing over me. Her golden eyes burned along with the stars above as she looked down at me. I could feel her warm patience as I muttered something incoherent and tried again to stand.

At last, I rose and sat facing her. A chilly wind ruffled my fur and whipped up the loose snow around us.

"Ah, I beg your pardon," I said, "I didn't detect your scent before, so I didn't realize that I was on your land. Please, forgive the trespass. I'll be going as soon as I'm able."

"No, no. This isn't my land," said the vixen, almost laughing. "I'm just staying here for the time being."

"Oh?" I asked, pausing a moment to sniff. "Where do you come from? Your scent is somewhat familiar, though I can't place it. Are you perhaps a neighbor of mine from the south?"

"No," she said. "I'm coming from the northwest, from the city, though I haven't lived there in about two moons. And, I'm sorry, but I don't recognize your scent at all. Do we know each other?"

"Well, if you're from the city," I said, "then, I'm sure you've heard of me. My name is Nimbus. I was part of Silver's team along with a few others. Our achievements are well known there."

"I'm Scarlet," said the vixen, "but I don't know who Silver is or about any achievements—"

"Of course you do," I interrupted. "We're admired throughout the city! There were five of us in our heyday, and we regularly did things other foxes never dreamed of— organized raids on food carts and things of that sort."

"Sorry," said Scarlet. "I'm not familiar with those stories. But I *did* hear about a fox called Nimbus once. He rescued my parents."

The shock shot through me again. "Rescued?"

"Yes. They were both being held in the animal park in the western suburbs. If you spent some time in the city, you may know it."

"Of course, I do," I mumbled. "I know it well."

Scarlet studied me for a moment. Then her eyes widened. "You're *that* Nimbus?"

"That's me."

"Then you also knew my mother as a child," said Scarlet. "She said she grew up around here and that the fox who helped them escape had been a friend of hers."

"Yes," I affirmed again, unsure of just how much Scarlet knew about my relationship with Aurora. "Your mother and I grew up as neighbors. We both ended up in the city by different ways and met there again by chance."

"In fact," Scarlet continued, "my mother spoke so fondly of her childhood home, it's why I wanted to move out here. She used to tell me about the exotic woods and peaceful farmland. It all sounded so beautiful and happy."

"It can be beautiful," I agreed, "but it's not so full of life at present." My stomach growled loudly to illustrate the point.

"Yes," said Scarlet, "I realize that. I know I'll have to wait for the spring, but at least the farm should sustain me till then."

"Have you found food here?" I asked hopefully. "And good shelter? I could use both at the moment." My stomach growled again.

"I see your point," said Scarlet. "I've been hiding in the stable for several days. It's quite warm and dry."

"And food?" I prompted.

"I've caught a few vermin. So far, it's been enough."

A frigid wind tore across the landscape rustling the bony branches above us. When at last the air calmed itself, I requested that we continue our conversation in the stable. Silently, Scarlet led me to a small path that the humans had cleared through the snow. We followed that for a few yards and then weaved around a conifer and continued till we reached the stable's far side. There, at the corner, one of the metal panels was loose. Careful not to cut her muzzle on the sharp corner, Scarlet lifted it just enough to slip inside. Mustering what I strength I could, I did the same.

I felt immediate relief. The earthy smell and gentler air filled my lungs and embraced me. Hunger still tore at my belly, and I felt faint again, but at least there was no biting wind or stark fear of exposure. Stalls of horses lined the walls. They watched us curiously with their large, dark eyes.

"I've got to eat," I said, lying down on the hard dirt floor. "My mind feels as weak as my body, and I'm not sure how long I can hold on."

Scarlet tilted her head and gazed at me with the pity that the young have for the very old. "You're welcome to stay as long as you like."

"If circumstances were different," I explained, struggling to keep my eyes open, "I would be most grateful and content with that, but I have to ask you for a much greater favor. You see, I have to get back home, not for my sake but for Amber's."

"Your mate?" asked Scarlet.

"My sister."

"Where is she?"

"We live about a day's journey from here," I explained. "At least, that's how long it would take a fox such as yourself in good condition."

"You flatter me," said Scarlet. "I'm certainly not at my peak right now."

"You're far stronger than I am," I said pointedly. "Believe me that I am not used to asking for help. Please, would you go to check on Amber? I won't be fit to return for days, and she's not well. She can't hunt for herself. Someone has to tend to her, or she won't survive."

"A day's journey," Scarlet repeated. I could see by her still expression that she was weighing the cost, but I also detected in her golden eyes a glint of generosity and the confidence of youth. "That's presuming that I can do it as quickly as you say. And, how long will you need to recover?"

"I don't know," I said with a moan. "If only I hadn't come so far in such bad shape."

"If *you* came here to find food, what guarantee do I have that your sister and I won't both go hungry?"

"There's no guarantee," I said, "but it's the place you're really looking for. It's where your mother grew up, and if you can hang on till the weather improves you'll see it in its glory and be welcome to stay as long as you like."

"It's really you," asked Scarlet, "the one who freed my parents, I mean?" She sounded hesitant.

"It's really me," I said. "Your mother's name is Aurora. Your father's name is Blaze, and his sister is River. River was also part of my team... while it lasted."

Scarlet seemed lost in thought. "That proves it," she said at last, shaking her head. "I suppose you'll tell me I don't have time to sleep on the decision?"

"I won't tell you anything," I said. "We both know the danger in every moment that passes."

"Yes," Scarlet said with a sigh. "I've been hungry before, and it's clear that I owe you."

"Please," I begged. "You're strong. You can make it. She'll die if you don't go."

"Let me think about it," said Scarlet. "In the meantime, I'll see if I can't find you something to eat. If your sister looks as bad as you, then the situation really is desperate. She may not survive the day it takes me to reach your den, assuming that I can even find it."

I thanked her for her consideration and closed my eyes. It felt like an instantaneous action, like blinking, but I must have fallen asleep again because a cold nose to my shoulder woke me with a start.

"Aurora?" I asked, sleepily.

"No, of course not," said Scarlet, puzzled. "It's Scarlet, remember?"

"Right," I said, shaking my head and struggling to sit up. "I'm sorry. It must be because your scent reminds me of hers."

"Well, in any case, I caught you a mouse. You must be lucky. I don't think there are many left here."

"All for me?"

"Yes," said Scarlet, tossing the creature on the straw before me.

Without hesitation I gobbled it up, crunching up the bones in the process. When I had finished, I sighed with relief. "Thank you," I said.

"I bet you're still hungry," said Scarlet.

"Yes," I admitted, "but I'll live a bit longer now, thanks to you."

"Well, I hope you can hang on for a long while," replied Scarlet. "I've decided to go and see about your sister. As I said just now, the food supply here may be running out. By leaving, I give myself and your sister a chance of survival, but that leaves you here. I don't suppose you have the strength to make it home?"

"No," I said. "There's no way I could go today, but you have to. You have to help my sister. Don't worry about me."

"All right," Scarlet said after I had given her directions to Amber's den. "Then I'm off. No time to waste."

"Thank you!" I exclaimed. "You've saved two lives today."

"Or lost three," she said grimly.

After Scarlet had begun her trip south, I tucked my-self beneath some straw in the corner. A place toward the center would have been warmer, but I wanted to avoid the horses. The stable held half a dozen. Their musty odor permeated the air. Each of them seemed content in its own stall. They all noticed me, of course, but no longer seemed interested. I prayed that Scarlet would understand my directions and even, with luck, find some nourishment on the way. I thought of Aurora, too, and chastised myself for not asking Scarlet about how her mother was doing. Totally spent, I fell asleep.

I couldn't say how long it was before I awoke to the slam of the large metal door followed by a hurried rustle of straw and dirt. A rollicking, rustling shuffle filled my ears. I licked my nose and sniffed, careful to keep my head low and hidden by the straw. A human odor, faint but distinct wafted through the stable.

There was a shout and a horse snorted loudly. I scrambled to get to my feet, but they failed me. In my panic, I twisted against the metal wall and rolled onto my side. My tongue lolled out of my muzzle from exertion as I rose to my feet. Even nourished by the mouse I had eaten, I would never get away.

A young boy ran to me and loomed down. If only I had remained still! Instead, my noisy movements had drawn him closer. Exhausted, I collapsed onto the dirt floor. No escape. I would be doomed to be this child's plaything or to have my pelt stripped off by his parents—fitting payment for my past mischief. Quivering amid the straw, I shut my eyes and waited for the cruelty to come.

"Please," I whimpered, though not to the child, who wouldn't understand me, "I'm afraid to die."

In dark silence I trembled. The boy did not move, did not make a sound. After a moment, I forced my ears, which had been thrust flat against my head, to stand upright. His breathing was regular and calm. I waited and waited, but nothing happened. Finally, I opened my eyes. Sunlight filtered in through the small vents in the ceiling.

Humans had gawked and stared at me many times in my city days, but none had ever watched me in the way this boy now did. Not since Aurora and I were cubs together had anyone looked at me with wonder. Amber loved me. I knew that, or, rather, I had come to realize it, but hers was a philosopher's eye, one that glances with an old, comfortable affection. The boy admired me as if I were a new creature, beautifully made.

At once it struck me. Nothing can live without wonder. Wonder, perhaps, is the definition of life. The wild flowers stretch toward a sun they can never reach as if enamored of it, and it is when they are closest to that sun, blooming wide and grand, that they are most alive. The soaring birds, the creeping ants, even humans—all of them are wondering beings.

Beneath that child's gaze, my fear began to change. I trembled not because I thought my life would end but because I was ashamed of what I would be at my final moment if it did. Had I once been like this boy, ready to befriend the world, relishing its secrets? Or was I corrupt from birth? Had all my pleasures sprung up from a twisted root? I cast my muzzle down, embarrassed to be watched by innocent eyes. How long I had been scratching out my own den! How often I had preferred architecting my own hell to being heaven's guest.

The boy rose to his feet. His eyes and rosy cheeks bulged from beneath his puffy hood, continuous with his red snow-suit. He almost looked like a fox. I felt he was no more than ten years old, though I had never mastered human ages as well as Silver. The child said something unintelligible but reassuring and then shuffled out of the stable.

When the boy returned, the scent of meat saturated the cool, static air. It drove me mad, and I pulled myself up. The boy laid several strips of bacon out on the floor in a neat pile, a treat I had not enjoyed since my time in the city. I gobbled them up and the child giggled from a few paces off, clapping his hands in excitement.

He ran back inside and repeated the offering, not with bacon but with bread that he tore apart and threw at me in little balls. I was too hungry to be indignant. I could sense that he wasn't doing it to humiliate me. I had played the fool before when creating a diversion for Silver or the others, but this was something else. This was pure, like a game, and I felt no resentment as I scarfed down each bread ball.

As he cast the last ball toward me, a cry came from far off, and the boy turned. I froze, leaving the morsel uneaten. I still didn't have the strength to flee outside, so I scurried as best I could and hid myself beneath the straw. It was the right choice, for at that moment an adult human, a female, appeared in the stable's large doorway. She surveyed the room, chattering something to the boy, whom I took to be her son. A horse whinnied, and she stopped to reassure it. The exchange between the boy and his mother lasted another minute or so, and then both left. Safe beneath the straw, I pulled my paws in tight and returned to sleep, my belly full at last.

I can't describe my dreams during that period in detail. There were no real images or sounds. I only felt at peace, like a cub in his mother's womb, who sees and hears nothing but still senses the life all around and within him, or like the fox cradled in the belly of his earthen den. I was a small part, the smallest part, of that web of living beings. The crawling insects, the deep roots that creep through the earth, everything joined together. I had never been alone. Life was all around me.

I hid in the stable about four days, sleeping often. The horses tolerated my presence fine, even when I drank from their water. The boy continued to bring me food. He liked to watch me eat, so I often stayed in view rather than retreating when he came.

He tried to touch me once, while my head was down. I had been chewing on a tough piece of cold ham. When his hand got close, my fur bristled and I sprang away. He fell backward onto the floor, his face crumpled, and I thought he might cry. Instead, he dusted himself off and stood silently as I finished my meal. To make amends, I sat still and close for a few minutes, allowing him to study me in the filtered light. He smiled and seemed to understand.

Once I had regained my strength, the journey home was hard, but not impossible. The landscape seemed different upon my regress, more compact and unified, as if some great giant had moved every barren tree and snow-capped stone closer together. I pushed myself to make the trip in only a day. Thankfully, the weather was clearer, and the snow was starting to melt. I prayed the whole way that Scarlet had found food and made it to Amber in time.

I also thought of Silver as traveled. I realized that I had deprived him not only of life but of redemption. By my choice, he had died at his worst. I had not been born corrupt, and neither had he. We had both been innocent, and we had both been guilty. It hurt my heart. Why should I be given so many chances and he perish? Nothing in me deserved it.

At last, I crossed the last field and reached that familiar oak, its strong old branches bare but stalwart through the winter. The scents of Amber and Scarlet heartened my final steps. Sloshing toward the den's entrance, I yipped in greeting.

Amber called back to me from inside, "Nimbus? Is that you?"

"Yes," I replied as I squeezed through the root-knotted hole into the welcoming darkness. "I'm home."

# CHAPTER

## 19

# Old Songs

"Mom was right," said Scarlet. "The country is beautiful."

She, Amber, and I were lying out in the field. The setting sun shot rosy streaks across a clear spring sky. Fireflies flitted about, appearing and disappearing all around us.

Gray winter's fading and the winged return of starlings and geese on the first winds of spring had seen my sister's full recovery. Scarlet had taken me up on my promise and remained with us. Her humor and warm spirit had brightened up our household. Scarlet had told us all about growing up on the city's southern side. Her stories of cubhood pranks and mischief—like daring her siblings to eat coffee grounds—had me roaring with laughter. I could just imag-

ine the look on Aurora's face dealing with all those caf-
feinated cubs!

Amber and I had shared some of our past as well, though
my sister was prone to philosophical digressions. I mostly
told stories of my adventures in the city, but I didn't reveal
everything. Scarlet still didn't know that Aurora and I had
once been betrothed, only that Amber and I had both known
her mother as cubs. I was grateful that my sister had kept
that secret without my asking. I was also careful to leave
out the precise details of Silver's death and why my team
had later split up.

Scarlet was also smart and naturally inquisitive. She
grasped Amber's more abstract points better than I did, and
I was glad my sister had someone else to converse with on
that level. Overall, it felt right, the three of us staying together through the winter and into the spring. I had no desire to return to my old den by the farm, nor to move anywhere else. I had had my fill of adventures for a while.

"Yes," I agreed, my head resting comfortably on my
paws. "This was a good place to grow up. Just wait till the
rains begin in earnest and all this foliage bursts and blooms
with life."

"It sounds lovely," continued the young vixen. "You
know, it's funny. My mother was raised in the country, but
she's urban through and through. I remember her lectures
on the different types of vehicles and how to avoid them. I
never thought I'd remember them all."

"Did you manage to do it?" asked Amber.

"Eventually," said Scarlet. "Of course, now I don't need
that knowledge anymore."

"Well," I added, "your mother was drawn to city life from
a young age, well before she really would have understood
it."

"How long did you live in the city again, Nimbus?" asked Scarlet

"Two years," I said, rubbing a paw over my ear to scratch an itch. "Well, a little less."

"Based on your stories, it sounds like you enjoyed it. If you had so much fun there, why did you leave?"

"I thought I enjoyed it," I replied, "and on a superficial level I did." I glanced to Amber, who seemed lost in thought. "But I had to leave. I may have mentioned to you that there were some coyotes who wanted me gone and that my team had split up. Those factors drove me back here, but I think deep down I knew that I couldn't stay anyway. I didn't belong there. I had to make a fresh start."

"It's too bad you never ran into our family in the city," said Scarlet. "Mom spoke fondly of you. I think she would have liked to see you again."

"Really?" I asked, cocking my head.

"Are you surprised?" asked Scarlet.

"Yes," I said. "Well, I mean, your mother and I didn't part on the best terms. I was rather rude to her the last time I saw her." I sighed. "Of all the mistakes I've made in life, not saying goodbye to her properly has been a big one."

Scarlet's nose twitched, and her eyes narrowed in concentration. "Strange. I never got the impression you and Mom had had a falling out."

"It's true. I had a lot of anger back then. Aurora made a certain decision—a very reasonable one—and I resented it. I still think about it sometimes, though no longer with bitterness."

"It takes a while to make friends with regret," interjected Amber, "but once you do, it can be transformed, like when a wound heals and the skin is tougher for having scarred."

"I've had some wounds in my day," I said. "What you say is true, but the marks remain."

"I know it well," said Amber. "Signs of pain and of healing."

"There's no healing without pain," I added, "or growth."

Scarlet turned her golden eyes to me. "If it's any consolation, I'm sure Mom forgave you. I never heard a bad word about you from her or Dad."

"That helps," I said. "It speaks to her character, and that's the most important. Aurora has always been a practical fox, a realist. It's not her fault that reality turned out to be different from what we expected, and she had the maturity to accept it when I didn't. I'm glad I didn't spoil that in her."

Time passed as it always does. Before I knew it, summer had come. Spring had failed to bring the roaring showers of prior years, and only a few spotty trickles had watered the earth. Soon it was a drought. First the fields began to brown, then the forest. As the weeks passed, the prey species left for other regions or simply began dying off.

The heat was intense, the sun hurling down its oppressive beams with no relief. Even my thin summer coat felt hot and itchy. My throat was often dry. Amber, Scarlet, and I shared the hunting and foraging duties. I was grateful we had stayed together, though I began to fear it would not be enough for our survival.

Scarlet had formed a strong bond with Amber and had proved herself an eager student, ready to hear my sister's perspective on the deeper questions of life. In truth, I was glad that Amber had found another dialogue partner, especially because I felt a greater call to solitude and silence. I had struck a pleasant balance, hunting and meditating alone each evening before returning to the chatter at home. I found comfort in the routine and the little idiosyncrasies of my denmates: a yawn from Scarlet on waking or Amber's pensive stares. The vixens noticed certain mannerisms of mine as well and sometimes let me know it.

I got in the habit of visiting the farm in Aurora's old territory, not to steal food or terrorize it—I was still keeping my promise—but just to watch and reflect. Besides, there was water in their troughs. If I quenched my thirst there, what little water could be found near our den stayed available for Amber and Scarlet. So far, no foxes had moved near the farm, though from time to time I could smell that a coyote had been around, a sign that they, too, were venturing out farther than usual. If the scent smelled recent, I would make a cautious exit. No need to risk an encounter with those nasty creatures.

On one of my trips I witnessed the farmer digging, not in the fields, which looked pitiful in comparison to previous years, but out back behind the barn. He had an expression on his face that I had not seen among the humans before, at least not clearly. I had glimpsed it once or twice for a moment among the men who lived by the bridge but hadn't paid much attention. He looked weathered and sad.

I realized that he was burying the old dog. Raising my nose just a little, I sniffed. The smell hit me. It reminded me of trashcans in the city summer, not like a fresh kill but like meat that has been out in the heat for too long. I thought of Sturdy, that poor, intelligent creature, who had only wanted to know about things and people. He had probably lost his life because of me. And then there was Silver, who had certainly died through my fault.

I realized as I watched the man that he had loved his dog.

Burying the old hound's body was an act of reverence and loyalty, the expression of a life-long bond come to maturity. Besides his sadness, I sensed from the man's scent and demeanor a kind of longing. He seemed out of place without his companion. He seemed not at home in the world.

Was this what Amber had tried to explain to me? Was she in touch with this restlessness, this sense of the beyond? Had Silver been, in his own selfish way, just a restless and fearful heart trying to hang on? Humans were not so different after all. They were just like me, like all of us. They were beyond nature because we all are, or can be. Their failures were my failures, their fears my fears. I could only hate them by hating myself, and I realized that I no longer hated either.

I awoke with a start one morning, partly from the heat of my denmates' bodies and partly from my first nightmare in months. I struggled to get my bearings, shifting in the dark.

Amber stirred beside me. "What is it, Nimbus? Are you all right?" she muttered sleepily.

"I- I think so. Just a bad dream."

"I surmised as much. What was it about?"

"It was about someone I haven't seen in a long time."

"Not Aurora?" asked Amber, glancing over to make sure Scarlet was still asleep.

"No, someone I knew in the city. Silver. You remember?"

"Yes, I remember. What happened in your dream?"

"I saw his death."

"That's unsettling," said Amber.

"Yes, it was," I said, "but it was also different. Worse. It wasn't just him. It was you. And Scarlet as well. And, somehow, myself. Death came for us all. I don't understand it, but it was so clear and horrible. My heart is still racing."

"It's okay," whispered Amber and gave my ear a reassuring lick. "It's over. Do you want to talk about it?"

"No," I said and rose gingerly, taking care not to disturb Scarlet. "I need to catch my breath."

After I had paced around outside for a long time, feeling the dirt beneath my paws and the warming morning air filling my lungs, I didn't go back to sleep. Instead, I walked across the browning field to the old forest. Despite the drooping stalks and wilting leaves, I hoped it would bring some comfort. A few mushrooms at the base of a mossy stump served as my snack.

I thought hard but couldn't focus. In my mind's eye I still saw the ghostly vestiges of my dream. I saw Silver's cruel face twisting with fear in his last moments. I saw Scarlet's innocent, golden eyes widening before she was consumed by darkness. I saw the boy from the stable running toward me with laughter and then turning away in revulsion and horror. My heart ached, and I was beginning to come to terms with why.

The next evening Amber and I lounged at the entrance to our den, enjoying the breeze and trying to remain cool. The sun was sinking toward the horizon, and the shadows of distant trees cut through our field like deep scratches from an enormous set of claws. Scarlet had just left to go hunting for the night.

"I have to tell you something," I said. "It doesn't have anything to do with you, but I want to say it."

"If you want to tell me, you can."

"I'm afraid of what you'll think of me," I admitted sheepishly.

"I'll still love you," said Amber. "I choose to love you." She said it without passion. On the lips of another fox, it might have been an insult, but this was Amber's way. She was stating her love for me as a proposition, a fact that could be counted on and verified.

"Thanks," I said. "I love you, too, but I've done some really bad things."

"The raiding and looting?"

"Yes," I said, "and much worse. I'm responsible for Silver's death. Not that I killed him in a fight or anything like that, but I let him die when I could have helped him."

"I see," said Amber. "I remember that you told me a man beat him to death. And you think you could have stopped that?"

"I could have warned him. There was time."

"Why didn't you?"

"I didn't like him," I said. "I guess I also wanted what he had. I wanted to be the leader. And, if I'm honest, I think I just wanted to *do* something, to make a choice that mattered. It doesn't make any sense when I say it now, but I felt pretty helpless back then, and I would have done almost anything to gain control. The power to end the life of a fox I hated was too much for me to resist. But I should have resisted because it was wrong. Anyway, I had to tell you the truth."

"It's hard to judge intentions," said Amber. "Maybe in the moment you weren't thinking clearly."

I shook my head. "No, I knew what I was doing. I almost killed again to keep it secret."

"I'm glad you didn't do that," said Amber.

"Me, too," I said, "but I would have done it if Ash hadn't run away from me. I know I would have."

"That's a lot to carry with you," said Amber gently. "Are you sorry?"

"Deeply," I said. "Silver was a bad fox, but I don't hate him anymore. Now I pity him. He surrounded himself with other foxes and yet he was always alone. He and I weren't so different once. Until recently, I was just like him. I wish I hadn't taken away his chance to find peace."

"And, have *you* found peace?"

"I'm getting there," I said and licked my sister's cheek. "Be patient with me."

"You're wrong, you know," added Amber. "This does have something to do with me."

"Oh?"

"It's part of you, and so it's part of me. Let yourself be forgiven, Nimbus."

"I'll try," I said. "I really will."

"Regret is a wise teacher."

"You know, it's funny," I said. "I used to think Aurora was childish for going after those silly flowers, but she grew up long before me. I'm the one who's wasted my life on pettiness."

"You haven't wasted your life yet," said Amber. "No life is wasted till the last breath. It's who you are in the end that counts. Your whole story is leading up to that. Regret what ought to be regretted, but love what deserves to be loved."

"Well," I continued, "if there's one thing I've learned, it's that each of us is a wounded beast, lashing out and wailing in our own futile ways. It's deadly to forget that."

"True," said Amber, "But, it's also deadly to forget that we're so much more."

I pondered Amber's words for several days. The idea that I could be something more, that I was already something more than my parts and choices, brought comfort, but it also challenged me. More can't come from less. *More* was in me, and in Amber and Scarlet—and even in Silver and every miserable or magnificent creature I had ever met. I imagined Silver's skin, scooped up and hauled away as trash. Was it possible that something of him remained—something his skin and bones could not contain? I felt that if it was possible, even in the least, it was necessary. But what made it so? And I began to think of the sun in the sky, the fire that blazes and irradiates the world. It gives warmth and energy in such abundance that in some cases—as in the present drought—the fragile life of our world cannot bear it.

One night I was lazing around the den's entrance, scraping idly at the browning grass. Without realizing it, I began to sing under my breath as I waited for the others to return from their hunts. My own contribution to our food supply, a small and raggedy-looking mouse, lay in the dirt before me.

"Hey, I know that song!" Scarlet called, trotting up from the side.

"Oh," I said sheepishly. "Welcome back. Have you caught anything?"

"No," Scarlet admitted. "Nothing this time. But, don't try to change the subject. I was just saying that I recognized what you were singing. It's one of the old country songs. Mom used to sing them to us when we couldn't sleep or when we were sick."

"Old country songs?" I said and chuckled. "I suppose I thought they were quaint, too, at your age. You say that Aurora used to sing them to you? Which one is your favorite?"

"Hmm. I don't know," said Scarlet. "I'd have to think about it. What about you?"

"Oh," I said. "You know, I haven't sung most of them in a long time, but there's one I could never forget. It keeps returning to me over the months and years. It begins '*I saw my love.*' Do you know that one?"

"No," said Scarlet with a shake of her head. "I don't think Mom ever sang that one. How does it go?"

"You really want to hear it?"

"Of course."

"Well, you understand that my voice isn't very good these days, with it being so dry and all—"

"Just get on with it, Nimbus!" Scarlet chided, rolling her eyes.

"Okay, okay," I said, then cleared my throat and sang.

*I saw my love! I saw the rising sun,*
*Whose rays pour down and warm us from above.*
*The fire burns! It blazes as the seasons run*
*And ever turns the dark of night to light.*
*No merit earns, no skill or art devises it,*
*But in its sight all creatures learn to love what lies beyond.*

I had shut my eyes halfway through, embarrassed to have the young vixen watching me. When I finished singing and opened them, Scarlet was grinning warmly. "That was beautiful," she said. "I'm glad you shared it with me. Why is it your favorite?"

"I suppose because its meaning has grown up with me. When I was a cub, I thought it only meant that the love we have for one another is as important as the sun. That's true, but now I feel it isn't enough. Now I believe it much more literally. Love is grand, but not only because it matters to us."

"What do you mean?"

"We can stop loving," I explained, "We fail. I've failed many times. Love has to be more than something in us. If it's real at all—and I've come to believe that it is—it could only be something greater, just like whatever life we see in this world below comes from a sun that shines down from above." I paused to study Scarlet's face, her eager eyes and narrow muzzle. She looked keen and smart and, suddenly, older. She understood. "And," I added, "it's the great relief of my life to know that love doesn't stand or fall with *me*, that what moves and embraces all things will go on being what it is without me. I spent so long trying to make everything about me. I wanted to be important."

"You sound a lot like Amber," said Scarlet.

"Yes," I said. "I suppose I do."

"It's not a bad thing," she said then laid a black-socked paw on mine. "You know, you are important, to Amber and to me."

"Thank you," I said. "You're important to me, too. Life has turned out so different from what I first wanted and from what I tried to force it to be, but I'm glad that I've ended up here with the two of you. I think this is where I was being led, even though it took me so long."

We sat in silence for a few moments. The night was clear, and the stars were shining bright. I hoped Amber had had a successful hunt so that the three of us wouldn't have to share just my single mouse. But, although I was hungry and part of me was anxious about the continued drought, I felt content there with Scarlet.

After a while she asked, "Do you ever regret not having children?"

I felt a twinge of sadness and embarrassment. "I- Well, I mean, yes. I always thought I would have cubs, but I'm grateful to be where I am."

Despite my fumbled response to the unexpected question, Scarlet must have sensed that I wasn't offended. I still hadn't shared the details of my relationship with her mother, but I no longer felt such a strong urge to hide it or other truths about myself.

"It must be difficult," said Scarlet, "to reconcile gratitude and regret."

"Yes," I replied, "it's hard to be thankful for what is without devaluing what might have been."

"Anyway," she added softly, "I think you'd make a good father."

# CHAPTER

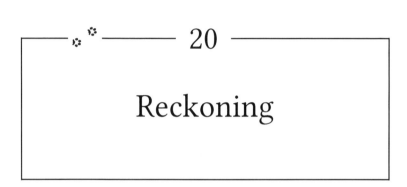

20

# Reckoning

By high summer, the last small ponds were only puddles, and the puddles had dried up. We needed water, and we had agreed that if any of us found a good source, we would have to move. There was one place I knew, and I was on my way there for the first time in years.

It was afternoon—not the best time to travel, but the situation was urgent. The sun beat down on me as I trotted south through arid fields. At last I came to the great highway. Till then I had avoided that region, where once I had mourned Aurora by the side of a frozen pond. I crossed the road, weary from thirst and eager to drink from the pond.

When I reached the bank, I lapped at the muddy water

without hesitation. The pond seemed smaller than I remembered, though whether this was because of the drought or because the whole world looked smaller to my mature eyes I couldn't say. I drank to my satisfaction and curled up in the shade of some nearby trees to rest. I had no desire to make the return trip in the heat of the day if I could help it. I was to meet Amber and Scarlet, also out looking for water, at our den by mid-evening. I hoped one of them would find a better place to relocate than this particular pond.

Sleep had come quickly, and I slumbered without dreams till suddenly my ears perked up and a shiver jolted me awake. Someone was hissing my name. Leaping to my feet, I realized that the air had changed. Storm clouds collided and growled in the late-evening sky. Had I slept so long?

A coyote, lean and rugged, stood just a yard away. Her stance was rigid, her yellow eyes trained on mine. She appeared to be in good health, certainly better off than myself. Her muzzle curled in a brazen smirk. She looked like she could have torn my throat already if she had wanted to. The stench of fury choked the air.

"Nimbus," she repeated, savoring the sound. "I had to be sure it was you. That's your name, isn't it? You said it that night." The words rumbled forth from somewhere deep within her shaggy belly, hardly interrupting her snarl.

"How—" I began, but a clap of thunder cut short my reply. I shuddered at the loud noise, but my interlocutor was unfazed.

"I am Ravenbone," she growled, "daughter of Sunstreak and Shadowpelt. You killed them many seasons ago. Not far from here, in fact. Surely you at least have the decency to remember." Her narrow eyes burned with concentrated energy, like the lightning crashing down across the horizon.

I probably should have bolted, but instead I answered her. "I do remember," I said. "And, you may not believe it, but I'm sorry."

"You're sorry?"

"I'm not sorry that I escaped with my life, but I am sorry that you lost your parents that way."

"On the great road! They died in unnatural agony, crushed and twisted, bleeding inside. You robbed them of an honorable death with your damned fox-trickery!"

"I'll say again," I repeated, keeping my voice level, "that I'm not sorry for escaping with my life. I didn't ask for trouble that night, and I certainly didn't ask to be the target of an impromptu hunting lesson. There's no need to reprise those events now."

"You foxes," she spat. "Crafty. You tried to talk your way to safety then, and you're trying to talk your way to safety now. It won't work."

"I wish I could convey to you that you'll never get over the pain this way," I said calmly. "I've tried it myself. It can't be done. Even if you kill me, you'll just feel empty. If you've been looking for revenge all this time, then you'll just go on being miserable when you get it."

Ravenbone threw back her head and cackled. "Don't flatter yourself. It's not like I've centered my life around getting back at you. Believe me, if I had you would have been dead years ago. Naturally, I never thought I would see you again after your escape. But I'm an opportunist, and when I got word that you were returning to this area, I had to see for myself."

"You got word?" I asked, puzzled.

"We coyotes have an extensive network, and we take our family bonds quite seriously—not like you foxes. Apparently, it was a raccoon who informed on you. I don't know the details, mind you, this has all been reported to me second-hand. But this raccoon knew all about a fox named Nimbus who came from these parts."

My fur bristled. Could Sturdy be alive? And, if so, had he *betrayed* me? "A raccoon?" I asked, trying not to let on that I really did know the animal in question. "How would coyotes understand him?"

"I told you I don't know the raccoon personally. Whether he traded information to save his own skin or whether he's a long-time ally of ours, I couldn't say. Somehow he spoke canid-language, and he told them everything. After my cousins forced you away from the city's outskirts, they relayed the message to me that you were heading this way. We have relatives all over these parts, and they've kept an eye on you. They knew I'd relish the chance to see you. Why do you think they let you go in the first place?"

The coyote's gaze reminded me in that moment no longer of lightning but of the lights at the front of human vehicles, whose piercing beams plow forward on their unrelenting course. Despite her denial a moment before, Ravenbone seemed obsessed. Another spidery streak of lightning flashed, and a deafening thunderclap followed at once. I was shaken but tried to stay focused, looking for an opportunity.

"You have a family?" asked Ravenbone.

There was no point in being evasive. Her tawny ears twitched, attuned and ready to pick out any double-talk. "Yes," I said, "of a manner."

"That's true," she said, inhaling. "Their scent is heavy on you. I won't ask their names, as I really don't care. They will soon be mourning you."

The coyote lowered her head just an inch, the beginning of a crouch. In that instant, I whirled around, whipping my brush into her muzzle as hard as I could and bolted. At once, I staggered. Sharp pain wrenched by leg. I had twisted too fast and caught my paw on a rough patch of earth. Ignoring the discomfort, I picked up my pace and dashed as fast as I could. My maneuver had earned me a few invaluable seconds. I prayed it would be enough.

"Damn you!" cried Ravenbone and leaped after me. I couldn't afford to glance back. The slightest wasted movement would cost me. Instead, I heaved onward, hurtling my chest forward with each bound. The joint at my rear paw burned. I could almost hear it cracking with each stride, but I had no choice.

I zigzagged, kicked up dust, anything to keep the lead. At last, after the second slobbering snap at my hindquarters, I had reached my goal—the highway. Unwavering and without pause, I climbed the steep embankment, practically dragging my leg over the dry grass. Ordinarily, even in a fight, I would have paused, would have checked for traffic. I could afford no such luxury. Without so much as a glance, I cast my body onto the road and darted across. The still-warm asphalt grated on my pads with each labored stride. A car ripped past me, creating a wall of air that blasted me toward the opposite side.

"A foolish try, fox!" Ravenbone yelled from the opposite side. "You think you can send me to the netherworld just like my parents? History won't repeat itself tonight."

I risked a single backward glance and saw that she was waiting on the far side of the road. For the first time, I detected anxiety on her face as she turned her head to and fro, ears erect, listening for approaching cars.

The continuous rumble of the storm made it difficult

to hear, giving me the chance I needed. I ran north, tearing across the plain. Another splintering flash of lightning rent the sky, followed at once by an explosion of thunder. I could no longer hear Ravenbone, but I had to assume she had crossed the road. I pressed on, racing through the pain, lame paw struggling against the dusty ground. I couldn't endanger Amber and Scarlet, so the den was not an option. I had to find another refuge. What I would have given then for Silver's trusty network of hiding places!

A heaving bark sounded from several lengths behind me, cutting through the din. Ravenbone was gaining. I veered right. We were already in my territory. The woods lay only a few hundred yards away. If I could make it there, maybe I could find shelter. Or, I thought, if I pushed my way through the woods, I could lead the coyote to the farm. Perhaps the human presence would deter her.

At last, I reached the woods, diving headlong into the foliage. The drought had prevented the vegetation from reaching its usual growth, so I was more exposed than I would have liked. Still, I crawled through the tangle, weaving around trees and logs. The coyote followed close behind. She was within range, but as long as I stayed low to the ground, the mess of vines and brush kept her from pouncing or lashing out. I had to keep moving. With every painful step, I told myself that I just had to take one more. To stop was to die.

I reached what Aurora and I had once called our clearing. I had to cross it or turn and fight. The brush no longer protected me. Overhead, lightning tore the black sky, thunder rocking the ground, the trees, and all around us. Just as I was about to cut hard to the right, I winced in pain. My leg trembled, and I froze. Even if it wasn't broken, it was badly sprained.

The coyote's eyes narrowed. "Looks like you won't get lucky twice," she growled, baring her teeth. "I am impressed, that you made it this far. Really."

I lowered my head to the ground, ears back. "I won't die without a fight," I hissed and showed my fangs. "You can kill me, but you'll have to work for it!"

Ravenbone padded toward me. "That's how we're going to play it, then? Fine by me. I prefer an honorable kill."

I squared my shoulders, bracing in case she pounced. The coyote glared at me as we circled. I had made up my mind not to strike first. I didn't have the strength. I would defend and parry as best I could, but I wouldn't waste my energy on attacks doomed to failure.

Ravenbone lunged at me, her jaws snapping. I lurched left, brushing against her side, and twisted myself, struggling for her throat. The thick fur slipped from my grasp as she reeled backward, launching herself upward. She knew I couldn't stand on my hind legs. Before she came crashing down on me, I rolled onto my back. Normally, this would have been a fatal move, exposing my underside, but it allowed me to thrust against her with my front paws.

I slashed as best I could, splayed out on the ground. It was enough to throw the coyote off balance and allowed me to wriggle free. In an instant, pain sliced through my muzzle, and I tasted warm blood. She had slashed my face with her claws, barely missing my left eye.

I roared. Flipping onto my feet once again, I stumbled, then lashed out with my fangs. Ravenbone dodged, trying to get behind me. I wheeled around, blinking fast to clear my vision, and rushed against her chest, knocking the wind out of her. She heaved and stumbled backward but quickly regrouped.

Before I could turn away, her jaws gripped the scruff

of my neck, and I felt her hot breath on my skin. I bucked upward as best I could with the power of my front legs alone and tried to shake her. The coyote hung on tight. I struggled, unable to wrest free from the hold.

Suddenly, I ducked, throwing my front end to the ground and flipped Ravenbone forward. I tumbled head-first over top of her with the momentum and smacked her hard in the face. Her muzzle opened, and in an instant I was free. She scrambled to her feet, and we began to circle once again.

I glared into the coyote's eyes. Both of us were bleeding from the snout. Each time she looked ready to strike, I barked a warning and she growled in return.

"Do what you like," she chortled. "I can see you dragging that leg. Pathetic. Each step must be agony. I can pad around like this all night. Go ahead, use as much energy as you please. When you're tired out, I'll tear your body apart at my leisure."

Ravenbone was right. Every step, every growl or hiss, depleted me just a little more. I couldn't beat her in a fight, I couldn't flee, and I couldn't wait her out. Before too long, I wouldn't even be able to make myself a nuisance to kill, I would just be a soft target ready for slaughter.

I weighed my options, keeping my eyes fixed on hers, trying to maintain a tough facade. Part of me still thought I might negotiate my way out of this predicament, despite Ravenbone's sensitivity to wily "fox-talk."

I halted and sat down, which caught her by surprise. "You know," I started before she could decide whether to attack, "when I lived in the city, I completed a detailed study of human behavior. I learned some very rare things. You live close to a human-populated area. Wouldn't you like to learn some useful things about them? I could teach you."

Ravenbone's expression relaxed and then widened into a lusty grin. "Now this I really like. I should have made you beg earlier. Actually, it's better that you do it on your own. It's more natural that way."

My face fell as I realized that she was toying with me.

"No, go on," the coyote continued. "Don't let me interrupt you. Bargain for your life. *Beg*."

"I'm being quite serious," I insisted, doing my best to steady my breathing and keep my ears upright. "I'm not trying to trick you. I can see quite well that you're not going to let me go, after all. If you're going to kill me anyway, perhaps you'd let me share what I know beforehand? That's all."

"And what do you get out of that?"

"Oh," I sighed, scratching behind my ear with my good leg. "A few more minutes of life? It sounds pitiful and desperate, I know. But, well, here we are. We both know that you've bested me, so what's the harm?"

"Are you that afraid to die?" The coyote wrinkled her dripping muzzle in disgust then jerked her head, flinging an arc of blood to the dusty ground. "I always knew you foxes were ignoble creatures. House cats. Surely no relatives of ours. But I didn't realize the extent of your cowardice."

"I'm at your mercy," I continued. "Everyone knows it or will. Word of your prowess will get out... even more than it already has, I mean."

Ravenbone's eyes narrowed again. "I'm vain, fox, but I'm not stupid. You'd better use your next breath to tell me some of this precious information you claim to have, or I'll see to it you empty your lungs in shrieks and whimpers."

"Ravenbone," I began, glancing all around, trying to conceal my trembling. "Some humans are as mediocre as any of us, but some are truly great. Do you know what makes them great? It's that despite their weakness, despite their stunted senses, despite everything that nature has marshaled against them... they refuse to settle!"

With what strength I had, I made a lame dash around Ravenbone. In other circumstances, she could have body-checked me with ease or lashed out with her fangs or claws. Instead the coyote stared dumbstruck as lightning flashed and thunder shook the woods once again.

I continued to limp away as fast as I could, hoping to regain my sense of direction. I sniffed hard. A strong odor stung my nostrils, one I knew well from the city. It grew denser by the second. I gagged, glancing back at Ravenbone as I realized what was happening.

Smoke. Fire! The eastern woods were burning. The perimeter of our clearing was going up in flames. Second by second, we were being surrounded. My eyes began to water.

Ravenbone wheeled around, cursing, then glared at me. Her eyes were filled with rage, but she hesitated. She could see as well as I could that there was little time. All around us, the brush and undergrowth lit up with a speed I would have thought impossible.

"Ravenbone!" I called. "Let's get out of here! We can still sniff out a way through to the west. You and I together can survive this!"

"Damn you, fox!" she roared, dashing toward an opening the flames had not yet reached. "If I can't choke the breath from you with my own jaws, I'll see to it that you die here nonetheless." The coyote positioned herself against the trees, guarding them, cutting off the last clear path.

I faltered. Ravenbone stood firm, seemingly unafraid. The consuming eyes, the intoxicated grin, her whole demeanor, told me that she no longer cared for her life. The coyote's only concern, her only interest, was my death. She would not budge, and I could not fight her. The only reason she didn't attack me, I suspected, was that I might then dart past her to freedom.

I had to find another way. I glanced all around looking for an opening. Lightning blazed across the sky again. The deafening thunder on its heels almost drowned out another sound. When I caught ear of it at last, my heart leaped. In the distance, beyond the spreading flames, someone was calling my name.

Ravenbone didn't seem to notice. I limped toward the sound, but as I reached the flaming perimeter, I paused once again and turned back to the coyote.

"Now," growled Ravenbone, almost cackling with glee, "I pay tribute to my ancestors. I give my life for their honor and set things right."

"You'll die for nothing!" I called, blood and smoke clogging my nostrils. "We can still survive this if you step aside. We'll flee the woods together and you can kill me another time."

"No, no, no." She shook her head violently. "No more talking. No more negotiating. Just watching, watching until the smoke strangles you and the flames lap up your flesh."

Despite the raging fire unfurling its wide wings behind me, despite the black smoke stinging my eyes and lungs, despite the stronger foe blocking the last clear escape, pity welled in my heart. In minutes, I might die, but I would die a free creature, not one possessed by hate. The flames would devour my flesh, but Ravenbone was devouring herself from within.

The barking from beyond the flames grew louder. Scarlet! I couldn't see her, but she was coming. Ravenbone was still so focused on me that she didn't notice.

"Please, Ravenbone," I pleaded. "I know what hate is. I know the pain, and I know the hollowness of revenge. I have no debt to you, and I will bear no guilt for you, but I would spare you, as I would any living being, the hell you've made for yourself. In a few moments, it will be too late, but it is not too late now. Make peace. If only in your last breath, make peace."

The coyote's eyes widened, blazing like twin infernos. She threw her blood-stained muzzle toward the blackened sky, as if about to shriek with a force to rival the storm itself. As she opened her mouth, a tremendous boom rang out. A blazing limb fell from one of the trees and crashed down upon her, casting sparks in every direction.

The surge of hope I had felt vanished instantly. Besides crushing the coyote, the burning limb had completed the circle of fire. The whole perimeter around me was blocked. At once, the flames seemed to double in size and intensity, folding into themselves and leaping back up again. I wavered on my weak leg. Again, Scarlet called to me. I couldn't see her, but my ears told me she was past the fallen limb, just beyond the flames.

My instincts took over. I ran toward the limb and leaped. I don't know how I did it, but I cleared the flames. The landing was excruciating, and I crumpled to my belly. Without rising, I crawled through the undergrowth as best I could, wherever the fire had not yet reached. I had no sense of direction, so I followed the sound of Scarlet's voice.

Little by little, I distanced myself enough from the heat and the smoke that I could breathe again, albeit with the occasional sputter. I blinked rapidly, wishing I could pause and rub the teary discharge from my eyes. I pressed on through the dry, scraggly brush until at last I caught sight of the vixen who was still calling to me.

"Nimbus! You're alive!" Scarlet cried before grabbing the scruff of my neck in her muzzle and, with a few heaves, pulling me from the thicket.

"Yes," I gasped. "I made it out, thanks to you."

"Are you okay?" Scarlet asked, nuzzling me sharply.

"Not exactly," I said, coughing, "but we'd better get out of here."

"Agreed," she said and thrust her head under my chest, pressing up and helping me to rise. Once I was standing she let me lean against her, and we started across the field.

"You've saved me again," I said once I had caught my breath.

"I was looking for you," she said. "When you didn't come back, I went out to find you, and then I saw the fire."

"It's funny," I said with a chuckle. "I was searching for water and I got fire instead."

"Well, you don't have to worry about that," said Scarlet. "Amber found a nice pool to the north."

"Amber found water, huh?"

"What did you think?" joked Scarlet. "That we couldn't handle it? It will probably take a few hours at this rate, but we can go there if you have the strength."

"With your help, I just might."

The fire raged in the forest behind us, spreading from tree to tree. Overhead, lightning still flashed at regular intervals, accompanied by the inevitable quaking thunder that shook the earth and sky. Left unchecked, the fire would soon spread to the field. I prayed for our den to be spared and the farm as well. The humans there were at the storm's mercy the same as the rest of us. It was a force greater than us all and beyond our control. And yet, as we limped safely across the field, I knew it was not the greatest.

✲

Before Scarlet and I could reach Amber, the pregnant black clouds began to release their rain. At first it was gentle, but soon we had to take shelter under a dense shrub. There was just enough room for the two of us, so we pressed up against each other for warmth and to stay as dry as possible. My body had grown so thin, it seemed, and I wondered if Scarlet noticed. My lungs felt worn out, and I still tasted the smoke with each breath.

"Who was that coyote you were yelling to at the end?" asked Scarlet as rain poured down all around. "The one who didn't make it out."

"I'll tell you the whole story," I said, eyes already shut. "But I don't have the strength at the moment."

"Rest, then," said the vixen gently.

With that, I let myself drift into a deep sleep. My leg had stopped spasming.

When at last I felt well enough to stay awake, I was very hungry. Scarlet was awake, too, watching me. The rain still fell lightly, but I could see from the earth all around us that it had fallen heavily through the night. It was nearly morning, and I sensed it would be a cheerful, sunny day.

"Do you think you could catch us something to eat?" I asked. "I'm pretty sure I can walk, but not without nourishment."

"Of course," said Scarlet. "We're not terribly far from Amber. Even at a slow pace, I bet we can get there by noon. Of course, now that the rain has returned we may not have to stay in the new location."

"Assuming that our den survived."

"Yes," she answered, "we'll have to go back and investigate eventually."

"All things will be well in time," I replied. "First we need to eat and rejoin Amber. Everything else comes later."

"Oh, I know," said the vixen, creeping from underneath the shrub and rising to her feet. She stretched out and opened her muzzle in a lively yawn. "How good it feels to stand up!"

"Don't get too wet out there," I teased as she shook moisture from her ruddy pelt. Before she could leave I called to her again, "Scarlet, wait. There's something I need to tell you."

"What's that?" she asked, turning back to me.

"It's about your mother and me. We were more than friends."

Scarlet sat down in the wet grass and gestured for me to join her. I rose, shook myself off, and sat beside her, blinking as the dawn struck my eyes.

"I know," she said softly. "You didn't just rescue my parents. You and my mother were betrothed once."

"Yes," I answered, "I knew your mother in those early days. She loved me, and I loved her, but she was never mine to keep."

"Well," said Scarlet, "if you had stayed with her, I never would have been born. So, I'm sorry, but I'm also grateful."

"I'm grateful, too," I replied. "But how did you know? Did Amber tell you?"

"No," said Scarlet shaking her head. "I figured it out a while ago. It's obvious how fond you were of my mother and even more obvious that you've been trying to hide that fact."

"Oh," I said, ashamed. "I'm sorry."

"I'm sorry, too," said Scarlet, "and I'm disappointed that you didn't trust me enough to tell the truth sooner, but I knew you would eventually."

"I'm sorry," I said again. "I was afraid."

"I forgive you," said Scarlet.

"Thank you," I replied, "I didn't start off trying to lie to you. At first the topic of my relationship with Aurora was just... painful. It's taken me so long to come to terms with my past. Then once I got to know you, I was afraid it would make things awkward between us. I didn't want to hurt our friendship. I really do appreciate your forgiveness. I'd hate to end things on bad terms. Sadly, I have a history of that."

"Why should things end?" asked Scarlet coyly.

"Well," I said, "You're a grown vixen with your life ahead of you. I don't expect you to stay with me and Amber forever."

Scarlet's gaze met mine. Her golden eyes were young and bright, but not naive. "What I want is to stay," she said, placing a paw on mine.

I was caught off guard, and it took me a moment to reply. "Are you sure?"

Scarlet laughed. "You're a good fox, Nimbus. Besides, a bird at paw is worth two in the bush."

"Your mother's pragmatism," I remarked.

"Maybe," said Scarlet, "but I'm *not* my mother, you know."

"I know," I said. "I wouldn't want you to be." We sat for a while watching the sunrise. Moisture on the grass and trees sparkled all around. The scent of refreshment and renewal filled the air. It was a beautiful day. "And," I asked, breaking the silence, "come the fall?"

Scarlet understood my meaning. "I'm not a slave to tradition," she said. "There's no need to run off anywhere. If our den didn't burn up, we can live there. Otherwise, the new place isn't so bad. I bet your sister would help tend the cubs."

"She'd love that." I said. "Well, in any case, there's still time. I used to be in a rush about these things, but not anymore. The season will come if it's meant to."

# Epilogue

Sometimes I make my way across the long field to where the forest once stood. My rear paw has healed, but it will never have its old strength, so the trip takes longer than I'd like. I sniff around and imagine the old clearing. I can almost smell those thick woods all around, and yet my mind clouds, too, and I forget the details and contours I once knew so well.

Several seasons have passed since the great fire. The surrounding countryside survived, including the farm, for which I'm thankful. Scarlet, Amber, and I returned to our old den shortly before my cubs were born. It has been only a few weeks, but all five have already grown so much. Scarlet minds them with such patience. I really admire her. Amber, too, helps with the hunting and cleaning. The cubs' eyes have just opened, and they are curious about everything! They watch me when I come and go, and I know they are eager to climb their way out into the sunlight.

One day, I will bring them with me and show them where the forest used to be. Only a few trees remain there, hardy trees that have weathered the calamities of many generations. Lately, when I go there, I see timid shoots creeping from the dark soil. They are just beginning to stretch and twist toward the springtime sun. These will be, I suppose, the tough old trees of ages yet to come. I marvel to think that my cubs will have no memory of the old forest. It has come and gone, and my generation with it.

I think of Aurora, too. I try to picture that rosy pelt flecked through with gray like my own. Foxes are noble creatures, but we cannot afford to be proud, or, at least, not to boast. The seasons turn and we with them, like so many plodding stars that march inexorably through the sky. I know that my soul is smiled upon by that eternal motion. There is a love that is not our own, one not achieved but given. I have lived a life I would not have chosen because that greater love, beyond all things and in all things, chose me. I am Nimbus, the least of foxes, and in my smallness I find peace.

Made in the USA
Middletown, DE
12 February 2022